Broken
image

Edited by Cynthia Rose and Lindsay McDonald.
Cover Design and Formatting by www.indyscribable.com
© Can Stock Photo Inc. / sjhuls

Disclaimer: This is a work of fiction. Names, characters, events, locations and incidents either are the product of the author's imagination or are used fictitiously. Any actual resemblances to actual persons, living or dead, or locales are entirely coincidental.

www.rdschultz.com

Praise for Broken Image

"...another winning story by Rene Schultz! She has knocked it out of the park with this one! I love that Rene has a message in each of her books and can't wait for the next book to come out!!! I am being honest when I say that she is amazing and that I love each of her books so far, even though they are all completely different, they all come together with a moral, a life lesson and an amazing journey!"
Stephenee Carsten
New Jersey

"I found myself talking to Mercedes and her friends a lot in this book. Rene's writing style makes you feel like you are actually there with the characters. You will absolutely love this book if you believe that beauty is only skin deep.... Broken Image is a book about 'body image'...how we see ourselves...and how others see us. Even though it's fiction, it's NOT fiction. The story plays out every day in our heads. Women, men, children...it doesn't matter."
Cynthia Rose
Tennessee

"I've loved this authors previous books and this was no different. Rene has such a great way with words that she pulls you right into the story. As always with Rene's stories there is a moral hidden in this book."
Philomena Callen; 2-Friends Reviews
United Kingdom

"There is a huge twist to the ending that I didn't see coming, as per usual Rene's lovely style of writing. ONE of the reasons I love this authors work is because she has a moral to every story. It's thought provoking, and sometimes, enlightening. This is a work of fiction, but like I say, it's also true to life."
Sue Ward; 2-Friends Reviews
United Kingdom

"WOW, this book is amazing I don't even know where to begin! This is a beautifully written story that anyone who has suffered from feelings of worthlessness or knows someone who does should definitely read."
Samaris Creech
Texas

"Broken Image by Rene D. Schultz is one book that I adamantly think that every woman needs to read. Our concept of 'beauty,' especially to the most recent generations in the US, is so shallow...almost as if we have tunnel vision...and there are certain prerequisites that every girl and woman must meet before they can be considered 'attractive' by society."
Lindsay McDonald; indyREVIEWS
Arkansas

Books by Rene D. Schultz

SEARCHING4MR.RIGHT.COM
BISHOP STREET
DONE DEAL
BROKEN IMAGE

A Note From the Author

AUTHOR'S NOTES:

Our younger generations have been pressured with an overwhelming message that achieving 'beauty' is mandatory in becoming successful in life, and it increases your personal value in the public and social scene. Thanks to the media, we have become accustomed to extremely rigid and uniform standards of 'beauty.' Seeing images of flawless, thin females everywhere makes it hard for women—or anyone—to feel good about their bodies. Our children are relentlessly encouraged and pushed by magazines, television, fashion, plastic surgeons and peer-pressure to obtain that beauty through different procedures of cosmetic surgery. Botox, Restylane, augmentation, and liposuction has become a common day occurrence amongst young people (mostly women) throughout the world.

Growing up with that overwhelming message places a lot of stress on our teens through peer pressure, and has created a lot of obsessive behaviors like eating disorders (Anorexia and Bulimia) and addiction to plastic surgery (Body Dysmorphic Disorder), that even the older generations have to deal with. Older women (over forty) have an increase of stress competing with younger women, forcing them to keep up with only acceptable 'beauty' standards. In many parts of the world it has deeply affected any success in their social life as well, as the work environment. Many movie stars are a perfect example of this obsession to stay beautiful. Aging as become discreditable and cosmetic surgery is their only way to keep themselves marketable.

The thin, athletic, sexy ideals of *beauty* have become the 'new normal.' That's frightening for the last few generations—not to mention the parents who are raising their young daughters in this environment of competition and judgment.

We deserve to be really angry about the current state of affairs that has a fashion and media industry feeding us ideals that cause us to feel guilty for our hungers, obsessed with our appearance, and hating the very bodies that we need to sustain us. The only real cure for plastic surgery, and this need to be 'beautiful,' is for people to realize that it is not the size of the nose but the smile on their face. It's not their appearance, but the accomplishments within their lives. It's not the outside, but the inside that actually makes us all who we are—Amen....

Broken Image is a glimpse into the world of the 'cosmetic' generations. Beverly Hills is the perfect example of the peer pressure of beauty.... There is a lesson to be learned!

My sister, Corky – Thanks for being there…

My cat, Sabby – On 04-25-14, my heart broke in two.
You curled up and laid by computer during my entire
writing career. I will always miss you!

Sue and Philomena – Your support means the world to me!

Linds and Cindy – You guys are the best!
You know what you know, and you always make me look good!

one

MERCEDES smiled to herself as she turned on the bathroom light and walked towards the sink. She leaned over the counter and glanced into the mirror. At nearly thirty years old, she still had beautiful unblemished skin like her mother. It was porcelain white and flawless, and it was her only admission of acceptance that she chose to acknowledge from her parent's gene pool. Leaning closer to the mirror, she frowned as she noticed small lines starting to form under her eyes, and creases near the corners. Her eyes were an unusual light green and surrounded by extraordinary long, naturally black lashes, and she didn't know where she got them from. Her father's eyes were blue; and her mother's constantly changed from hazel to brown, depending on her mood swings. But it was her nose that had been a disparaging state of contention since her childhood.

When she was ten she was playing softball with a group of schoolmates when she was struck in the face with a fastball. Her nose was broken and swollen for weeks. The school nurse told her, *'don't worry, it will heal on its own.'* Now, twenty years later, she ran her finger down her nose, sighing in frustration. It was visibly crooked, and had a good-sized bump on the left side. That bump, mixed with her flared nostrils, had become one of the least favorite parts of her body. Heading further down, she finally touched her lips. They were not full and luscious, like the ones that always flashed on the television screen during lipstick commercials. Full, luscious lips would be one of her dreams, along with higher cheekbones. But as she got older, she was forced to realize that life was not always what you wanted. God had given her what he thought necessary, and that was something she felt obligated to live with.

Her fingers pushed back her shoulder-length, wavy light-brown hair with processed blonde streaks as she continued to stare at herself in the mirror. Mercedes knew she was not beautiful, or stunning, or even close to either. None of her features were delicate enough, when blended together, to create anything dramatic or striking. She was plain, simple, and ordinary. Not at all close to what society considered *'beautiful.'* And definitely nothing compared to the magazines that cluttered all the newspaper stands.

Sometimes it made her blood boil when she walked past the magazine aisle at the store. She would ask herself questions like: *Why was beauty based on perfection? How did those women get so gorgeous? Was it in their gene pool, or was it because of living in California—where plastic surgeons were a dime a dozen and on every corner?* She was a bright young woman who knew the obvious answer—but refused to acknowledge it.

To Mercedes, the fashionable trend of plastic surgery started years ago, and hit close to home when her best friend in High School got an augmentation for her sixteenth birthday. In high school, Jennifer Lang was still slowly developing breasts when her mother initiated her into the world of 'perfection.' Mercedes thought Jennifer was already one of the most popular and attractive girls in the school with her tall, slim figure, and beautiful long legs. All the boys chased after her, including the quarterback of the varsity football team. Her long, thick blonde hair flowed down her back, and she always looked like a graceful ballerina. That wasn't enough for her mother. Her mother was addicted to plastic surgery, and had been diagnosed with a disease called 'body dysmorphic disorder'. It was a disease where an individual became preoccupied with a slight or imagined abnormality in their appearance, and the only way to fix it was through corrective surgery. After twelve surgeries, her mother continually found fault with her body, which changed on a daily basis. Mercedes and her friends watched this from a distance, but they were too young at that time to recognize the problem.

In those days, cosmetic surgery was just starting to *'rear its ugly head'* all over the media. Talk shows became the rage where the cosmetic surgeons displayed their sculptured divas. Within a few years, movie stars, both men and women, were lining the halls of the vast growing groups of Beverly Hills *plastic surgeons*. Jennifer's mother patterned herself after the famous movie stars who felt surgery was their only means of attaining physical 'perfection.' It had become acceptable and more commonplace in society, amongst those who could afford the 'pricey' procedures. At first, it was more of the aging starlets and wealthy women that indulged in this extravagance. As the cosmetic surgeons began to push the perfected face, the sculptured bodies, and introduced new beautifying procedures, the young began to participate more. Mercedes and her friends thought starting in high school was pushing the boundaries for young women. Unfortunately, Jennifer's sixteenth birthday present had physically started her down the same path as her mother—addicted to 'beauty.'

Looking back, Mercedes realized it had also created a lot of dissention amongst her group of friends. The acceptance of Jennifer's decision to enlarge her breasts left a big wedge between the girls. In addition, it caused a lot of angry parents to make rash decisions that eventually divided the group up. Jennifer had been a dear friend of Mercedes' since grade school, and when the group divided, she had sided with Jennifer. Not because she believed in enhancing one's self to be socially acceptable, but because she believed that every person was entitled to do whatever made them happy.

Now, years later, Mercedes looked down at her tiny breasts in the mirror and shook her head. *"Oh well, I guess I'm not perfect!"* she muttered to herself and picked up her electric toothbrush. The radio turned on again, and Mercedes began to hum to the song that was playing. Swaying her hips and shuffling her feet, she continued to brush her teeth. After a few spins around the bathroom with her toothbrush, she turned on the shower, and continued her rituals of the morning.

An hour later, Mercedes was sitting at her kitchen table sipping her first cup of morning coffee and planning her day on her iPad. With all of her notes neatly typed into the small electronic device, she shoved it into her backpack, took her last sip of coffee, and walked out the door of her condo. Parked in the driveway was her economical four-door car. It was nothing to look at, and definitely not like the fancy ones her best friends raced around town in. Mercedes loved her beat-up rattletrap because of the high gas mileage and low maintenance it demanded. She could care less if the heater didn't work, her speaker on the driver's side was out, the gas tank didn't register anymore, and a few other minor problems had appeared over the last few years. It was a great choice for her when she bought it and a constant source of ridicule from her friends. She unlocked the door, slid onto the seat, and started the car. With the sun shining, and the birds chirping, she thought, *"What a wonderful day it is going to be!"*

On her way to work, stuck in bumper-to-bumper traffic, she thought about Christina and their dinner plans. As a frown crossed her face, she wondered why she always set herself up for this demeaning form of punishment. She loved her friends, but lately it seemed harder and harder for her to deal with their enormous amount of criticism. *Why couldn't they mind their own business and leave their opinions to themselves? Why did they constantly try to change her? Why couldn't they just understand that she liked who she was and didn't feel a need to be like others? Why were her friends so shallow with their addiction to beauty? Why did they always make her feel vulnerable?*

Two

AFTER seven miles of nail-biting traffic, and a

progression of nasty expletives—Mercedes finally made it to her employer's underground parking lot in Los Angeles. She pulled her car up to the small glass cage, stopped and waved her parking pass at the attendant, and gave him a big smile. He looked at her with a somber, dismissive nod and pointed to the rising gate. Somewhat irritated at his response, she entered the structure, looking for a parking spot.

"*I wonder what ticks in that little brain of his—that he always looks so gravely disappointed with life,*" she said to herself. Mercedes always tried to border on the side of positive. It was hard for her to comprehend negative people, especially coming from where she had been.

She parked her car, shut off the engine, and looked in the rearview mirror to make sure her lipstick wasn't smeared. Then she picked up her backpack filled with all the things she needed for this new day. She got out of the car, walked to the underground elevator, and waited for the doors to open.

As the crowd began to gather around the closed doors, Mercedes caught the eye of one of her coworkers and gave him a nod. He casually nodded back and continued texting on his cell phone. Within minutes, the glass doors opened and everyone started to crowd the elevator. Mercedes moved to the back and pressed deep into the corner. She closed her eyes and waited for the door to close. Both hands gripped the railings with white knuckles and she held her breath. With a lurch, the elevator ascended to the fourteenth floor, where her office was located.

Ever since Mercedes was a child she had a fear of heights. And now, standing in the back of the elevator, she could still remember the exact day and time that fear began to manifest. It happened one summer when she was just eight years old.

She was on her way to Colorado with her mother, Betty. Her mother had just been fired from her recent job as a housecleaner. That night, packed with the little worldly possessions they owned, she crammed them into her old beat-up car and took off. This had been their fifth move in the past four years. After seven hours on the road, they were driving through Arizona on their way to her mother's new job that she had found in a newspaper from Colorado. Suddenly, her mother pulled into a 'scenic lookout' overlooking the Grand Canyon as the sun began to rise in the beautiful blue sky. Mercedes thought it was one of the most beautiful sights she had ever seen. Not that she had seen much in her young life except poverty, squalor, and her mother's inability to provide for them. The Canyon, with all of its majestic splendor, brought a big smile to Mercedes' face, and her excitement was hard to contain. Mercedes shaded her eyes as the car came to a complete stop, then with one small hand she grabbed Scruffy, and with the other, the door handle.

Mercedes did not understand the tumultuous divorce, or why her mother was filled with uncontrollable anger that was constantly directed at her. When Mercedes got out of the car, she was holding her favorite stuffed toy that had been by her side for the past four years. It was the only gift her father had sent her after he left—four years earlier. The little dog was her best friend, security blanket, and quiet listener during those difficult times of her young life. She held on to 'Scruffy' with a tight grip as she came to the edge of the short wall that stopped any sightseers from getting too close to the edge of the cliff. Looking over the rim of the cliff was frightening to her, so she stood back. Betty stepped forward and pushed Mercedes closer to the wall, so they could both admire the Canyon.

Releasing a long, slow sigh, Betty boasted, "Isn't it a beautiful sight?"

Mercedes leaned over to look, then pulled back and closed her eyes. "It's scary to look down, Mommy," she whispered. "Scruffy wants to go back to the car."

Suddenly, her mother grabbed Scruffy from her small hands. With an angry, vile look on her face, she threw the stuffed dog as far over the cliff that she could. "There! How scared do you think that damn dog is now? It's just a stuffed carnival doll!" she screamed out loud.

Mercedes began to panic. She took a step toward the wall, and began to climb over it. "No, Mommy... why did you do that? I love Scruffy!" She looked down, and the fear of the steep cliff caused her heart to pump wildly. At that very moment she wanted to jump—but her eyes looked down as the bile began to rise in her throat.

Her mother immediately grabbed her arm, and started pulling her toward the car. "I'm tired of you dragging that dog everywhere we go. You are eight years old now, and you don't need a silly stuffed toy constantly at your side!" she yelled.

Mercedes began to cry hysterically. "Please help me get him, Mommy. I love him...he's my best friend!"

Betty narrowed her eyes. *"No! He's gone. Goodbye and good riddance to him!"* She turned and pointed her finger as she continued. *"If you don't quit your sniffling, whiny crap, I will throw you over that cliff just like Scruffy!"* She turned her toward the cliff and gave her a small push. Mercedes' face lit up with fear, and immediately Betty shoved her toward the front passenger seat of the car.

Mercedes was crying and looking back as they drove off. From that day forward, Mercedes had developed a fear of heights.

Or...was it the fear of looking down and not seeing little Scruffy at the bottom of the cliff?

For years Mercedes had nightmares of that horrible day, and it was only one of the few hurtful memories she still stowed deep in her heart. The elevator doors opened and Mercedes waited for the rest of the riders to get off before she slowly walked toward her destination. *"I wonder what made me think of poor little Scruffy today?"* Her childhood was filled with a lot of taunting moments. And some of those moments just came up when she least expected it—others she continued to work out through years of therapy.

Mercedes opened the beautiful mahogany doors to the suite of offices. On a big brass plaque attached to that door was a list of employees that worked in the office. Her name was at the bottom, but that didn't bother her. She knew if she worked really hard, and did really well, eventually her name would creep up to the top—just like her boss, Jarrod Rosenberg. She worked in a private banking group in Beverly Hills that specialized and catered to all the financial needs of its wealthy clientele. She was the only woman banker in this fast-paced office, and was considered on the 'fast track' to success. Her knowledge and consistent ability to deal with any given situation was scrutinized continually. Over the years, she had established a flawless reputation that was highly regarded by her company and her peers.

There was only one thing missing, and Mercedes thought it was a big point of contention. She was never considered, or invited into the good-ol boys' club that had formed within their ranks. Her coworkers, Michael Lu, Zackary Steele, and Alexi Alferov were within her generation; and yet they would go out together for lunch, and she was never invited. Sometimes, she thought it was because she wasn't pretty enough and they only liked to hang with the 'superficial' women of Beverly Hills. She knew what that was like. She had a few friends that placed a lifetime of value on their beauty, but she was smarter than them. She had learned to trust her gut instincts, be intuitive, and to think outside the box. Mercedes was beyond that point of shallowness. She always looked beyond the surface. It still bothered her that Michael, Zackary, and Alexi were still young, single, and foolish enough to be pulled into that delusionary world of Beverly Hills.

"Morning, Mary." Mercedes said as she walked into the office and noticed Mary standing next to her desk. The short, stout older lady, with gray hair tucked into a bun, was concentrating on sorting through the mail. Her matronly dark skirt hung six inches below her knees and looked flawless, along with the cream silky blouse that had a big bow tied around her neckline.

She looked up as the door closed, and smiled. "Isn't it a beautiful morning, Mercedes? My...don't you look very becoming in that outfit. Are they new?" Mary asked with a twinkle in her shiny blue eyes.

Mercedes looked down at what she was wearing. "I bought it on sale at the end of winter last year at Nordstrom and had to wait for it to get cold enough to wear it. The black turtleneck sweater is a few years old."

Mary walked over to where Mercedes was standing and touched the petite belt. "This little tooled silver belt around your waist is delightful, and it really makes this outfit. Is that new?" she questioned.

"No...I've just never worn it in the office. But thanks for the compliments. I appreciate that you noticed my new purchase. Well, except for my new short leather boots. Aren't they cool?" Mercedes lifted up her pants' leg slightly, so Mary could take a better look at her new boots.

"Those are so you, dear, and so lovely. When I was your age, we could never wear pants and boots to work. Amazing how things have changed." Her friendly smile was warm and sincere.

"The past twenty years have kept my head spinning in circles with all the changes. I can't even imagine what it's been like for someone your age, Mary! Technology is almost second nature to us. To your generation all this technology is so hard to absorb." Mercedes spun around in a small circle and laughed.

"I hate technology and constantly having to update our lives. I come from the age of black and white televisions, phones attached to a wall, and Swanson TV dinners. I loved my years growing up and the simplicity of it. We didn't have 'big brother' watching over us through cell phones, websites, and grocery stores where they can monitor everything you buy." Mary sighed. "Now, I just want to retire and enjoy that simple life again!"

Mercedes laughed. "Anything I need to know before all hell breaks loose in the office?"

"No, everything is calm and quiet this morning. Would you like some coffee? I'll bring it back in a few minutes."

"Thanks, Mary. That's very sweet and appreciated."

Mary Dugan was the private secretary for Mercedes' boss, Jarrod. She was a lovely lady, in her sixties, had been a secretary for over forty years. She had been in this office for the last twenty-two years, and was a great friend and mentor to Mercedes. Her knowledge was invaluable and Mercedes had learned so much from her. Now at the age of sixty-seven, her sights were set on retiring in the next year, and enjoying her later years with her husband and twelve grandchildren.

Mercedes and Mary had a great relationship, and every payday they enjoyed going to lunch at the trendy restaurants in Beverly Hills. On many occasions, Mary had expressed to Mercedes how bright and astute she was compared to her other associates in the office. She was very impressed with how Mercedes handled the clients, how she managed her accounts with extreme ease, and she always let her know it. Over the years, Mary had to clean up a lot of messes left behind by some of the young men on the staff. She covered their behinds and made it a point to reprimand them, as if they were her own children. They didn't care about work ethics as much as Mercedes. They were too busy trying to balance their social life with their heavy workload. Not Mercedes, she didn't have much of a social life; and they all knew it.

The other secretary was Sally Puttin. She was there to service the younger associates in the office. Sally had only been with the company for seven years, but she was an expert and knew just how to handle Mercedes' three partners—Michael, Zackary, and Alexi. She was hardnosed and didn't take any disrespect from anyone in the office. Sally kept everyone in line, kept that office moving smoothly. Except for recently, since her husband had been diagnosed with terminal cancer. Michael, Zackary, Alexi, and Mercedes never complained when she took off from work to nurse her husband. It left a big gap in the office, at times, and an overload of work for Mary, but Mercedes was always there to lend a helping hand to keep things going.

Mercedes sat down at her desk and started sifting through her mail. Zackary poked his head in the door and said, "Hey, Mercedes, can we talk later? I'm having a problem with Jim Smith and his mortgage loan. He's being a real shithead!"

She looked up, "Sure. I have an appointment at 3:00 p.m. Once I leave the office, I won't be back. Let's do it before noon. By the way, do you know where Sally is? I haven't seen her today."

Zackary looked at Mercedes with a sad look on his face. "She's at the hospital. I think her husband took a turn for the worst. His blood count is low and they might have to start him on different medications. That poor lady is going through hell right now. That's why I asked you for help. I had no one else that knows about mortgages, more than you."

Mercedes was quiet for a few seconds. "Maybe we should send her flowers or bring over some platters of food from Canter's Deli on Fairfax Avenue." Mercedes voiced her concern. "She's been such a loyal secretary to all of us, it would be nice to do something nice for her."

He stared at her with questioning eyes. "I thought you only do that when someone dies?"

"Nope. Flowers and food always make your friends feel better." She smiled.

He looked at her matter-of-factly, then in a condescending tone he said, "You women get so emotionally involved and always try to smother everyone."

Mercedes took offense to that comment, you could see it on her face. "Are you talking from experience, or observation? Or are you just spouting off out of those 'macho' lips of yours?" Her nostrils flared out a little when she sucked in air. "I was going to say something, but I'd better not, because you won't like it. I already said I would meet with you and discuss your problem with Mr. Smith. So if you're going to push my buttons any more, my suggestion is that you get the hell out of here."

"Sorry, Mercedes, I didn't mean to offend you. And I really do need your help today!" He tapped the wall three times with his finger. When Zackary was nervous, or confronted about something, he had a habit of tapping the wall or tapping anything his fingers could find. This was his way to acknowledge he was leaving a conversation or room. Mercedes didn't understand it at first. She grinned and thought about his little eccentricity and wondered how it ever started. Zackary slowly turned and began to walk down the hall to his office.

Mercedes got up, rushed to the door, then she loudly said, "You offended all women, not just me!" With a smile on her face, she walked back into the office and began to work.

Toward noon Mercedes picked up her cell phone, put it on speaker and dialed.

"Hey, Mercedes, what's up? Are we on for tonight?" Christina asked.

There was a short pause. "Oh...I don't know. I've had a tough day at the office."

"Holy shit, you sound like Alisha's boyfriend! Every time he comes out with us, the first thing he says is 'I've had a shitty day at the office!'" She started to laugh.

Mercedes' lips pursed at the comparison and she became defensive. "Well, it was a tough day.... Look, Christina, I'm not here to make excuses—I had a horrendous day!" Mercedes sighed.

"Hell, it couldn't be any worse than mine. I dropped a whole plate of salad on the lap of a fucking bitch!" The anger in her voice was noticeable.

The visual was enough to make Mercedes laugh, but she refrained. Christina was a waitress and wannabe actress, waiting for her big break. "I know, I would be a 'fucking bitch' myself, if I went out to lunch and had a...*what kind of salad was it?*" She put her hand over her mouth to stifle any hysterical laughter that might come out.

"It was an Italian chopped salad with extra dressing. It just slipped out of my hand." Suddenly, Christina began to laugh uncontrollably. Once those two started to laugh, they didn't stop for a while.

"Chopped salad? Holy shit, crap-o-la...that's like picking up a zillion pieces of vomit off your lap! No wonder she was pissed!" Then they were both hysterically laughing again.

Christina started to beg, "Come on, bitch, and go out with us tonight. If you could make me laugh over my crappy day, then I can force you to indulge in a little social life. How long has it been since you've been out with us ladies?"

"It's been really crazy at work. Plus, having my kitchen remodeled was the worst headache ever! I've been cleaning up for months trying to get the dust and debris out of the whole house." Her voice had dropped down a few octaves, as she whined through the last sentence.

"Answer my question! How long has it been?" Christina demanded.

There was a moment of silence. "Okay, a few months. There, now I suppose you want to put bamboo under my fingernails to make the pain of answering that question hurt worse!" Mercedes picked up her Starbucks and took a sip.

"No, pain is when you sit across from Jennifer with her size triple-X boobs! You haven't seen her new 'ladies' yet, have you?" Christina listened to a commotion on Mercedes' end of the phone. "What the fuck are you doing?"

Mercedes continued to cough and choke, and could barely catch her breath. Tears were streaming down her face when she finally answered. "Gagging on my coffee!"

Christina giggled. Then she said, "Well, should I call the paramedics...?"

Mercedes shook her head in silence. "No..." She sucked in a deep breath, and exhaled slowly. "Okay Christina, I'll meet you there. Who else is going, so I can prepare myself for the barrage of bullshit I know I'm stepping into?" she said with a long sigh.

"Jennifer, Tessann, Alisha, and maybe Emme. Who gives you bullshit?" she raised her voice with a touch of anger.

Mercedes moaned. "All of you! It really hurts sometimes sitting amongst the beauties, and I always feel like the 'ugly duckling.' Then you all tell me how I can change, and constantly criticize me," she whispered.

Christina paused and said quietly, "I always wished I had the wisdom and brains that you have. You are so bright, and so sweet, and so kind...and your beauty shines on everyone you know. Beauty is only skin deep my friend. Always remember that, dear Mercedes," she said the last sentence with the sincerity and genuineness of a good friend.

Tears began to accumulate in Mercedes' eyes, "What time?"

"Half past a monkey's ass!" They both knew what that meant. It was something they'd always said when they were in high school. It was silly, it was stupid, but it always made Mercedes feel better . . . .

Three

MERCEDES had the valet park her car and wondered how he liked driving her old beat-up Honda compared to the Ferraris, Corvettes, Shelbys, or Vipers he regularly parked. Most of the cars that lined the streets and parking lots cost more than the small condo she had bought five years ago. She walked down the street and noticed the line to the dance club was filled with people waiting to get in. As she walked closer, she noticed a hand waving in the air near the front door of the club. She took a closer look and realized it was Christina. When she finally reached the entrance to the club, the bouncer looked down and frowned with displeasure.

"Sorry, Miss, you need to go to the back of the line," he said with a stern look.

Mercedes pointed her finger to Christina. "But my friend is right over there."

He looked up and noticed Christina, then he flashed her a big smile. Christina blew him a kiss and jiggled her boobs. He turned and looked at Mercedes again. It took him a few seconds before he removed the rope that blocked customers from just walking in. "Okay...today is your lucky day!" he said sarcastically.

"Oh gee, thanks!" Mercedes wanted to kick him in the balls, but it would have suited no purpose, except to get her permanently banned from the club. *On second thought . . . . It would be worth the ban, watching his balls swell to three times their size!* She giggled to herself at the visual.

Christina ran up to greet her. Her Hispanic heritage produced flawless tanned skin, big brown eyes, plumped lips, and perfect shiny brown hair down to the middle of her back. Her small petite figure was adorned in a shimmering, sequined mini-dress. Her cleavage was almost to the point of being obscene, and her six-inch stiletto heels made her as tall as Mercedes' five-foot-five height.

Christina Lopez was in the small group of Mercedes' elite friends. She was a young and striking woman with a *'hot tamale'* temper. She was also one of Mercedes' friends from high school that no one liked to hang around with. Everyone knew that her mood swings were enough to generate an enormous amount of drama and angst amongst their small group of friends. At times, her tongue would lash out verbally, piercing her friends with sharp barbs, and leaving everyone stunned and angry. Other times, she could be that angelic angel she physically looked like. For years the girls had taken turns with her abusive tantrums, trying to make sense of her abundance of anger. Mercedes, of all her friends, knew where it came from and always tried to pacify the group from pushing her out. Luckily everything changed the past year after Christina's doctor had started her on psychotropic medications to ease that heavy anxiety she had carried around with her since childhood.

Mercedes never could understand the need for those kinds of drugs, but in Christina's world, that was the only thing that could keep her mood swings level and steady.

Over their years of friendship, Mercedes had seen what devastation Christina's rages could do. She had not been able to hold a job for any length of time. Her inability to control her anxieties had left her in many situations that included unemployment, homelessness, and left her friendless. The past year had changed, with the medications, and the only way Mercedes could explain it was very simply— Christina was on her road to recovery. With the new medications kicking in—Mercedes was happy; the group was happy; and Christina had finally mellowed out.

Christina looked at her friend, grabbed her hand and crooned, "Oh baby, it's so good to see you. It's been awhile. Come on, we have a great table inside."

Mercedes' eyes scanned her gorgeous friend up and down. "I bet you do!"

Christina ignored her friend's comment, or maybe she just didn't hear it because of all the noise surrounding them. The club was packed with people, like a can of sardines. Trying to push their way to their table was like navigating through L.A. traffic—at a snail's pace. A few times, Mercedes caught herself apologizing for bumping into someone, or being pushed into someone, but no one ever seemed to be bothered by the disturbance. It was almost like they were immune to the invasion of their space—unless there was a spilled drink. Mercedes hated to navigate through any crowds, but the club environment was even worse—the level of intoxication was prevalent and it was just like a game of human bumper pool. For just that reason alone, Mercedes never felt comfortable, and rarely liked to frequent the club scene with her friends.

Christina pointed to the group halfway across the room. "Jennifer is here, and so is Tessann, and Emme. Alisha already had plans with her boyfriend," she yelled over the rambunctious crowd.

Mercedes just stared at Jennifer and her two big assets. "Oh, that's too bad. I wish the whole 'gang' could be here. Then we'd have a whole bevy of beauties," she said sarcastically.

Christina pouted and said, "Come on Mercedes, don't be a party pooper. You know you could be anything you want—if you wanted to! That's the nice thing about having, and making choices in life."

"Okay, I'm sorry. It's just hard being the only *ugly stepsister* all the time." Mercedes put her arm around her friend and they began to walk through the crowded club. "Let's go have a nice evening." A smile crossed her face as they walked closer to the table.

When Mercedes and Christina finally made it to the table, the girls all got out of their chairs and gave each other a hug. Tessann Chen was the first to hug Mercedes. Her exotic Chinese features and short, spiky black hair could have been on a cover of any high fashion hair magazine. Her petite body was draped in a silk kimono, tied only at the waist, and it displayed her perfect augmentation. Her skin was as smooth and unblemished as her silk dress, and her flat strapless sandals showed off her cherry-red painted toenails with rhinestones.

She backed away from their hug and said, "Gosh, Mercedes, long time—no see! You look terrific!"

Mercedes started to laugh at the last sentence. "How can I look terrific when I'm still wearing my work clothes and I haven't put a comb through my hair since I left the house this morning?"

"Some people are just naturally beautiful. In my eyes, you are one of the lucky ones!" leaning over again, she gave Mercedes a small kiss on her cheek. At that moment, the music began to blast throughout the club. Mercedes could already feel a headache coming on as the rhythm vibrated through the room and the strobe lights began to flash. The disc jockey entertained the crowd. Everyone was eagerly waiting for the band that wasn't going to be there for another few hours. Mercedes had never heard of the band that was booked for the evening. It didn't much matter, because she knew that eventually she would leave and nobody would ever notice, except perhaps the bouncer out front. Smiling down at Tessann, and taking a good look around the room, Mercedes knew it was going to be a long evening. She pulled out the stool next to the table, and was just about to sit on it, when Jennifer appeared at her side.

Jennifer pushed Tessann aside, and could barely get her arms around Mercedes. Her body had changed again in the past few months, and more than Mercedes had imagined. A few months earlier, she had had her third augmentation and so much Botox—making her struggle to smile almost impossible. Her blonde hair was long and woven with hair extensions for fullness. Her body was lithe and firm—more so now, than in high school, and that was because of all of the liposuction. It had become very evident, to all the girls, that her mother's 'dysmorpic disorder' had transferred itself to Jennifer at an early age. Since high school, her nose had been done twice; her breasts three times; her lips were plumped; she had cheek implants; and everything from the neck to her toes had been through liposuction. With her itsy-bitsy dress, stiletto heels, and a neckline that left nothing to the imagination, she wrapped her arms around Mercedes. She looked like a Barbie doll, and prided herself with all the attention her body received. You could see her eyes continuously scanning the room while hugging Mercedes.

Jennifer was standing on the longest legs Mercedes had ever seen. "I've tried calling you for the longest time Mercedes...where have you been?"

Mercedes' eyes went directly to her breasts. "Evidently not to the same places you've been hanging!" Mercedes' sarcasm was back.

Jennifer pushed her two large breasts together and jiggled them. "Don't you just love my 'new girls'?"

Mercedes started to laugh and tried to choose her words wisely. "Yes, it looks like they could be friends with Dolly Parton's!" she said condescendingly.

The music was so loud, Jennifer screamed, "I'm sorry Mercedes, I didn't understand what you said."

"Oh, it wasn't anything worth repeating or anything with great meaning," she yelled back.

Jennifer started to giggle and gave Mercedes a kiss on each cheek, "I wish I could stay and catch up with the girls, but Tommy over there is waiting for me." She turned around and pointed to Tommy, who looked very preoccupied, sliding his body up another big breasted woman. When he finally looked up and noticed Jennifer, he blew her a kiss. "Doesn't he look like Channing Tatum? He's such a hunk!" She tapped her hand-on her breast to simulate a heartbeat.

Mercedes nodded her head in agreement, but what she really wanted to do was gag. "Yes, he does. Well, you have a fabulous evening with 'Boy Toy.' I mean...Tommy Boy, and we will catch up soon!"

"Thanks, Mercedes. I love your boots. Maybe I can borrow them sometime. You know, like when we were in high school!" Those were her parting words.

"Oh...sure," Mercedes said, and she blew Mr. Boy Toy a kiss with her hand!

The music must be getting to me...or was it Jennifer's stupidity?

Years ago, Mercedes finally came to the realization that Jennifer had never matured, or got past the point of high school. She wasn't the brightest of Mercedes' friends, but she was definitely the *'most developed.'* Somewhere along the road, her life had come to a standstill and she never moved past her obsession with beauty. Some people were like that. They could never get past a vulnerable part of their life. Or they just felt the place they had gotten stuck in was more comfortable than moving forward. Jennifer was one of those.

Mercedes turned around and found an empty chair next to Emme Martex at the large table. Once seated, she twisted around, and flagged down a waitress with her hand. When the waitress came over, Mercedes bought a round of drinks for all her friends. Sometime later, the drinks finally made it to the table.

Emme held hers up in front of Mercedes and the girls. Then she gave a short, but sweet toast. "To good friends...." Everyone clinked glasses around the table. Emme doubled clinked with Mercedes and they both sipped their wine.

Lucky for Mercedes, the music had stopped and there was a semblance of peace and quiet, even if it was just for a few minutes. The crowd had filled the small club to capacity. Not an inch of space was unoccupied and the constant chatter of voices began to sound like the hum of a beehive.

Emme turned to Mercedes and shrugged her shoulders. Mercedes got the feeling that Emme could see, in her eyes, how overwhelming this was for her. She was the artist of the group, and you could definitely see that. Every time Mercedes saw her, Emme looked so completely different from the time before. She wasn't tall and she wasn't short—she wasn't paper thin and she wasn't overweight. She wasn't gorgeous, but carried a very unique beauty of her own. There was a distinctive look that separated her from most of the crowd. It was once defined as 'European,' but nowadays, it was considered more of a rocker-grunge kind of look. Coming from a French background, and a family filled with Artisans who migrated from Southern France, she was the most interesting of Mercedes' friends. A slight French accent added to the mystique. Mercedes liked her the best. Mercedes and Emme always got along and nothing ever seemed to get in the way. They were both successful, bright, and the quiet ones of the group. However, she wouldn't call Emme conservative, by any means. As an artist—her style of dress; her sense of color; her need to be different; and her unusual taste in men really separated her from the other girls.

Emme reached over and laid her hand over Mercedes' hand. "How is my sweet friend doing nowadays? It's been a few weeks, and I'm really surprised to see you here," she said with kindness shining in her eyes.

Mercedes took a sip of wine. "I've had better days, but I really can't complain. Work is going great, my refurbished kitchen came out perfect, I'm not addicted to alcohol or drugs yet, and I still have my same old junkie car!" Mercedes laughed, and so did Emme.

"Well, that sounds good to me. I'm on my fourth car in the past two years—two accidents and one stolen!" Emme lifted her eyebrows. "My life constantly seems like it's always changing dramatically, including my cars!"

"Are you still seeing that rocker with the thousands of piercings? What was his name? I always had such a hard time hearing what he had to say, because he always mumbled!" Mercedes bent closer and whispered, "Secretly, I nicknamed him 'Mumbles!'" Emme started to giggle with Mercedes. "I didn't mean that in a condescending way, trust me, it just came out one day in a conversation with Tessann when I couldn't remember his name!"

"That is so funny! I actually did call him 'Mumbles' one day, after Jennifer asked him to quit mumbling, because she couldn't understand a word he was saying—not that she understands or comprehends anything anyone says!" They both started to laugh. "Actually, give *her* a few drinks and I call her 'Mumbles' too!"

Mercedes slapped the table, she was laughing so hard. She began to choke and had to take a sip of her wine.

Emme waited to make sure Mercedes could breathe and then she said, "I'm not seeing Striker anymore. He did too many drugs, and his temper was erratically out of control. He was killer in bed, and a good ride while it lasted!" They both put their hands up for a knuckle-bump. "What about you, Mercedes, are you seeing anyone?" Emme questioned.

Mercedes opened her eyes wide and in a silly voice said, "Who me...? Who'd want an old, plain fuddy-duddy like me?" Emme could see the pain in Mercedes face that went with that response.

Emme pointed her finger at Mercedes and swung it back and forth like a pendulum. "Now, let's not go there again. You've got so much more going for you than you really know. I can't believe how you underestimate yourself. That makes me really sad." Emme produced a sad face to go along with the swinging finger.

"That's not what my mother used to say. She used to call me her worthless 'ugly duckling.' And if that wasn't enough for a young child to swallow, she insisted that my middle name was 'dumbass.' How's that for my initiation into the hard, cold world of childhood?" Mercedes said with tears gathering in her eyes.

"Well, your mother was a fucking lunatic. We all hated how mean she was to you. She was a selfish bitch whose only way to get even with the man who left her was to emotionally hurt his kid. We didn't know that then, but we are old enough, and smart enough, to see that now!" Emme announced with conviction. "Where is that bitch nowadays?"

"I really don't know. I haven't seen her in two years. When I heard from her then, she was living in a trailer, in some God-forsaken desert town, running a pet grooming business. She moves continuously, and I always lose track. Of course, unless she needs money or something that's the only time she ever calls me." Mercedes' eyes opened wide, and she grimaced. "I think my phone number is wired to her checking account. When she is out of money, my phone rings. The last call came when she was going to be thrown out of her trailer and needed some rent money," Mercedes said nonchalantly.

"Did you send it to her?" Emme closed her eyes, scrunched up her face, not wanting to hear the response, but knowing what it was.

Mercedes took a deep breath in, and then exhaled slowly. "Look. She gave me life. That's about all she ever gave me, but I am here because of her. I owe her something."

"Well, you're a better person than me. I would have changed my phone number and let her find her own way out of the hole, like she did for you at seventeen."

Mercedes turned and noticed that Tessann and Christina had lost all concentration on their conversation; instead they were surrounded, with lots of guys competing for their attention.

Mercedes sighed. She needed to change the subject for her own wellbeing. She leaned over and touched Emme's hair. "I just want you to know that you look fabulous tonight. I love the two-tone pink and black hair. That look doesn't work for many people, but I think it fits you perfectly." Mercedes leaned back in her chair and let some of that built-up tension leave her body.

"Oh, that's so sweet. You actually just made my day. My sister did the color and cut a few days ago. I wasn't so sure about the one-shaved side, with the other one really long. The way she blended it came out pretty cool!" Emme began to laugh. "And you know me, I like different and artsy-fartsy!"

Mercedes smiled. "I probably know you better than any one of our friends. And I've respected your choices, and your wonderfully creative approach to life. It makes me wonder how I've survived in this group, with such a conservative attitude and lifestyle." She placed her hands in her lap.

"Don't ever underestimate yourself, Mercedes. Out of all our friends, I find you to be brilliant and strong, and you always know what direction you are going. You never let anything or anyone step in your way, or block your path." Emme looked directly into Mercedes' eyes as though she could see into her soul. "Your conservative approach to life didn't compromise your values, and your moral compass never wavered. You are a rare gem in its own setting."

Mercedes narrowed her eyes and took a sip of her drink. "But I don't have a boyfriend, I work long hours, and I rarely step out of the circle that keeps me a prisoner."

Emme picked up her glass and clicked it against Mercedes'. "I don't have a boyfriend...I work long hours...and I've created my own little circle that keeps me a prisoner." She mimicked Mercedes, but the meaning was head-on! She took a long sip of her drink. "So, how are you any different from me, with the exception of this...?" Emme pointed to her hair and then one by one she pointed to her piercings. She had a small sparkling diamond in her nose, two pierced rings in her eyebrow, a small diamond on her cheek, and two bars of rubies, each about an inch long, bringing her clavicles together below the neck bone. Her ears had more holes and earrings than Mercedes could count. And whatever laid below, or under her clothes, remained hidden most of the time. Not to mention the sleeves of tattoos that were also hidden under her clothing. She was the only one of her friends to completely 'step out of the circle' and make an artistic statement of who she was. And for that, Mercedes really respected her friend. The freedom of 'not caring what other people said' was displayed all over Emme's body.

Emme may have been filled with colored graffiti and steel, but she also was a very astute and successful business woman. Eight years earlier, she had gone to Mercedes for help in getting a small business loan to open her own clothing boutique. With a written foundation and strategy, Mercedes and the bank worked hard to make her dream come true. It was a small-scale clothing shop when she opened it, compared to today. Now, it was not only a successful business—it was one of the hottest and trendiest clothing shops in Los Angeles, and frequented by the rich and the famous. Her shop started with one small store and grew into nearly half of a block on Melrose Avenue. Thanks to Emme's store, the street had become one of the trendiest areas around, over the past years, and it was located right in the heart of L.A.

After a few hours of stop-and-go music, rounds of drinks, and an endless circulation of people stopping at their table, Mercedes was ready to call it a night. Her friends were never without a large rotating group of young men standing around, trying to get their attention. Mercedes sat there the whole night feeling more insecure than she had in a long time. Not once did any of those men stop to talk to her, or draw her into a conversation. Not once was she asked to dance.

Emme looked at Mercedes and said, "Why the sad looking face, my friend?"

Mercedes looked across the table toward Christina and Tessann, and said, "I just think it's time for me to leave. I think I've had enough punishment to last me for the next few months! The past few weeks I've felt this awful depression. And coming here tonight has nearly sent me over the edge. The girls are surrounded by men, and I haven't had a man pay attention to me in years."

Emme looked back at Mercedes. "I don't think you would like any of those young studs who are just looking for a great set of jugs, a one-night lay, without the complication of a relationship. I, personally, know none of them would interest me, so I can't possibly see how they could interest you!"

Mercedes looked at her with questioning eyes. "Why? They all look very handsome and are built like Studly Dudley Do-Right! Maybe, for once in my life, I would like to feel what it would be like to have men vie for my attention."

Emme squinted her eyes and looked deep into her friend's face. "Vying for attention is not enough for you. You need more. You need brains, humor, thoughtfulness, prosperity, and independence." She smiled and paused for a moment. "Every one of those '*boys*' have none of the above. They are all just losers, trust me!"

"Maybe they are. But, for once in my life—I would like to see what it feels like to have all that special attention surrounding me."

"Someday, my friend, you will find your match. But this is not the place he will be." She patted Mercedes on her back and said, "Come on, I've had enough; and I certainly know you have too. Let's get the hell out of here!"

Mercedes hopped down off her chair. "Best idea I've heard all evening, not that anyone can hold a decent conversation in this place with all the noise."

Emme followed and hopped down off her chair, also. "What does the noise have to do with it?" She stood there and looked across the table again. "Most of these people are just here to expose their insecurities. Half of them are 'Trust babies' and have no clue what one day of hard work is really like; and the other ones are 'wannabes' that are filled with fucking bullshit!"

Mercedes walked around the table and hugged Emme. "Thanks for shoving the reality of this place into my face, I need that sometimes!"

They said their goodbyes, as quickly as they could, and pushed their way to the exit. When they finally got to the bouncer at the front door, he looked at Mercedes with dissatisfaction and asked, "How the hell did you get in?"

Emme jumped in front of her friend, looked directly at the bouncer with a fierce angry face, and screamed, "Because your sac of balls doesn't have anything in it except a bunch of hot air. That's what all the women in this place are saying about you! So, go fuck yourself, asshole!" Emme grabbed Mercedes' elbow and with a straight back, and all the dignity she could muster, she began walking toward the valet stand. Mercedes turned around and he was still staring at them—his face was redder than a tomato. She lifted her finger and flipped him off!

four

MERCEDES pulled up into her driveway,

pushed the button and waited for the garage door to automatically open. Exhausted from the long day at the office, and an even longer evening at the club, she leaned over, picked up her purse, opened the car door, and got out.

"Thank God I don't burn the candle at both ends very often," she muttered to herself, barely able to walk into the house.

She opened the door leading into her newly renovated condo and walked in. She had bought her condo five years earlier when the real estate market had busted, and foreclosures were flooding the marketplace at an astronomical rate. The real estate bust had nearly taken down the country, and many people lost their jobs and life savings, along with their homes. It was a greedy time in our country when banks and mortgage companies became deregulated; they took advantage of the false market, and enticed unqualified homeowners with creative financing.

That was just the beginning of this growing bubble. Mercedes was in the banking industry, and tried her best to keep her wealthy clientele clear of the growing bubble.

At the time, it wasn't obvious that the financial structure of our country was headed towards disaster. It wasn't until four years later, that the leading economists finally stepped forward and determined the root of the disintegrating economy. The four main causes were the low mortgage interest rates, low short-term interest rates, relaxed standards of mortgage loans, and irrational greed. Everyone had jumped on the bandwagon. Then, all of the sudden, the housing bubble burst and this caused the whole structure of the economy to go into a tailspin. Some people survived it, others were not so lucky. Mercedes had received a lot of recognition from her employer for steering her affluent clientele away from the imminent disaster. Unfortunately, many of the clients from her office had invested in the stock market and when the economy dumped the stock market plummeted as well.

Mercedes had saved money for years, hoping to put a down payment on a home. With the bubble growing, rising inflation, and prices of homes skyrocketing, it had slowly pushed her out of the real estate market, until the big bust. During that bust, most home prices in California had nose-dived by fifty percent or more. Lucky for Mercedes, this had pushed her right back into the vulnerable market. Investors were snatching up foreclosed homes at cut-rate prices, while banks were holding on to them, to try to recoup their losses.

Mercedes was a first-time buyer with a large down payment, an impeccable credit score, she was one of the fortunate ones who was able to dip into the foreclosure market, and she found her perfect home. It was everything she was looking for, in spite of having to do a few renovations. The price she paid was considered a steal for this desirable area. It was a block from the famous shopping center, *The Grove,* and located in the heart of Los Angeles.

Broken *image*

The condominium complex had offered a lot of amenities, including major security, a pool and spa area, and tennis courts. It was only a few blocks from the trendy area of Beverly Hills, where Mercedes and her friends worked and shopped. It was the perfect location for a young woman of her age, and it gave her access to everything she needed within walking distance. Large malls, great restaurants, movie theaters, and plenty of places to frequent became her playground during the weekends.

Mercedes walked through the door and entered her kitchen. She flipped on the switch and two overhead lights came on. She turned off her alarm, then she put her purse down on her interesting granite countertop. Her kitchen had just been renovated a few months before, and she was glad to get rid of all the dust and mess it had produced. But most of all, she loved her new kitchen and the amazing look the designer had created.

After giving it much thought, Mercedes finally hired an interior designer to help her renovate her kitchen and master bathroom. Even though Mercedes was a very gifted and successful young business woman, none of her expertise centered on interior design. Leigh Rosen, a reputable designer in the area and a friend-of-a-friend, took on the task. Her reputation for meeting all the expectations of her clients was flawless. The one thing that made her stand out from the rest of the designers that Mercedes had interviewed was she liked her clients to put their own personal emphasis or mark into their restoration.

Mercedes wanted a cozy kitchen with a cottage look, like she had seen in a magazine. She asked for an open kitchen, with plenty of light, and a gathering place where she could hang out with all her friends. She didn't want the formal dining room the condo came with; so Leigh had the wall removed and extended the kitchen to make it even larger. Leigh then gave Mercedes a list of antique stores from all over the city, and the task of finding an old piece of furniture for her kitchen island. Leigh loved to mix old with new and create an ambience of decadence; she also wanted Mercedes to take part.

On Mercedes' hunt, she found a perfect large, dark weathered wood buffet. Leigh had her craftsman add a solid granite top. With two drawers and an open area below, it increased the room's storage and brought a homey feel. To keep things warm and cozy, Leigh brought in darker wood cabinets throughout, and granite countertops with ribbons of earth tone colors. The countertops blended with the stacked rock that was used on one accent wall and in the backsplash. The appliances were stainless steel, and the stove was professional, top-of-the-line. Even though Mercedes rarely cooked, she thought it was still a good resale investment.

The mix of warm colors and texture gave the kitchen a comfortable and cozy feel. The stacked rock added architectural character to the space and a beautiful dark table and eight chairs made this Mercedes' comfort zone. With the functional plan, a slight European flair, and a seat for everyone, the new room became the heart of her home— and the life of her party. And although it came with a hefty price tag, Mercedes didn't care. As a child, she dreamed of a place of her own that would finally give her a feeling of security.

Security and stability was something she never had in her childhood. Her mother and her constantly moved around and never stayed in one place too long. Except when she was in high school. After her father had disappeared, Mercedes' mom couldn't find a job. When she finally did, she didn't hold on to it for a very long time. Her mother didn't have an education past the eighth grade, and her skills were very limited. Her abundance of anger issues always seemed to leak into her jobs. This left Mercedes with a very unstable home life, and they were always moving from city to city, from state to state for years.

It was a two-story, three-bedroom home with a decent size yard and a nice size patio. The great room, office/den, and half-bathroom were downstairs. The three bedrooms and two full bathrooms were situated upstairs. The floors throughout the home were dark, textured hardwoods that were there when she purchased the house. Mercedes smiled, as she felt the unevenness of the cool wood floors on the bottom of her feet.

She climbed the circular staircase and when she got to the top, she turned on the hall light. There was a catwalk that went across the whole top floor and allowed everyone to look down into the great room with the massive fireplace, the office, and the entry.

Mercedes entered her bedroom and turned on the light. Her bed was placed diagonally between two walls and became the center of attention with the tall black headboard that towered over the stack of decorative pillows. She used the color black, with splashes of red, to give her room a suggestive Asian ambience. And after almost a year of rummaging through small antique stores, garage sales, and the interior design center in Los Angeles, she was finally done and could not be happier with the results. Her favorite piece in the house was the immense black buffet, centered on a solid wall that faced her bed, with her large flat screen television sitting on top. She had found the buffet at a flea market on Melrose Avenue, a few years earlier, and was determined to make it her *'once-a-year repurpose project.'* It was very heavily carved and quite the unique piece. Mercedes had unknowingly walked by it as Emme and she were combing through seller's stalls filled with one-of-a-kind items. Emme turned and saw it. Instead of buying it herself, she begged Mercedes to consider painting it black and giving it the new rustic grunge look. With a push from Emme, she bought it with the idea that one day she would refinish it and put in her home. Now, nestled in her comfortable bedroom, it looked amazing.

Emme was a very artistic and creative woman that always kept a watchful eye for friends. On many sunny California days, you could catch her frequenting the local flea markets or garage sales. Emme had learned early on, from her mother, how to take something old and repurpose it into something beautiful with just a little hard work and some paint. For years, she watched her mother use her creative intuition to supplement their family's income by reselling refinished furniture. It became a hobby, and something Emme and her mother always enjoyed doing together on the weekends.

Emme had acquired an eye for interesting antiques; and she used it well, in her store, in displays to showcase her clothing and accessories. Her shop on Melrose catered to the trendy, classic vintage customers. When Mercedes and she were out and about, she always looked to pick up fashionable odds and ends like purses, hats, belts. Other times, she enjoyed repurposing small pieces of furniture she sold to the clientele in her store. Half of the clothing merchandise in her popular shop was new. The other half was selectively bought at big estate sales or auctions, usually donated by the rich or famous celebrities.

Mercedes pulled back the comforter on her bed, turned on the light on the night table, and walked into the bathroom. Mercedes loved the large bathroom that consisted of all tumbled travertine. Mercedes called it her 'rock cave.' The light-colored tumbled travertine had the most electrifying veins of black running through it and looked very mystical. Leigh agreed; and even though it was a little more expensive than Mercedes had counted on, there was no hesitation. Now looking at it, Mercedes liked it just as much tonight as she did when she found the sample in the little shop outside of town. The large oval spa-tub, the extra-large shower, and the floors were all done in the stone. Leigh had hired an amazing stone craftsman from Guatemala that customized the entire bathroom. And it was Mercedes' favorite place in her whole house. Sometimes, you could catch her relaxing in the tub filled with bubbles, just appreciating her beautiful rock room.

Tonight, she was having a tough time, and even in the sanctuary of her own home, she felt on edge. It had been a lousy day; and one of her clients had given her a hard time over interest rates and he wouldn't let up. When she finally did leave work, she had skipped dinner and then decided to punish herself more by going to the crappy nightclub with her friends. By the end of the evening, she was thoroughly depressed, and felt like the weight on her shoulders was insurmountable. Her friends, who were so wrapped up in their own good time, never realized her discomfort, except for Emme. Christina and Tessann had a constant flow of male testosterone surrounding them. They danced all night and there was always a drink in their hands, from some admirer. They were doused in attention and loved every minute of it. On the other side of the table, Mercedes sat quietly, listening to the music and getting more and more depressed, until she had had enough and finally decided to leave. She was thankful for Emme keeping her company, otherwise the rejection would have been more than she could handle.

Mercedes walked up to the sink and bent over and looked in the mirror. With pain shining in her eyes, she touched her crooked nose, and a tear began to slide down her cheek. *"Why had God given me brains, but skimmed on my looks?"* she asked out loud.

There was no answer. It was a silent audience, and Mercedes could only question 'why'? It was so painful to be simple, plain, and unnoticed. And yet, she could change her crooked nose. Nothing stopped her from improving her looks, except herself. Wasn't that what her friends kept telling her? *'You have options...'*

"Maybe I will start a diet and lose those twenty pounds that have crept up on me the last five years. Then I will consider having the bump taken out of my nose."

Mercedes opened the drawer in the cabinet and pulled out the bottle of pills. She never took medication unless she really needed it. Even antibiotics and aspirin were on her 'no-go' list. It had been a long time since Mercedes had felt so miserable and overwhelmed. Tonight was one of those nights; she felt an 'obsessing' evening coming on. Years ago at the University, the school doctor had written her a prescription for Xanax. He specifically told her to take it when she felt the need to fixate on negativity. Since her unhappy childhood, she would get in these fits of hopelessness, and obsess about certain areas of her life. It wasn't until one evening, when she felt this urge to commit suicide, that she forced herself to take a hard look at herself. It also forced her to finally face reality and to see the school shrink. After a few years of intensive therapy, that helped her get through college, she had finally found peace with most of the rejection that her mother had wrapped around her young shoulders.

She hadn't taken a whole pill before, she had always cut them into halves or quarters, and yet tonight, she wanted a good night's sleep. She knew one pill was guaranteed to knock her out for days and tomorrow was Saturday; she didn't have any special plans. She changed into her favorite motorcycle T-shirt, and a pair of pink flannel pants, and brushed her teeth. She washed her face, put on some night cream, and took a pill out of the bottle. Tonight was enough and she didn't want to lay in bed thinking about anything— not her friends, not work, and definitely not some of her hurtful memories. She just wanted to fall into a deep slumber. Without a second thought, she slipped the pill into her mouth, sipped some water from the sink, and turned off the light.

She climbed into bed, wrapped the comforter around her, and fell deep—deep into sleep.

MERCEDES turned over and laid on her back.

She loved her comforter made from down feathers, and how warm it made her feel on cold wintery mornings. This morning, for some reason, she felt physically exhausted, and could barely remember the night before. She knew she had gone somewhere with her 'beautiful' friends, but everything seemed extremely blurry at the moment. She kept trying to shake the cobwebs that seemed to consume her memory. Instead, she just laid there for a few moments in the silence and warmth. At first, she couldn't understand why her alarm hadn't gone off, but then she remembered it was Saturday. She immediately relaxed her shoulders and a big smile crossed her face, knowing this was her free day she could do as she pleased.

Still tired and drowsy, she tried to remember what was on her schedule. *Was there anything important that she had on her calendar today?* Normally she wrote everything down, because her memory just couldn't remember it all anymore.

Her calendar had become her 'bible,' and anything that was important was marked down for God, and her, to see on a daily basis. Why was she having a hard time remembering today?

Life had been chaotic for the past six months. Weekends were just as stressful as weekdays, because of all the construction she had done in her home. The dust was dreadful and the noise was like the constant pounding of a headache. For months, she endured the inconvenience, but in the end, it had been worth it. Her beautiful kitchen and bathroom made her safe haven so comfortable, that most of her weekends were spent relaxing at home in her small garden, or catching up on the movies she missed. Today, the silence was golden. The sun streamed in her window and she raised her arms above her head and gave a long, slow stretch. Outside somewhere, she could hear a dog barking. Then it stopped.

She smiled as she listened to the silence. Odd, she never heard a dog bark before. She wondered if someone in the area had gotten a new dog, or if she had just been too busy to hear it before.

Mercedes didn't have any animals to take care of. She always loved her friends' pets, but for her, the responsibility was overwhelming. Having another living being to be accountable for was something she knew she wouldn't be good at. Her life had always been filled with spontaneity, so the thought of having to live on a schedule was scary to Mercedes. Especially an animal that depended on his master to be fed, bathed, and walked. Big or small—it didn't matter. Cat or dog—it was still a liability. So her devotions to enjoying animals had her spending a day at the zoo, or enjoying her friends' pets from time to time.

Amongst all her friends, they had a menagerie of pets. Christina has one of the littlest Chihuahuas that Mercedes had ever seen. 'Nippy' was seven inches tall and weighed barely two pounds, but he was named 'Nippy' for a reason.

Broken *image*

The minute you walked into Christina's house, he constantly nipped at your heels. For a small dog, he made quite a bit of noise and backed that up with a bite that could draw blood. That pampered pooch went everywhere with Christina, except the nightclubs.

Tessann had a male Siamese cat, *Seal Point*, that Mercedes thought was absolutely beautiful. Its piercing light-blue eyes caught your attention immediately and that was why she named him 'Blue.' He would stand at the door until she would let him go outside and check out the wildlife and hone his hunting skills. On a good day, he would bring home a dead bird or lizard and leave it at the front door. The first time Mercedes saw a dead animal laying by Tessann's front door, she knew that cats would not be her pet of choice either.

Emme, by far, had a menagerie of animals that floated in and out of her life. At one time, she had two identical cats, but they wreaked havoc in her house, shredding almost every piece of furniture. Another time, Emme had a miniature pot-bellied pig, named 'Miss Piggy.' Mercedes thought she was adorable, but the smell in the house was more than Emme's friends could handle. Miss Piggy was supposed to be a miniature, by no means was small, and she was growing at a rate that any butcher shop would consider her 'prize bacon!' She was litter box trained like a cat, but her snout was into everything. Her playful rampages knocked off cabinet doors, pulled up the carpets, and her favorite thing was rummaging through all the trash cans. Eventually, she became more than Emme could handle and she wound up at some farm outside of the city. Emme had learned lots of lessons involving her pets. Over the past few years, she had gone to the zoo many times with Mercedes when she needed her 'animal fix.'

Mercedes thought she would get up and go to the deli for breakfast and then head over to Emme's shop. She had promised Emme for weeks that she would stop by, so today seemed like a good day to do it. Besides, she thought, maybe she should treat herself to something new to wear. Emme had a great eye for fashion, so that was the perfect place for her, but not before she fed her addiction to coffee.

Dressed in faded jeans, a turtleneck sweater, and a casual jacket, Mercedes walked out the door. Her favorite deli was down the street, and in a trendy little shopping center. It was a hangout for most of the locals; and the owner was a charismatic and attractive young man a little older than Mercedes. On occasion, when the place was not busy, he would come over and talk with her. They had a lot in common; and for some reason, Mercedes always got shy around him. Especially last year when she came in for a quick cup of coffee and she noticed he was no longer wearing his wedding band. The year before when Mercedes first started to frequent the deli, he had worn the shiny gold band and Mercedes had once made a comment about the beautiful lattice pattern. Now it was gone, and so was the beautiful young woman, who on occasion, had been sitting in the back booth.

Divorce was pretty common in the younger generations. They didn't know how to hold a marriage together, nor did they try. They were too busy with their fast-paced lifestyles, and had too many distractions in the real world to keep them from trying harder. Out of all Mercedes' friends, only two were in committed relationships. How committed? One never knew, not until the nasty rumors began to circulate.

Jennifer was married once, for a short time, when she was very young. Paul was the quarterback of the high school football team. When Jennifer got her augmentation her junior year, not a single boy in school could keep their eyes off her—including Paul. They dated for a year, and when he went off to play football for a nearby University, she followed. The next year they got married, but their lives never settled down. He was in the spotlight, on the football field, and she was jealous. To make up for her insecurities, she continued down the path her mother had taken. The more 'beautiful' she became, the more fights occurred. For those two years, he constantly battled the men who would vie for her attention, in spite of the fact she was married— and she couldn't curb her flirtatious nature. Finally, one day, she moved back in with her parents and the marriage was over.

Christina was engaged once, for a long time, but Jorge never seemed to be able to finally commit himself to a marriage. He was a sports fanatic who loved to watch and play soccer and football on the weekends with his friends. Christina didn't like outdoor sports; she was too busy, clubbing, dealing with a hangover, to even notice that he had packed his bags and moved out one weekend.

Tessann liked to swing both ways, and was having too much fun in the single life. She loved to travel, loved to meet people, and had never found that right person to make a solid commitment. Alisha was a different story, she came from a very large, close-knit family. She was the most solid of all the girls. Her family values gave her stability.

Alisha and David had been college sweethearts. For nine years, they had been in a very solid relationship. They bought a house together, lived together, had a baby together, but never married. Alisha was a good mother; and Mercedes loved their two-year-old daughter, Makayla.

Emme was the most interesting of the girls. She'd been in a lot of superficial relationships, but never found the right guy. Most of them were either drug addicts, alcoholics, unemployed, or they had heavy anger-management problems. At first, it seemed like she found the men that needed to be 'saved.' Other times, it seemed she was just had bad taste. Emme had a personality and lifestyle that was definitely not conservative, nor did she fit in with the doctors, lawyers, or businessmen. Her tastes gravitated toward a very diverse group of men from Hollywood rockers, wannabe movie stars, or motorcycle clubbers.

She was a dedicated business woman whose success had spoiled many of her relationships, because of her unrelenting commitment to her popular store—Rags. Her dedication and commitment to Rags left little time to delve into a deep relationship—with her headstrong and very opinionated personality, most men just backed off. For Emme, she could care less if she had a man in her life; she was just one of those happy people who could find pleasure in just about anything she did.

Most people judged Emme visually, by her tattoos and piercings, but that wasn't really a fair analysis of who she was. She looked hard and tough on the outside, but underneath, she was by far the most sensitive and giving of Mercedes' friends. She was always there for friends, strangers, anyone who needed a helping hand or kind words in their hour of need. She was the chairman of an annual charity event that donated its proceeds to sponsor children that lived in crime-infested areas, and fed the old and the hungry. She believed that young children were the only innocence left in the destruction of the world's crumbling morals—and that circumstances sometimes dragged them into a life of crime and hatred.

Her neighborhood and the people that lived within it were important to her, and during any holiday, you could find her in the soup kitchens, serving and cooking for those in need-Emme's charitable acts of kindness continued to grow more and more with all of the great success she was experiencing.

Mercedes walked those three blocks with a bounce in her step. She opened the deli door and walked in. There were only two open seats at the counter, so she walked over and took one next to an older man who was reading a newspaper. She sat down and pulled out her cell phone from her purse. Like almost everyone in the small deli, they had their cell phones either in their hand or right next to them, on the table. It was a new way of life for the younger generations. No one was talking on the phone because posted on the wall in big, bold black letters was a sign for all to see: 'Please put your phones on vibrate if you need to talk . . . GO OUTSIDE! Thank you, Saul's Deli Management.'

Mercedes loved that sign because it assured her that some idiot would not be screaming into his cell phone and creating a major disturbance in the restaurant while everyone was trying to enjoy a meal.

Josh came over and took his pencil from behind his ear, pulled out his small pad of paper, as though he was going to take her order. "Morning, Mercedes. Nice to see you today. Looks a little brisk outside, but I bet it turns into a beautiful day," he said.

"Nice to see you too, Josh! Looks like you're having a typical Saturday morning rush." Mercedes smiled as she glanced around the room.

"I think just about all my regulars have been in this morning, including you! You want the same as you usually have?" he asked.

"Of course, I'm a creature of habit. Nothing changes with me, except my underwear!" For some unexpected reason, that comment popped out of her mouth of its own volition. Mercedes laughed, and then her face turned bright red. *Why did I say that?* she silently questioned herself.

Josh started to laugh out loud, attracting some attention. "You are too funny. Right when I think I have finally figured you out, you throw in a zinger like that!" He casually placed his hand on her back and patted it.

The hand on her back nearly sent her over the edge. Mercedes held up the menu to cover her face. "I will have what I always have, a cup of cappuccino, toasted bagel and maybe I'll 'eat a little crow.'" Sometimes she enjoyed her, 'colloquial idioms.'—*Eating a little crow fit into her vocabulary a lot lately.*

He was laughing even harder now. Josh pulled the menu from her hand and tucked it under his arm, and then he said, "Then you won't be needing this to hide behind. Let me go to the kitchen and see if I can find that 'crow!'" He walked away, laughing out loud to himself.

Sometimes I actually think he is flirting with me. Why would he play with me that way when he could have anyone of these gorgeous, hopeful starlets that come into his deli?

His deli was the hangout for all the hopeful beauties who came to Hollywood, waiting for their big break into the movie industry. Like everywhere in Los Angeles, it was filled with struggling actors and actresses—except for Mercedes. She had found her place in the world, and was very happy where she was at.

When Mercedes was done with breakfast, she went up to the cash register to pay. She handed him a credit card and smiled. "Thank you."

"It was nice seeing you this morning," Josh said, handing her credit card back to her.

Mercedes blushed slightly, "I bet you say that to all the regulars."

He came from behind the counter and leaned against the front and relaxed his body right next to Mercedes. "Nope, only the ones I find interesting."

"Well, that leaves almost everyone who comes into this place. It's a Mecca of 'interesting people.' That's why I hang here!" Mercedes laughed and started to walk away. Then she turned around, "Best 'cappuccino and crow' in town!" She walked out the door and headed down the street. Josh just stood there and stared for a second, and then the biggest grin splashed across his face.

Mercedes walked down the boulevard with a smile on her face. He was so cute, but so untouchable. *He could have anyone he wanted,* thought to herself. *I bet his bed is filled with beauties from all over Los Angeles.*

Mercedes had almost reached her destination as she walked along the street in the warm sun and passed a few of her favorite places. The outdoor flea market, on Melrose Avenue, was filled with lots of vendors and buyers. Mercedes enjoyed walking through the market with Emme. For hours, they would browse through all the new and used items. Mercedes couldn't help it as she drifted toward one of the vendors who faced the street. It was a merchant who sold all kinds of cheeses. Mercedes knew what Emme's favorite cheese was, so she purchased a block of cheese and a French baguette. She loved to surprise her friends with thoughtful little surprises, and today was no different.

Mercedes stood in front of the popular clothing boutique, Rags. It was located on one of the most famous streets in Los Angeles and it attracted tourists from all over the world. She loved to look in the big storefront windows that had the most artistic displays, catering to the new wave of younger generations. She opened the door and walked in, listening for the bell that let the salespeople know a customer had just entered the store. Rags was filled with shoppers and Emme was standing behind the counter with a customer. When the bell rang, Emme looked up and a big smile spread across her face. Within seconds, she called over a salesperson to help her customer, so she could go greet Mercedes.

Emme jogged up to the front of the store and hugged her friend. "What a wonderful surprise, Mercedes. I'm so glad to see you. You look fabulously happy today."

Mercedes settled her eyes on Emme. "I look fabulous? You must need new contacts!" Mercedes handed Emme the bag with the cheese and baguette. "If you have a bottle of wine, we could have a little party. It's not too early to drink, is it?" Mercedes giggled.

"No! That sounds great. I think I have a bottle a customer brought in a few weeks ago." She grabbed Mercedes' hand and tugged her toward the back where there was a small employee lounge.

As they were walking toward the back of the store, the front bell rang again. Emme, out of habit, turned around to see the new customer. A big smile lit up her face, then she stopped walking. "She's right on time for our party."

"Who's in time for what?" Mercedes turned around to see who Emme was waving to. "Oh, we are having a party, and look who's here!" Alisha walked up and gave each of the girls a hug.

"Wow, Mercedes. I'm so happy to see you. You look fabulous!" Alisha said.

"Oh brother, you guys had this planned, didn't you?" Both of the girls looked confused. "First Emme says I look fabulous and now you!" Mercedes started to laugh.

"If we planned something, you would know it! And I meant what I said...you do look fabulous and it's nice to see you're not in hibernation mode." Alisha said with sincerity.

Emme took both of the girls' hands and started walking to the employee lounge. "I'm so glad you're here Alisha. I've been dying to see you and see how things went. Plus, I got some new clothes in that I think you'll love."

Mercedes looked puzzled. "How things went? What did you do or where did you go now? Did I miss something?"

Mercedes and Alisha sat down on the couch, and Emme went to get the wine. Mercedes opened the cheese and yelled across the room, "Bring a knife and plate for the cheese, Em!"

Alisha was part of their group, a stunningly beautiful girl who had a white mother and a black father. Her light-brown skin was flawless. She was taller than the other girls and could have been a double for Halle Berry. Her big blue eyes and long straight hair fit her complexion perfectly. She was engaged to David and they had a two-year-old daughter who took after Alisha.

Emme entered the room, this time carrying three glasses of wine and a cheese plate and knife. She handed the girls a glass and then sat down on an overstuffed chair.

"Well..." Alisha began.

Mercedes look confused again. "Well...what? Gosh! Why do I feel like I'm in a dream?"

Emme started to laugh, at the same time, she got up and put her face really close to Alisha's. "I think he did an awesome job!"

"Awesome job?" Mercedes stood up. "Okay I'm leaving...you guys are making me nuts today!" She put her hands on her hips and said, "Well...what the fuck are you talking about?"

Alisha and Emme started to giggle. "Alisha had her nose done a few weeks ago...doesn't it look great!"

"What..." Mercedes plopped down on the couch and took a better look. "Wow, it's perfect now..." she sighed. "But then I thought it was perfect to begin with."

Emme ran her finger across Alisha's improved nose. "How does David like it?"

Alisha shrugged her shoulders and laughed, "I don't even think he cared one way or the other, or if he did, he didn't say anything! It was me who hated the small bump on the bridge and my flared nostrils."

Envy shined in Mercedes' eyes. "Who did it? The doctor you work for? He did a wonderful job. I wish mine didn't look so crooked and have a big bump on it. Look..." She turned her profile toward them and sadness dimmed her eyes.

"How many times have we told you, if you're not happy with your nose, to have it corrected? You know I work for the best Beverly Hills cosmetic surgeon there is, and he's willing to give you a discount!"

Emme turned to Mercedes and took a sip of her wine. "How many times have I said, 'have the bump taken out,' hmm?"

"Well, I just am too scared to do any of that stuff. You girls do it on a daily basis and that's just not who I am." Mercedes sighed again.

Emme took her hand and squeezed it. "But you've hated your nose forever. It's just a simple procedure...."

Alisha stood up and angrily crossed her arms on her chest. "That's it! I'm setting up an appointment for you to see Jeffrey! He's the best, and it's really an easy procedure."

"No, I don't think so. After nearly thirty years, I've become used to this bent nose with big nostrils that flare like a horse, with its bump the size of Mount Everest!" Mercedes exclaimed.

"Really...?" Emme probed.

Mercedes took a bite of cheese and smiled.

Six

MERCEDES stood up and starting pacing around the waiting room. "Oh, for Heaven's sake, sit down, Mercedes!" Emme interjected.

Jennifer was sitting in a chair next to a table piled with magazines. "Yeah, it's going to be fine. I've had two of them and look at me, I survived!" Jennifer pointed to her nose.

Emme started to laugh and she said, "You've had two or three of everything, and now you look like Barbie!"

Mercedes' eyes opened wide at Emme's comment and stopped pacing. She knew what was coming next.

Jennifer stood up and looked angry. "What's wrong with looking like Barbie?" she demanded, pouting with her huge lips that were filled with Restylane.

Alisha came around the corner to stop the bickering. "Hey, knock it off, or I'm afraid Mercedes will dart out of here." She halted Mercedes and patted her back.

The nurse came around the corner and announced her name, "Mercedes Simon." She looked at all the ladies and smiled.

They all stood up at once and stepped forward, except for Mercedes. She remained rooted to the spot.

"I only want Mercedes!" the nurse declared with in slight agitation.

Everyone else sat down and waited for Mercedes. Mercedes finally took a deep breath and approached the nurse.

"Follow me. We're going to prep you and then you'll be done in a few hours or so. The rest of you scoot out of here. Leave your cell numbers and we'll text you when she's done."

Mercedes started to slowly follow the nurse. She ran her finger along her nose, felt the crooked bump, and then she turned around and waved. "If anything happens to me...."

Emme stood up and pointed. "Go."

Mercedes was groggy and felt like she was in a dream. Emme was quietly sitting in a chair next to her bed in the recovery room, holding her hand.

The nurse walked in and went to the bed. "Okay, Mercedes, it's time to wake up," she murmured soothingly.

Mercedes opened her eyes and whispered, "I don't feel any pain. I just feel like I have a stuffed nose."

Emme smiled as she stood next to the bed. "That's because it is stuffed—with gauze—and you're heavily drugged.

Alisha smiled at Mercedes and said, "Don't worry, you're going to feel a little groggy because the complete anesthesia hasn't worn off."

Mercedes lifted her hand slowly toward her face. Emme pushed it down to her side and gave Mercedes a stern look. "Your nose is stuffed with gauze, so don't try to breathe through it. And...don't touch it or try to take it out."

Dr. Jeffery Schwartz came in and sat down next to the bed. He had a big smile on his face as he began to explain the procedure. "Everything went picture perfect! I used the 'open' technique for your surgery. I made a small incision in the columella. That's the bridge of skin between the nostrils, and another incision inside the nose. Everything looked great. I took a better look at that bump when I directly opened the bone and cartilage of the nose. Then I manipulated the shape and made the nostrils smaller. I think you're going to love your new nose." He patted her hand that still had the IV tube in.

"You doctors always seem like your speaking in a foreign language! All I care about is if you straightened it and got rid of that lousy bump!" Mercedes whispered.

"I did exactly that!" he said reassuringly. "I'm glad you took off next week. That will give you a full ten days to recover. After that, you should be completely back to normal. Besides, Christmas is around the corner, and you can get a little shopping in, providing you don't do too much and don't mind walking around with a taped nose."

Still unsteady, Mercedes raised her hands and felt her bandaged nose. "What about this?"

Dr. Schwartz smiled and said, "Nasal sutures are usually in place for five days. I also placed a plastic splint and tape on your nose to support the new shape and prevent bruising and swelling." He touched the nose lightly. "I've packed your nose with gauze and I'll take that out in a few days. You will have bruising and swelling, but this can usually be covered with makeup. Improvement will be seen early, but it may take up to a year, or longer, to see your final result."

"What? A year? Really?" she stuttered.

"I tell that to all patients, but usually it takes just six weeks to get a pretty good result." He patted her hand. "Look how great Alisha's nose looked after only a few weeks!"

Emme stood behind the doctor and said, "I bet you're going to look awesome!"

He lifted his fingers and touched around her eyes, "Why don't we set up the appointment to return in a few days and we'll take out the gauze and take off the bandages," his voice was assuring. "And we should put some Botox around your eyes and forehead to relax the muscles around the nose." He raised his hands in surrender. "I know how you feel about any kind of cosmetic stuff; I'm just making a suggestion. Think about it."

"Botox. Really?" Mercedes questioned, sounding skeptical.

Emme stepped forward and so did Tessann. "Oh, for God's sake, Mercedes, you live in the caveman days!" Tessann teased. "All of us have been doing Botox for years! You're the only holdout! It'll stop your crow's feet that are accumulating around your eyes that I've been noticing lately."

Mercedes' eyes opened a little wider, even with the bandages hindering them. "You have? Well, I have noticed them too, but I'm not as neurotic as you guys with appearances!"

Dr. Schwartz stood up and threw his hands up in the air again. "Whoa...I'm out of here. You ladies can hash all this up with each other. I don't want any part of it." He started to laugh as he exited the room. Just before he was out of sight, he turned around and said, "Just let my staff know what you want to do before you come in so we have enough time to do it!" He held up his hand and waved. "Bye, ladies!"

Emme, Tessann, Jennifer, and Alisha all looked at her simultaneously, and then Mercedes said with an edge of anger, "The next thing you ladies will tell me I need to do is plump out my lips!"

Jennifer stepped forward and said excitedly, "What a great idea! Your lips are so slim that they are almost nonexistent! They say, as you get older, you lose them!"

Mercedes was really angry now. "Really...Jennifer? You can't be that stupid to think that! I'm only twenty-nine, so where do 'thin lips' and 'older' fit into this conversation." Mercedes tried to sit up and laid back down. "Will someone please help me get dressed before I scream!"

Mercedes was sitting in her kitchen having coffee. It had been a long six days of just lounging around, and recuperating from her surgery. She was never one to sit around idly and do nothing, so Mary, her secretary, secretly brought over some work Mercedes could do. The first time she came over, she didn't tell anyone in the office, because she knew that Mercedes didn't want them to know why she had taken a personal week off. But after a few days, Alexi called to make sure she was okay and not on her deathbed. Mercedes was excited when he called, and tried not to show it. She was also saddened that Michael and Zackary hadn't made any effort to check on her.

Mercedes picked up the phone. "Hello."

The male voice on the other end of the phone sounded concerned. "Hello, Mercedes, this is Alexi. I was calling to see how come we haven't seen you at work in a week. What's up? They said you took a personal week off. I got pretty nervous, because in the four years I've been at the office, I can't remember you ever taking one day, let alone a whole week off!"

Mercedes laid back on the couch and closed her eyes and smiled. He was right, she had never taken a sick or personal day off in years. "That's cool of you to call, Alexi. I'm doing fine. Since I hadn't heard from Michael or Zackary, I figured you guys were doing just fine without me!"

"Well, you know Michael and Zack...they are both in a world of their own, and only come out when it's something they need or want. I try to do better than that," he said humbly.

"Thank you, I appreciate your call, and most importantly, your honesty."

In a low, kind voice he said, "I heard a rumor that you had surgery. If you did, I sincerely hope it went well and wasn't anything serious."

Mercedes laughed out loud. "Alexi, I didn't have brain surgery, or an amputation! I've had a hard time breathing at times, because my nose was once broken. This week the doctor just fixed my septum and got rid of the little bump while he was doing that."

Sounding relieved at her answer, he teased, "Little bump? It actually looked like a huge mountain!" He started laughing.

Mercedes' face turned bright red at his hurtful remark and she remained silent as a form of punishment.

Alexi stopped laughing and in a serious voice he said, "I hope you know I was just teasing you, Mercedes." There was another long pause then he said, "In all honesty, I never noticed any bump. I always thought you had a really nice nose."

"I've been extremely sensitive about it lately and that is why I decided to do something. But thanks for the apology," she said in a low, deep voice.

After a slight awkward pause, he asked, "When are you coming back to work?"

In a very serious tone, she quietly said, "I resigned last week!"

"What...!" was the only word he yelled into the phone and the outburst could be heard across the room.

Mercedes began to giggle. It was her turn to tease. "Are we even now?" After another slight pause, she said, "I'm coming back this Monday."

At this moment, a restrained voice blurted out, "I always knew you had a mean streak in you. That was really mean!"

She took her last sip of coffee, and walked over the dishwasher and placed her glass inside. "Who plays fair anymore? Definitely not you guys at the office."

Alexi didn't comment on her question, he just said, "I'm glad everything went okay and I can't wait to see you at the office soon. And, of course, your new nose!"

"Why, did you miss me? Or just the knowledge I bring to the office." Mercedes knew how to throw 'zinger comments' around when she wanted to.

He acknowledged her comment, "Both! Enjoy your days off, your desk is stacked with work! So get your track shoes out!"

"Thanks for the heads-up. See you Monday." She hung up the phone. She knew she would have piles of work on her desk. None of the men in the office ever put themselves out to help her, unless she asked for it—and she wouldn't.

Alexi Alferov was more considerate than her other two coworkers. He was a brilliant young Russian immigrant that had lots of responsibilities, besides working long hours. Four years earlier, just when his life was beginning to take shape, everything fell apart. His parents died in a car accident in Russia while visiting their families, and now he was raising his two sisters by himself. The entire office had been stunned. Only Mercedes had stepped in to lend a hand with his workload, while he tried to reorganize his life. The last four years had become extremely complicated. At the beginning, he held down two jobs because his parents had left behind no assets. His parents were hardworking people who had come to the States to make a better life for their children. It was hard enough losing the parents he loved. It was even harder trying to support and put both his sisters through college. With impeccable work ethics, and a steady income, his life-saving survival tools had finally gotten him over his crisis. Fortunately for him—his two younger sisters still retained some of their parents' Russian values, and they both did what they could to help.

When he started at the office, Mercedes noticed that he was also the most sensitive of the three male coworkers. He was the only one who appreciated the help that Mercedes gave him when he had a problem with a client, or he needed a favor. Sometimes he would ask Mercedes to cover for him if a family emergency came up, or he got behind in his work—she was always there to help. He, in turn, would help Mercedes when he had a chance. Like when her car was being repaired. That whole week, without fail, he picked her up and took her home from work, even though it meant going out of his way. Michael and Zackary could care less, and their suggestion was that she take a bus. It was an unbalanced office, and there was still the good ol' 'boys club' mentality, and Michael and Zackary only included Mercedes when it was required of them.

Michael Lu was spoiled and pampered by his overindulgent Chinese parents. They immigrated to this country with great wealth just before Michael was born. With an ego the size of Mount Everest, he maintained his bragging rights to his dual citizenship, and his million dollar high-rise apartment on Wilshire Boulevard in the heart of Beverly Hills. *Spoiled and a playboy*, is how Mercedes would characterize him, but he was also brilliant in the business world and knew exactly how to play the game with his clients. He didn't like working, and would have preferred to be a partying playboy, but his parents had threatened to cut off his inheritance if he did not maintain an honorable position within the bank.

On the other hand, Zackary was a wannabe. He came from a middle-class family, with six siblings and two working parents, who barely made ends meet. He was very envious of Michael. Yet they were great friends who loved to party and have a good time. When Zackary was hired in the group, he maintained two jobs for over a year. He was drowning in student debt, and continuously pushed to build his clientele to where he could afford to quit his second job. For over a year, he went from the long hours in the office to waiting tables in a small restaurant in Hollywood. That was five years ago, and now since his clientele list was overflowing, he was content that he had more free time to enjoy the finer things in life. On Friday and Saturday nights, he and Michael kept up a very active social life outside of work. Clubbing was the rage for their generation of fast-movers and shakers—and they belonged to that group. The music and alcohol never stopped until the clubs closed, and sometimes it even continued until the next day.

Mercedes remembered many times when Michael and Zackary would come into work barely functional. For a while Mercedes considered them functioning alcoholics, but she never said anything. Everyone noticed, but nobody said anything when they watched the coffee and Visine begin nonstop. They were party boys who knew how to balance, but sometimes they still teetered on that edge. Alexi didn't have that luxury of no responsibility, and never tried to keep up. Although they were friends in the office, it never spilled into their social life. Alexi had different principles and obligations.

After hanging up the phone, Mercedes decided she needed to get out of the house for a short time. Christmas was only a few weeks away and she needed to do some shopping. She went upstairs, put some makeup on her yellowing bruises under her eyes and got dressed. The day before, she had gone to see Dr. Jeff. He took off her bandages and unpacked her nose. There wasn't as much swelling as she thought, and what swelling there was had gone down considerably. Looking in the mirror for the final time, she felt good about her decision—she loved her new nose. It wasn't a significant change, but enough to finally make her happy. The bump was gone and her nostrils had visibly slimmed down and the only thing left to acknowledge the surgery was a small butterfly bandage across the bridge.

With hunger gnawing in the pit of her stomach, and with a slight skip in her step, she headed down the street to her favorite deli, looking forward to a cappuccino. It was late afternoon and the traffic was slowly creeping down the city streets. People were walking, cars were honking, and kids were skateboarding down the sidewalks as she enjoyed the city life and the Christmas decorations. She placed her hand on the handle of the door leading into Saul's Deli and pulled it open. She walked in and looked around for a friendly face and a place to sit. At this time of day, it was empty and quiet and she almost had the place to herself.

This is pretty unusual. Most folks must be at the big malls doing their shopping for the holiday. Mercedes thought as she continued to look around.

She took a seat in a small booth and waited for the waitress to come over and take her order.

Out of nowhere, Josh walked up and smiled. He took the pencil from behind his ear and held the order book. "Hey, you, long time no see. Happy holidays to you and yours."

Mercedes' nose was in the menu looking to see what she wanted to order. "Thanks, same to you," Mercedes said and then looked up with a big smile. "It's pretty quiet here today. Where's your waitress?"

He smiled. "What am I...cheesecake?" he teased her. "We had a tough morning, with all the early holiday shoppers, so I gave her an extended break." Looking disappointed, he said, "Do you want to wait for her? She'll be back in a little while. I just thought I'd come over and say 'hi' and take your order."

His disappointed look threw Mercedes off slightly. She blushed and said, "No...No...I...just needed to get out, so I took a walk and thought I would stop in for a cappuccino, and see what's going on at the shopping center. I wanted to stop in that small bookstore down at the end of the center and find a good book to read over the holiday."

"Are you okay, I mean, you look a little different today? Have you been sick?" He moved closer and took a deep look into Mercedes' eyes, as though looking for something. His look of concern was touching and Mercedes slightly turned her head away.

After a few seconds, she turned back and said, "I've been home for a week. I'm not sick...I've had a difficult time breathing lately, so the doctor fixed my nose and that stupid little bump I hated!" She rubbed her finger along the bridge of the nose, looking slightly embarrassed.

He sat down across from her in the booth. "What bump? I thought your nose was perfect. Well, as perfect as any nose could be. Look at my nose. It's been broken three times and it's as crooked as a dog's hind leg!" He pointed to his nose and laughed.

Mercedes started to laugh. "Oh really...well...I have this great doctor...." She was feeling more comfortable and decided to tease him back.

"Nope...I like this big hunk of bone on my face!" He smiled and said very genuinely, "I like your new nose, it looks very nice...And if you're happy, that is all that matters!" He lightly laid his hand on hers.

Feeling a little awkward with his hand laying on hers, Mercedes folded her hands together on the table. "Can I get that cappuccino? It's starting to look and feel a lot like Christmas, and I need something hot to warm me up for my walk to the mall," she said innocently.

His eyes opened wide and his eyebrows wiggled up and down. "I've been known to be hot and warm!" he teased.

Mercedes blushed a bright red. It wasn't like she was a prude or anything, it was just, he was so cute, and she actually was attracted to him. She wasn't good at flirting like her friends, who could jumpstart a man with one sultry look, or cut them to the quick with a sharp word. Mercedes was too naive and inexperienced at the mating game. Her uneasiness always kicked in when she was teased or confronted.

"Look, you're blushing. That's what I enjoy about you, Mercedes. You're not as socially aggressive as most of the women around this area. Had I teased any of my regular wannabe actresses, they would have been giving me a 'lap dance' by now," he said with honesty.

"Well, I hope it's not disappointing to you. And believe me, it has nothing to do with you...it's me. I just never learned a lot of flirting skills because I was too busy living on my own and putting myself through school. I must have missed that lap dance 101 class!" She smiled and her face was hotter than ever, at that moment.

He laughed out loud and stood up. "It's getting cold and windy. Do you need a ride home? I'd be happy to take a break and take you home."

"That's very sweet, but I need to stretch my legs, walk over to the mall and do some shopping. That was the whole idea of coming down this way. I've been cooped up for a week." She could see his rejected look.

"One cappuccino and bagel coming up." He walked away and into the back kitchen.

Five minutes later, the waitress came out and delivered her coffee and bagel. When Mercedes was done, she placed her bill with a large tip on the table and left. Josh never came back out front and Mercedes felt slightly disappointed.

She left and walked down the street to the mall. On her walk, she looked up and stared at all the big and versatile billboards that cluttered the street. Billboards were an important outdoor type of advertising in and around the city. Mercedes lived in the trendiest area of town that attracted thousands of tourists, so billboards were commonplace. Companies wanted to reach everyone on the move, and this was their strategic way of marketing their brands. Major companies targeted specific demographic areas, such as income and ethnicity, and where Mercedes lived was the perfect location. Near Beverly Hills, around the corner from Hollywood, was a marketing heaven to these companies to draw in the attention from driving and pedestrian traffic.

Each billboard consisted of beautiful women showing off designer clothes, liquor, perfume, television shows, movies, clubs, and just about anything that was marketable. Although Mercedes had walked by these billboards all the time, it constantly reminded her that 'beauty was what *'turned on'* America.'

The billboards always flaunted sexuality and models for everyone to see. It was what the companies and corporations banked their sales on. Gorgeous men and women paraded their perfect bodies, some dressed, others barely—all exuding sex and beauty to sell products. Everyone wanted to be part of the party, and almost every billboard had that party on display.

Mercedes continued until she reached the shopping center. The festivities were in full swing and the holiday season had fully arrived. From a distance, she could see the large decorated Christmas tree that adorned the middle of the shopping center. Holiday music was drifting through the PA system and people were enjoying the evening under the stars.

It had taken Mercedes a while to acquire that festive feeling of this time of year. In her younger days, her mother never celebrated anything and gifts were nonexistent. While her friends partied and enjoyed what the season had to offer, Mercedes was at home only dreaming of what it would be like. Her childhood didn't allow for the frivolous displays of affection or include celebrations of any kind. This time of year had been hard on Mercedes, and being alone and without siblings, she had no way to vent or any way to change things. Without a backward glance, she blended into the crowds of shoppers and enjoyed the beautiful lights and merriment of the season.

The next day Mercedes busied herself with cleaning up and doing laundry. When the phone rang, she picked it up.

"Hello." Mercedes said.

"Hi, Mercedes. How are you doing?" Alisha asked.

"Oh, I'm doing great. The swelling in the nose and my cheeks is going down day by day. It's really starting to look much better," she said with enthusiasm.

"That's great. I wanted to confirm you're coming in for your final appointment tomorrow. Then Dr. Jeff can release you for work."

"Yep, I have it on my calendar. One p.m. Right?" Mercedes smiled because she remembered she had written it down on her calendar.

"Why don't you come early and we'll go to lunch. There's this really cute little sandwich stand down the street and they have the best tuna melts...yummy!" Alisha asked.

"Sounds great." Mercedes countered.

There was a slight pause. "Listen, Mercedes, I was talking to the doctor and he thinks you should have just a little Botox done between your brows and on the corners of your eyes. Not a lot, just a little. He said he could see the creases deepening in your skin. What do you think?"

Mercedes' hand went to the corner of her eye and felt the creases. "Really? *What ever happened to 'growing old gracefully'?*" Mercedes asked.

Alisha laughed. "That was your mother's generation! Our generation is the 'all about me.' We don't want to age. Seventy percent of our clientele are our age. Most not only use Botox, they use fillers and other stuff. Look...Mercedes, it's only Botox. But...if you don't want it, that's fine. I just needed to book his time out so he could do it."

There was a silent pause. Being put on the spot always ruffled Mercedes' thought process.

"Mercedes, are you there?" Alisha sounded slightly nervous.

"Okay, book me for just a little Botox. What if I have a reaction to it? I heard Botox was a form of 'botulism.' That's a pretty scary word!" She sounded very concerned.

Alisha started to giggle. "First, it is botulinum toxin...big difference. This toxin is non-invasive. Botulism is a form of food poisoning and could kill a person. This is approved now with the FDA and is not harmful. I have it done every time he has extra left over from a patient," she continued, "besides I would never do anything to hurt you...you're one of my best friends."

"I know you wouldn't, but I wouldn't bet a dollar on Christina or Jennifer!" Mercedes chuckled. "Okay, sweet Alisha, I will be there early for lunch." She hung up the phone.

The next day, Mercedes pulled her car into the underground parking structure and found a parking spot. She walked out to the front of the building and waited for Alisha.

While she was standing there, two hands came from behind her and covered her eyes. "Guess who?" the squeaky voice announced from behind.

"My mother?" Mercedes' two words dripped with sarcasm.

"Ewww... that was mean!" Tessann bounced in front of Mercedes and gave her a big hug.

"What are you doing here? Are you going to have lunch with Alisha and me?" Mercedes asked with surprise.

"Yes. I had some time between my clients. Alisha and I usually go to lunch on Friday." She smiled.

Tessann looked stunning in her long black tunic and jean leggings. Her knee-high, black leather boots with six inch heels made her almost as tall as Mercedes. She was one of the most beautiful women Mercedes knew, and she always looked meticulous. Her thick Asian hair was cut geometrically and framed her face to perfection. Her makeup was flawless and her red lipstick highlighted her jet-black hair. Feeling very inadequate at the moment, Mercedes looked down at herself and felt frumpy. She was wearing a baggy pair of jeans, a white ivy-league blouse, and a pair of her favorite penny loafers—without the penny. Her light-brown hair was wavy and hanging a little longer than her shoulders and there was no significant cut or style. The only thing she did do before she walked out the door was put on some mascara. Even now, that was feeling minimal compared to her two attractive friends.

"I'm so glad you could come," Mercedes reached over and hooked her arm into Tessann's elbow.

"I booked light today. I know I'm going out tonight and I didn't want to be exhausted." Then she said disappointedly, "Tomorrow is the one Saturday a month I work. Ugh!"

Mercedes looked at her with questioning eyes. "When did you stop working Saturdays?"

Tessann smiled, "Just recently. I built up my clientele so that I work all week now and have most Saturdays off."

"How is the haircutting biz going? I noticed you were in a big stylist magazine the other day. Bravo for you!" Mercedes clapped her hands together.

"I have some big name stars, but they are always such a pain in the ass and so time consuming. I've learned to stroke more of their egos, than their hair!" Both girls giggled.

Mercedes shook her head. "I get that. This is a tough town to live in. The gigantic egos are a dime a dozen, and man-o-man, some of them are the biggest babies! I have a few famous clients, and I always dread the phone calls, or their need to come in."

Alisha walked up and surprised both the girls. "Hey, did I hear something about babies?" she asked.

Tessann was quick to say, "Not from me, Alisha. I'm on a dating spree with women this month. Babies are impossible!" All the girls laughed. They knew Tessann bounced back and forth, from one gender to another, with her dating games. Mercedes had seen some of her beautiful lady friends and could understand why.

"Well, let's get going, I have to get Mercedes back to the office for her checkup and Botox after lunch!"

Tessann looked shocked, "What...? Botox...? Are you kidding me? Our little lady over here has decided to indulge in a little toxin. Oh my God, she is stepping out of her circle, and dipping into the 'beauty world'?" Tessann started dancing around on the sidewalk like a little leprechaun. "Maybe I can finally get her into my chair and give her a decent hairstyle. Something adventurous, so she doesn't look like an old granny! What do you think, Miss Mercedes?" Tessann stopped her dancing and stood directly in front of Mercedes and starting groping her hair.

Mercedes pushed her fingers away. "I think you had better shut the fuck up before I pick up that small gorgeous body of yours and throw you as far as I can!" She grabbed her hand and started tugging her down the sidewalk. "Come on, I'm hungry now!"

Tessann looked at Mercedes and shook her head. "Botox...wow! I can't wait to tell Emme!" Mercedes rolled her eyes and started walking faster.

Together all three began talking nonstop as they walked down the street.

It was Saturday morning and Mercedes' attempt to sleep in was unsuccessful. After having the week off to recuperate, she was glad she could do some early Christmas shopping today. She was sitting downstairs having coffee in her new kitchen, running her fingers across the different colored veins in her granite countertops and laughing. She was remembering the day when the girls came over to celebrate the new renovation. They were sitting on the barstools with a glass of wine when Mercedes started to boast about her skillfully designed room. As she was chatting about her new granite and running her fingertips across the smooth surface, she inadvertently called it 'orgasmic!' What she really meant was *'organic.'* For months whenever they came over, they loved to tease Mercedes about her slip.

Then one morning, when Jennifer, Christina, Tessann, and Emme were sitting on the barstools having a cup of coffee before they went to the movies—'orgasmic' was brought up again. They were all laughing at Mercedes and her sexual choice of words she used to describe her granite.

Unexpectedly, Jennifer climbed up on the countertop, laid on her back and spread her legs. "How long do I have to wait for the 'orgasm,' Mercedes?" She stuck her hand down her pants and playfully vibrated it back and forth. Ten seconds later, she sat up and said in her sexiest voice, "You're right, Mercedes, that was the most amazing experience!" Then she started laughing so hard she got the hiccups.

The girls were hysterical at the crazy antics of their friend. They looked at each other, and didn't know whether to believe Jennifer, or if she was just joking. Jennifer was not 'the brightest bulb in the bunch,' and they all knew that. To mix things up a little, she would do the strangest things at the oddest times that completely threw them off balance and added to her charm.

Mercedes always looked at Jennifer with a skeptical eye. She was never sure if she was totally brainless, or if it was just an act she hid behind. Usually she placed her on the side of brainless. However, every once in a while, a reasonably intelligent woman would peek out. That morning Mercedes began to question her highly amusing actions again. *Could she be fooling everyone? Was there something behind that façade? But why would she hide?* One day Mercedes was going to put her through the gauntlet and see how she really matched up.

Mercedes got up, rinsed out her coffee cup, and put it into the dishwasher. She wasn't really a neat-freak. She actually thought she was an interesting creature of habit, because she had a cleaning lady once a month to dust, vacuum, and clean. The ridiculous part was that she pre-cleaned the house the day before—for hours. Emme would laugh at Mercedes and ask her why she had someone to clean it if she cleaned it herself. She never had a good answer. It was just something she felt compelled to do, and that was just who she was.

Mercedes got dressed and walked down to her favorite deli. She walked in and ordered a cappuccino to go. Josh walked out of the kitchen and nearly bumped into her.

"Good morning, Mercedes," he said politely.

Mercedes thought he appeared a little distant by his distracted look. "Hey there, Josh. How's it going?"

He nodded his head and walked off. Mercedes tapped her hand like a drum on the cashier counter while she waited for her coffee. When she saw Josh coming toward her again, she hooked his elbow and forced him to stop. "You're not angry with me, are you?" she looked very confused.

"No, not at all. I just have some heavy crap in my life with my ex-wife, and I'm pretty distracted right now. Sorry."

"Anything I can say or do?" She tried to lift her eyebrows but they wouldn't move. The Botox had numbed her whole forehead.

Josh squinted his eyes to take a better look at her brow. Then he laughed out loud. "I used to love when your eyebrows lifted and caused that little crease on your forehead. When did you get the Botox?" He looked closer. "Must have been recently, I can see the little needle holes that run along the ridge of your brow and down the corners of your eyes." He touched it with his finger.

"Caught in the act. My girlfriends talked me into it yesterday. I went kicking and screaming." She looked away, not wanting him to make judgment.

"Well, I've got to go, lots to do today. It's beautiful outside, I hope you enjoy the day." And he took off.

Mercedes felt empty with all his curt responses, and she was also embarrassed that he actually noticed her change. She thought getting rid of *'those character lines'* in her face would make her more attractive.

She turned around, left some money on the counter, picked up her coffee, and walked out the door. She started walking down the sidewalk and headed toward the hottest shopping center in Los Angeles. The Grove housed a hundred and ten high-end designer stores and more than thirty restaurants, plus the 1941 Clock Tower that was a famous Los Angeles landmark. Its pseudo-European façade, cobblestones, marble mosaics, and pavilions were packed with regulars and tourists, especially on weekends and holidays. It was packed with tourists and locals shopping for Christmas. That didn't bother Mercedes, hanging out at the center was one of her favorite things to do. On sunny

California days, she enjoyed riding the steel-wheeled Red Car trolley. The trolley would carry shoppers two blocks through the farmers market and the large outdoor shopping pavilion. Back and forth, it went slowly and sometimes Mercedes would ride it for hours just watching the people and enjoying the unique area. Mercedes and the girls loved to go there after a tough day at work, or sometimes to browse through some of the most elite stores the area had to offer. Mercedes' favorite place to hang was the three-story bookstore. She would sit in an overstuffed chair and browse through fiction novels for hours, as music floated throughout the store. Walking toward her destination, she knew exactly what she was doing for the next few hours.

Mercedes opened the door and walked into the office. After a week off, she was terrified to see all the work that was piled on her desk. Mary was sitting at her desk sipping on a cup of hot tea.

She looked up as Mercedes walked in. Then she stood up and walked around her desk to greet Mercedes. "Good morning, young lady. Come here, let me take a look at that beautiful new nose of yours!" She bent close to Mercedes' face.

Mercedes looked into her light blue eyes as they scanned her nose. "The swelling is a lot better and my bruising is almost completely gone."

She backed up and smiled. "Yes, he did a great job." She switched to a mock-stern frown and said in a deeper voice, "Sorry. But that doesn't get you off from taking care of all the piles of work you have, dear!"

The door opened and Michael walked in. "Morning, ladies," he said politely. Then he continued to walk toward his office.

Alexi walked into the room and saw both women. He nodded to Michael as he passed him, and stopped in front of the ladies. "Morning, Mercedes, glad to have you back. I'm afraid we've all been too busy to help you with any of your work." He turned and picked something off of Mary's desk, then said, "Nose looks great." He was gone within two seconds.

Mary laughed and shrugged her shoulders, "When I was young that would have been called 'disrespectful.' But your generation is on a fast track to nowhere and so that is acceptable behavior." She sighed and walked around her desk and sat down.

Mercedes smiled at Mary. "I completely agree with you. The men in my generation are spoiled, inconsiderate buffoons! That's probably why I don't date very often."

Mary lifted her eyebrows and asked with humor, "You date?"

The rest of the week was grueling with all the work she tried to catch up on. It was Friday and the office was quiet at the end of the day. Everyone left early, except Mercedes. She had made progress on her backed-up work, but could not see the light yet. She was sitting at her desk when her cell phone rang.

"Hello." Mercedes said as she hit the speaker on her cell.

"Where the hell are you?" Christina's voice screamed through the phone.

"Where I need to be. If you remember, I was off of work for a week and I have a lot of work to catch up on!" Mercedes smiled and sat back in her chair.

"We're all meeting at 'The Club' tonight at nine...you coming?" The background noise was drowning out her voice.

Mercedes lowered her voice, sounding a little guilty. "No. I'm really tired. It was a grueling week."

"Are you fucking kidding me, Mercedes? Don't you ever like to have fun? You're going to dry up and die a lonely old maid. Work can wait and you can sleep in tomorrow. Get your ass to the club!" she demanded as she screamed into the phone over the background noise.

Mercedes looked at the phone and tears began to well. Christina had hit a nerve and it hurt deeply. "Hello... hello...hello...." Mercedes pretended the connection had cut off. She didn't feel like dealing with the girls tonight. She shut off the phone, stood up, picked up her purse, and walked out of the office. When Mercedes got home, she barely made it up the stairs. She went into her bedroom, stripped off her clothes, and was washing her face in front of the mirror.

She tried in every way to make her face scrunch up, but nothing moved. "Oh dear Lord!" A look of incredulity crossed her face. *"How long did the doctor say this stuff was going to make my face motionless?"* she mumbled to herself. Then she looked at her nose and a small smile peeked out. It was something she had wanted to change for years.

She loved her new nose and now her mother could not say anything more to hurt her. Those constant nasty comments about her crooked nose never stopped. Every time she'd see her mother, without fail, she would sit in fear of her destructive comments.

She lit a small candle on her dresser, shut off her light, crawled into bed, and waited for her dreams to take her away from the despair that was slowly creeping up on her.

seven

M ERCEDES' cell phone began to ring and she slipped her arm out of the warm comforter to see whose number was on the small screen.

With a slight smile she said, "Good morning to you, Emme!"

"Wow, you sound in a good mood. I thought for sure you had worked all night!" she said.

Mercedes rolled over and looked at her clock. "Why the hell you calling me at seven a.m.?"

"Because I'm going to drag your ass to the gym with me so we can do a Zumba class. The new instructor is amazing," she sounded excited.

Mercedes sat up in bed and prepared to do combat. She knew what was coming. "I am not going to your gym or any other gym. That is not something I have any desire to do! Zumba, what the hell is that? It sounds like an African war dance!" Mercedes screeched into the phone. "You're not going to hang on a rope, roll all over the floor, or bang on drums like they show on the Dr. Oz show, are you?"

"No, it's like fast salsa dancing! And you don't have to worry, you don't need a partner, because you dance alone!" Emme said impatiently.

Mercedes laughed heartily. "You're so right, Emme. I don't have to worry, because I am not going!"

Emme continued to push Mercedes. "Yes, you are! Don't you think, now that you're turning thirty, you should get into shape and get healthy?"

"I am healthy! I may be just a few pounds overweight, but healthy!" Mercedes pinched the fat around her waist and ran her hands down her thighs. "My doctor told me that just before I had my nose done, so there!"

"I know you're touching those chunky thighs of yours…I'm picking you up at eight, so be ready." Emme hung up the phone.

Mercedes looked at the dead phone, lay back down in bed and groaned. "I am not going to some frickin' sweat hole where I have to compete with all those perfect bodies!" she screamed to the walls. Mercedes flopped back onto her pillows and closed her eyes. Within a few minutes, she opened her eyes and looked at the clock. Immediately, she jumped out of bed and ran into her bathroom to brush her teeth, comb her hair, and find something to wear.

"What the hell am I going to wear? I'm not a gym rat and I don't have anything. Shit!" A whole slew of expletives came out as she rummaged through her closet. She settled for an old, neon orange nylon jogging outfit she bought a few years back when Tessann tried to get her into running in the park.

Mercedes jogged to the door when she heard the incessant pounding. "Okay, I'm coming!" she yelled.

Then she swung the door open and stood there with a big smile. "Good morning," she said in a condescending voice. She stared at her friend, who looked like a model out of a health fitness magazine. She was wearing black formfitting yoga pants, a tight fitting wife-beater T-shirt that exposed her full sleeves of tattoos down her arms, and her bright red hair this week was clipped up on the top of her head and dangled down in all directions.

Emme strolled into the house and stared at Mercedes. "Oh my God, I can't take you to my gym looking like an Orangesicle!" Suddenly she thrust a pair of black yoga pants at Mercedes. "Go put these on with a plain old T-shirt. I picked them up from my store on the way over, just in case!"

Mercedes slammed the door, marched upstairs, and came down minutes later. "Is that better?" she said disdainfully.

"Much! Let's go, or we'll be late!" Emme grabbed her hand and they were out the door.

Two hours later, they were driving in Emme's car after the class. Mercedes was wiping the sweat off her brow with her sleeve. "I feel like I'm going to die, right here in your car!"

"I must say, *'you did keep up with the best'* and I think the instructor was impressed." Emme giggled and patted Mercedes' leg.

"Don't touch me, you bitch. My body hurts all over." A slight smile arched her lips.

"Well, get used to it. And go out and buy some more pants. I'm picking you up every Saturday morning until you drop those twenty pounds you've been bitching about for the last ten years!" Emme slammed on her brakes in front of Mercedes' house. "Get out, I have to get to work! Now you can enjoy your day, my friend!"

Mercedes slammed the door and Emme took off in her sleek black two-seater Mercedes Benz without another word.

The next few weeks went by in a flash. With the New Year just beginning, the stock market taking off again, and the real estate market making a recovery, Mercedes found herself knee-deep in demanding clients. Every day, she came home exhausted and barely able to keep her eyes open. Saturday mornings were spent with Emme, in the Zumba class, in the gym she now belonged to. She was beginning to enjoy the exercise and wasn't sure if it was the endorphins that flowed through her body that made her feel good, or slowly feeling her body begin to shape up.

Emme and Mercedes had just finished their Zumba class and were on her way to Starbucks. "Come on, Mercedes, one little tattoo is not going to hurt you!" Emme laughed.

Mercedes looked at Emme's tattooed body with eyes open wide. "Evidently, one wasn't enough for you! Look, I don't want or need a tattoo, Emme. Isn't going to the gym with you on Saturday mornings enough for you?" she shook her head and clinched her eyes closed, waiting for the constant haranguing.

"Oh, for Christ's sake, you can put it where no one will ever see it." Emme tried to rationalize to Mercedes' negative issues.

Mercedes grabbed the door handle and looked directly at Emme. "I will see it!" her voice raised a few octaves. "And that is one person too many! So take your crap, and leave me alone, or I will open the door and jump out!"

Emme smiled sweetly and said, "You can't because you have a hair makeover this afternoon with Tessann. She charges big time if you miss an appointment, so take your hand off the door handle!"

"Why do all the girls have to come this afternoon? I don't know why you called them. It's only a haircut." Mercedes slowly shook her head. "Everyone always looks at me as if...."

"It's not just a cut— it's a style! And God knows you've needed this for years. How does a person who has beautiful, thick hair like yours, let it hang drably down her face?" Emme pulled into a Starbucks' drive-thru.

Mercedes sat quietly.

"What do you want, a latte or cappuccino?" Emme asked.

"I want to be left alone...." She turned her head toward the window as tears gathered.

Hours later, all the girls were sitting in the high-tech beauty salon where Tessann worked. Zoe's Salon was located in the high-end neighborhood of West Hollywood, a few blocks away from Beverly Hills, and just down the street from Mercedes' house. Zoe's was a well-known salon that catered to exclusive clientele, and at any time, you could catch celebrities enjoying one of its many services. Zoe's was recognized in the fashion industry for its artistry and trend-setting styles that were constantly splashed across the covers of fashion magazines.

Tessann had been there for years, and was part of a group of elite hairstylists that were regularly recognized for their unique and edgy cuts. She loved her work, and her wealthy and famous clientele were just the perks of her trade. For years, she had tried to get Mercedes into the salon for a new trendy cut, but Mercedes was happy with just a shoulder length blunt cut. It was an easy cut to take care of, and had very little maintenance. Mercedes was the kind of person who usually settled for fast and easy. And it had been almost ten years since she updated, or changed her simple look.

Mercedes never felt comfortable in salons. She had never been in one until she was on her own at nineteen. Her mother's idea of a haircut was getting out the sewing sheers and whacking off Mercedes' hair—only when she needed it. When she was young, her mother would give her a 'bob' with bangs cut straight across. It was definitely not stylish and there was no technique or skill involved.

When her friends introduced her to beauty salon treatments, it was something she didn't feel at ease with either. There were too many choices of services and products that she had never considered. Tessann's spa-like salon offered: hair styling, color, skin treatments, waxing, massage therapy, hair extensions, manicuring, Brazilian keratin treatments, and almost anything one could think of. Mercedes was always behind the times, and it wasn't until a few years ago that Mercedes put away her eyebrow tweezers, and settled into waxing. She hated the pain when they ripped the wax off, but it was definitely easier than sitting in front of the mirror trying to pluck one at a time.

Mercedes had gone to visit Tessann many times at the shop—rarely did she stick around. Although it was a welcoming and hip environment, it always reminded Mercedes of a streamlined, futuristic surgical room. The spacious salon had a minimalist, loft-like industrial design. The sleek white space specialized in relief and renewal. It was distinctly unique, and the modern edgy look was flooded with natural sunlight from the warehouse-style windows that faced the busy, famous street. Everything was white except for the chairs the patrons sat on—those were black leather. There were mirrors everywhere and dangling lights hung from the high ceilings generating lots of light. If you had any flaws, the abundance of light brought them out for everyone to see clearly—there was no hiding anything.

Jennifer and Christina loved to hang out with Tessann, and enjoyed that atmosphere and pampering. Emme was a different story. She had her own store for fraternizing with the famous clientele, and was not the least bit impressed with who walked in the doors. She was also simpler, like Mercedes, although not to the extremity as her friend. She always knew what she wanted—knew exactly how to get it— and when to get it. She didn't waste time stroking her ego, or emptying her pocketbook on frivolous things. Nor did she let anyone tell her what she needed—she was extremely independent and set in her ways.

Mercedes walked down the street to her favorite deli to order a cappuccino to go.

She opened the door, walked in, and went to the cashier counter to order it. She looked around; and her eyes caught a glimpse of Josh sitting at a table with a very pretty young lady. He caught her eye, and raised his hand to wave. Mercedes smiled and waved back. She immediately turned around and looked in the other direction feeling slightly disappointed, and almost like she was invading his privacy. A few seconds later, Josh tapped her shoulder, and Mercedes turned around with a big smile on her face.

"Hello, Mercedes. Is Stella getting your cappuccino?" he asked.

"Yes, thanks for asking. You didn't need to come over, Stella's got me covered," she countered.

"Just wanted to say 'hi.' I haven't seen you around for a while, or at least not on Saturdays. Glad to see you out and about."

"I've been doing this silly Zumba class with my best friend on Saturday mornings. She picks me up just to make sure I go!" Mercedes laughed.

"I bet it's fun and you just don't want to admit it!" He gave a smug look, and then asked, "Why the big rush today? Usually, you sit down and enjoy the coffee."

"I'm on my way to get my hair cut." She flung her long hair with her fingers and laughed.

His two fingers reached up and touched a few strands in a very intimate way. "Really? I think your hair looks beautiful like it is. You women are never happy with easy and simple." He laughed, but his remark hit a nerve.

"Wasn't my idea. My friends seem to think I need to shake up my life a little. One has me going to the gym on

Saturday mornings; and now Tessann, who's a hairdresser, thinks I need a new 'do'!" She rolled her eyes and started to laugh.

"Well, good luck. Stop by and let me see what a pair of scissors can do!" At that moment, Stella, the waitress, handed Mercedes her coffee. She said goodbye and left.

Mercedes sipped on her coffee as she walked down the street, headed towards Zoe's Salon. She was thinking about the woman who was sitting with Josh. Once she saw the shop come into view, she began to get nervous. When she got inside, in the corner, she could see her friends all sitting around the waiting area, laughing and having a good time. Emme saw her first and stood up, walked over, and gave her a hug. Then the other came over and did the same.

Tessann pointed to Jennifer's new hairstyle. "Doesn't she look awesome!"

Mercedes' eyes opened as wide as they could with all her Botox, and she turned around to walk back out the door. Emme grabbed her arm and swung her around, "Tessann said she would be very conservative with you. I made her promise!"

Jennifer's hair was blonde—kind of. It was cut in a very long, severe shagged-out style. The underneath was a very dark brown, the overlay was blonde and the roots were really dark on purpose. All-in-all, it was a very 'in-your-face' trendy look. Jennifer wore it well, but Mercedes knew that could not possibly work for her. She was not going to compromise all her penchants.

"Don't go, Mercedes." Emme begged.

Mercedes stopped and looked directly at Emme. "I don't want any color change, okay? And I don't want to look like a punk rocker!"

Tessann came over and hugged Mercedes, and said, "I'm only going to add a few little highlights. If you don't like them, we can immediately take them out. And I'm just going to give you an easy style and show you how to maintain it.

Okay? I came in especially for you today, don't go. Let's make you pretty."

'*Let's make you pretty,*' hit a nerve, and those words hurt Mercedes immensely. She didn't show it—or let them know it. She closed it off in her head—the same way she ignored her mother when she ranted about how ugly her daughter was. Terrified, she walked slowly over to the chair and sat down. *What was she thinking when she showed up? How could she put her hair in Tessann's hands?* Those hands just punk'd out Jennifer's hair, and she wasn't sure how, or if, she was going to survive the afternoon. Over the past few months, she had given in to some changes that were difficult enough to live with. A new nose, a forehead that didn't move anymore, the gym, a ten pound weight loss, and now her hair. The list was getting bigger every day. *Thank God I was strong enough not to add 'a tattoo' to the list!* she thought to herself.

When they finally let Mercedes look in the mirror, she went into shock. Not sure if she liked it, or not—she knew it was different from anything she had ever had. Her biggest fear now was not knowing if she could maintain it. It was shagged and shorter, it had some soft blonde highlights, and the bangs were a little spiky in front. It was a sharp trendy look and the girls loved it. Mercedes was stunned into silence. She stood by the mirror with her fingers touching her hair and admiring its texture.

Tessann came along side of her and tapped her nose. "Well, what do you think? I didn't want it too radical, but I think the change has given you an awesome new look. What we need now is for Liza, my makeup lady, to highlight that beautiful new nose of yours, and put a little color onto your cheeks!" She leaned over and kissed her cheek. "The transformation is unbelievable. See what a little change can do?"

Mercedes smiled at her friend and said, "I hardly recognized myself in the mirror. Thank you, Tess, for not making me look like a punker! I actually think I could get used to this." She carefully lifted her hand to her hair and gently touched it.

"Let's go out and celebrate Mercedes' new look!" Christina blurted out to the girls.

Jennifer got excited and jumped up and down, clapping her hands. "Yes! I can't wait to show off my new 'do,' too!"

Christina and Emme rolled their eyes at the same time. Tessann got angry. She looked at Jennifer and sliced her hand in the air across her neck, and said, "Cut it out, Jennifer. This is not about you today!" Jennifer got the message and looked down at the floor.

Mercedes gave Tessann a hug and teased her. "I think I'll just go home, stare at myself in the mirror tonight, and make sure it's really me!"

Tessann looked at Mercedes and said, "I get that. You've had a long day, and the changes can be overwhelming to some." Then she turned and tweaked Emme's hair and swatted her ass. "Not to this little 'hottie' friend here, she changes her hair color and cut like you change a baby's diaper—constantly!"

Emme pushed her hands away. "It's people like me that keep you employed, you brat! Besides, I really like this bluish color this week. It might stick around for a while."

"Come out with us tonight, Emme." Tessann said as she started cleaning up the area around her.

Emme turned and hugged Mercedes, "As much as I'd love to girls, it's been a busy month with the holidays and I've given some of my staff a break. So, I'm closing the shop tonight. So I'm out on those plans—sorry, ladies. But you have fun without me!" Then she looked at her dear friend and said, "You look beautiful. So different and so unique."

Mercedes' eyes had a soft puppy dog look. "Thanks, Emme."

They all had an enjoyable afternoon together. Mercedes had more excitement then she could handle for the day, so she headed home while the others went out to the clubs for the evening.

When she got home, she grabbed a bottle of water from the refrigerator and went upstairs. She changed into an old pair of flannel pajamas and walked into the bathroom. She stared in the mirror for a few minutes. Then, she went back into her room, crawled into bed, and turned on the television. This was her typical Saturday night, only now she had a new hairdo. Just before she fell asleep, she touched her hair for the last time and hoped it would look decent in the morning. New hairdos were like that. When you left the shop they looked great, when you got up in the morning—that was another story. It never looked the same after the first day.

EARLY Monday morning, Mercedes turned into the

underground parking lot to park her car for work. As she was pulling in, the attendant raised his hand to stop her.

"I see you every morning, but I'm not sure what office suite you're in? My name is Amed." he said with a big smile on his face.

Mercedes wondered why after years of ignoring her, he suddenly stopped her to ask such a silly question. *Why does he have that asinine smile on his face like some love-struck puppy?*

"I'm on the top floor, in the Private Client Services Suite," Mercedes grinned and said politely. She didn't want to encourage him, or give him any reason to believe that she was interested.

"Oh! I like your new haircut, looks great!" He removed his arm and let her by. Once Mercedes' car had passed him, she rolled her eyes and sighed.

Mercedes parked, gathered her briefcase and purse, got out of her car, and walked over to the underground elevator and pushed the button. While she was waiting, she pulled out her cell phone to check for messages. Suddenly, there was a tap on her shoulder and she turned around.

"Oh my! I thought it might be you, but I wasn't sure, you look like a stranger! My, oh my!" Mary Dugan just stood shaking her head and stared, as though she had seen a ghost.

"Is that all you're going to say?" Mercedes waited for an answer.

Unable to give a coherent answer, Mary finally just lifted her fingers and lightly touched Mercedes' hair.

Impatient to hear an answer, Mercedes asked, "Well, is it a thumbs up, or a thumbs down?" Mercedes slipped her phone in her purse. "Still waiting for an answer."

"Why...sweet Mercedes, you look absolutely... positively...very different!" She couldn't take her eyes off of Mercedes.

"I surely don't want to turn this into twenty questions. Well, do you like it?" She said, beginning to lack the confidence she had when she walked out of the house twenty minutes earlier.

It wasn't only the hair style that had transformed Mercedes, but she was wearing a little foundation, some light green eye shadow, to set off her beautiful green eyes, blush to add color to her cheeks, plain lip gloss to add some shine, and her hair was perfectly manicured. The elevator door opened and Mercedes held it while Mary continued to stare at her.

Once they were both inside of the elevator and the doors were closed, "Okay, Mary. I get your point. I'm probably not wearing the right color eye shadow, but it's all I had! At least I gave this new look some extra time in the morning!" Mercedes said, feeling a bit embarrassed.

"Good, I'm glad you got my point! You look absolutely stunning today. I'm shocked beyond belief, but not the least bit surprised. You're a beautiful girl, and you just made a little more effort to show us today. I bet those friends of yours put you up to this change."

Mercedes touched her hair and finally smiled. "I just think it was time for some changes. I was tired of being 'the ugly duckling!' And now that I'm turning thirty, I thought it was better late than never!"

"You were never *ugly*, nor a *duckling*, Mercedes! I think this change was long overdue. Somewhere in that awful childhood, you didn't recognize any of your beauty." Mary patted her hand.

"Thanks, Mary, you're right! And your opinion means a lot to me."

"My opinion means squat! You need to grow some backbone."

They got out of the elevator and walked into the office. Mary put her stuff down on her desk, and walked down the hall to make some coffee in the small employees' kitchen. Mercedes continued down the hall and into her office. She turned on her light, walked over to her desk, put down her briefcase and sat down. The light was blinking on her phone, signifying she had some missed calls. Her day had just started and she could tell already that it was going to be a long one.

Ten minutes later, Alexi popped his head into her office and his eyes opened wide. "Wow! What the hell happened to you? You must have had one hell of a weekend!"

"Not really, I stayed home on Saturday night and watched movies with popcorn." Mercedes laughed, sounding a little naïve. They all knew, in the office, she had no social life except an occasional outing with her friends to the movies or a club.

"I have to say. With that new nose, makeup and hair...you look great!" He did a wolf whistle and walked down the hall, continuing to whistle.

Mercedes' face turned bright red. She was not used to all the attention and a little uncomfortable with how Alexi had stared at her.

Over an hour later, she heard Michael and Zackary talking as they walked down the hall. They always came in late, and then it took them a while to settle in. They hung out at the Starbucks down the street before coming into work. They always explained to Jarrod and Mercedes, that with Wi-Fi, they started their work on their computers while having coffee. But in reality, it was the triple shot of caffeine that jumpstarted them in the morning after long nights of a hefty social life.

The morning was almost over, and Mercedes was concentrating on her desk computer, when she heard a finger tapping on the wall. She looked up, and both Zackary and Michael were staring at her.

"What's up, Mercedes? Wow, you look great. You must have had a good weekend!" Michael said.

Mercedes looked a little bemused. "Like I told Alexi, who happened to say the same thing—it was a boring Saturday night at home. With the exception that my girlfriend, Tessann, cut my hair at her salon that morning."

Michael lifted his eyebrows. "You mean that cute little Asian girl that hangs at the clubs with you? I keep asking you to introduce us, but you keep ignoring me!" Michael laughed, and leaned against the door, crossing his hands over his chest, waiting for a reply.

"She's really not your type...trust me! She'd eat you up and spit you out in pieces. Besides, I refuse to mix business with pleasure! I can see how that tears apart an office in minutes." Mercedes nodded her head. She wasn't about to tell him that her girlfriend went both ways and was a wild child. That would just excite a 'metro-clubber' like him even more.

"Well, she did a great job with your hair, and I must say...you look much better!" Zackary finally stepped into the conversation. And his finger kept tapping against the wall.

"Thanks, guys! I'm pretty busy, so I'll catch up with you later." She looked back at the computer and that was their signal for them to leave. She didn't have time, nor did she care to chitchat with those two *bozos*. Mercedes was feeling extremely self-conscious at this moment, wondering if there was an ulterior motive. Michael and Zackary rarely ever said much to her. As long as she could remember, they never complimented her on anything, other than work. The party boys never considered her attractive; she could tell by the way they acted around her. Now, after a little haircut, they were suffocating her with compliments. *What was up with that?* She wondered.

The day went pretty smoothly. It seemed very redundant when everyone commented on her new haircut, including the concession stand lady in their lobby. It was late afternoon when Mercedes finally placed her phone in the office on hold and sat back to relax for a moment. The past few days had been a real whirlwind. Mercedes didn't know how to take everyone's reactions. *Was it a good thing, or bad?* Not wanting to delve into something that would never have an answer, Mercedes left her office.

As she passed her boss' office, she knocked on his door.

The voice from behind the door said, "Come on in."

Mercedes opened the door and popped her head in. "Hey, Jarrod, I know you've been really busy since you just got back from vacation, I just wanted to say 'welcome back.'"

Jarrod was leaning back in his chair, his eyes showed his exhaustion. "Thanks, Mercedes. Thanks for holding down the fort. I'm actually glad to be back. After one week with my wife and two young children, I need another vacation!" They both laughed.

"I get that!" She smiled and nodded.

He sat forward, opened his eyes wide, and nodded his head. "By the way, I like your new look! It's very attractive." He stood up, took his suit jacket off the chair next to the desk, and started to walk toward Mercedes. He was close to six feet tall, and had an athletic body that showed off his muscular chest. His brown hair had a dusting of gray around the temples, and he was a very handsome man in his forties. His smile lit up his face, it was one of his best assets. "I say we both get the hell out of here, I'm exhausted."

"I just saw Michael and Zackary leave a few minutes ago. I don't know how those two make it all day, after partying all night."

"Youth! Give them another ten years and they will have burned out at both ends!" They started walking down the hall.

Mercedes stopped and grabbed his elbow. "Whoa...I'm their age and I feel it now!"

"Yeah, but I bet if you got into those clubs and mulled around, your adrenaline would spike like theirs!" Then he shook his head and laughed. "You can only do that for a few years. Ask me, I know!"

As they approached the front office, Mary was sitting at her desk still working.

"Go home, Mary!" Jarrod said, waving his hand toward the door. "Whatever it is...it can wait until tomorrow. It's half past five...."

Mercedes and Jarrod walked over as the elevator door opened, they got inside, and went down to the parking level.

"Have a restful evening." Mercedes said, as she started walking in the opposite direction.

He put his hand up to wave. "You too, see you tomorrow. I have a client coming in at nine I would like you to meet. He's very wealthy and I think you can help him with his accounts." His voice got lower as they continued to walk to their cars.

Mercedes gave him a thumbs up.

The next morning, Mercedes had a hard time with her hair, it was tweaking out, so she used some spiking gel that Tessann had given her. It worked really well. But when she was finished, she looked like she could have been Joan Jett from the rock-and-roll group in the eighties. Walking out the door, she approached her car; she looked at her reflection in the window. She reached for the door handle, and started to laugh at her unrecognizable image. Overwhelmed with her changes, she asked herself, *Where the hell did Mercedes go?*

She arrived to work earlier than the rest of the staff, so she went into the kitchen and started the coffee. Minutes later, she went into her office and sat down to start her day.

At ten to nine, she was buzzed on the intercom by Jarrod. He wanted her to come down to his office for a meeting with his client. Mercedes knocked on the door and nonchalantly entered the office.

She looked at Jarrod sitting behind his desk, and never turned and noticed the gentleman sitting in front of the desk.

"Good morning, Jarrod. What's up?" she said before she turned to her side to sit down. That's when she noticed there was a man sitting in the other chair.

Jarrod stood up, and and so did the man who was seated. Jarrod said, "Mercedes I'd like you to meet a client of mine, George Johnson."

Mercedes reached for George's extended hand. "It's a pleasure to meet you. Jarrod has said some wonderful things about you, Mr. Johnson." Mercedes lied. She didn't know who he was, or anything about him, but she knew enough in the business world that you put that 'schmoozer' face on and stroked the client's ego.

George slowly released her hand and sat back down. He indifferently crossed his legs and folded his hands in his lap. He was a short man, small in stature, with a thick head of gray hair. He was casually dressed in creased jeans, a crisply ironed shirt, new tennis shoes, and a leather jacket. As a man well into his sixties, he appeared a lot younger than his age he was very distinguished looking.

Jarrod broke the silence. "Why don't you have a seat, Mercedes? I brought you in here so that you could be part of our discussion. Mr. Johnson and I were just talking about his new business venture. He has an active merchandising franchise and he's looking for financing. I told him you were the best."

Mercedes smiled and said, "Thank you, Jarrod. I'd be more than happy to help." She turned toward Mr. Johnson and gave him a warm smile.

Hours later, Mercedes was sitting in her office trying to figure out what had just happened. Jarrod had never brought her into a meeting with a client. He always brought in Michael, because of his prowess with handling high-end businessmen. Or, sometimes he would bring in Zackary, or Alexi, because of their dynamic personalities that could carefully entertain the client's needs. That never bothered Mercedes, nor did she really care. She knew she was the best of the four, and she had built up her own collective group of substantial clientele over the years, and they constantly kept her busy. From a distance, she silently watched as the good ol' 'boys club' passed off clients to each other, and never included her. There was nothing she could do. She worked hard at her job, and she made a great salary catering to her own clients.

Alexi poked his head into her office and said, "Nice job, Mercedes. I hear Jarrod's new client was extremely impressed with you!"

Mercedes looked at him in surprise, "Really?"

"Yes, really! It must be that new look you're sporting! That's really a hot haircut and that new hot pink sweater looks great." He did another wolf whistle that could be heard throughout the whole office.

Mercedes looked down at her sweater and then back up at him. "It the same old sweater I've been wearing for years. Even the same old black skirt and black pumps." A look of confusion crossed her face. "I think he was just impressed with my thorough business plan and how I presented it."

Alexi shook his head. "I don't think so...." He began to laugh as he left.

The day was finally over and it was time to go home. Mercedes was exhausted and just wanted to hibernate in her own space, where nobody could touch her. She picked up her purse and slung the strap over her shoulder, grabbed the handle of her briefcase, and walked out of her office.

As she walked down the hall, she could see that Mary was cleaning up her desk and getting ready to leave. "Long day, Mary?" Mercedes smiled.

"Much too long. One of these days I'm going to have to call it quits and succumb to retirement like my husband!" Mary picked up her purse and said, "I don't know why you and I are always the last ones to leave. Doesn't seem fair. Come on, we'll walk to our cars together."

They walked out of the office and into the open elevator. Mary looked at Mercedes and said, "Have you been losing weight? You look wonderful."

"I think I've lost a few pounds, but I'm not really sure. I don't have a scale at home. Those things scare me. But I am going to Zumba classes, with a friend, on Saturday mornings. It nearly killed me the first few weeks!" Mercedes began to laugh.

Mary raised her eyebrows and gave her a wink. "Well, young lady, it is definitely working." They walked out of the elevator and said their goodbyes.

Mercedes was tired and hungry, and didn't feel like cooking, so she decided to go to Saul's Deli. She got into her car and drove off. After trolling the small parking lot in front of the deli a few times, she finally parked her car and walked inside. It was packed, as usual, and all the regulars were out in force, leaving only one spot open at the counter. Without hesitation, she quickly walked over to claim the seat. As her hand reached for the back of the seat, another hand pushed hers away.

Mercedes pushed the hand away and said, "Sorry buster...this chair is taken!" Ready to defend her rights to the seat, Mercedes narrowed her eyes, pouted her lips, and fiercely turned around to see who belonged to that offensive hand.

"I'm sorry, I don't recognize you. Do we know each other?" Josh said dramatically. "I was saving this seat for my friend Mercedes, with the long, beautiful brown hair." Josh started to laugh out loud. Then he turned the chair to the side to let Mercedes slide in. "Do you know where she might be?" He mockingly questioned.

Mercedes shook her head and answered boldly. "Nope! And...if she does show up today, it will be a fight until death over this chair!"

With a serious tone in his voice, Josh lifted his hand to her hair and touched it. "I barely recognized you. What a nice change. I like the blonde highlights—very interesting."

"Thanks. Tessann is my dear friend and the hairdresser who is responsible for this messy 'do.' She said it was time, and that I needed a change. She said I was behind the times, and looking very frumpy and matronly." Mercedes admitted.

With a surprised look on his face, he said, "You're kidding, right?"

Mercedes cast her eyes down and whispered, "No...."

He poked her arm and she looked up. "I thought you looked fine before...I never considered you frumpy or matronly."

Mercedes picked up the menu, and put her nose into it, to hide her reddened cheeks. She was on the verge of tears.

In a soft voice Josh asked, "Tough day, huh?"

Mercedes nodded her head. "Very! And yours? I'm pretty lucky, mine is over. I can see yours won't be over for quite a while. Why the big crowd tonight?" she asked curiously, and was thankful to change the subject from her new haircut.

"I think there was an actor's workshop down the street and every student came in famished. Must have been an all-day thing. When they finally let those starving students leave, they either darted for the nearest watering hole, or here to eat. You know how that goes." He took out his order pad and then the pencil from behind his ear.

"Actually, I don't. Never wanted to be an actress. And personally, I don't have those shocking good looks that all the studios are looking for!" She placed her purse on the counter and looked up with a grin.

"I don't know what mirror you've been looking in, or who's filled your head with garbage, but you are a very pretty young woman!" He jotted down what her finger was pointing to on the menu. "Just chicken soup and a small side salad, that's it?" he asked.

"Yes, thanks...."

"You on a diet? Because you look like you've lost weight." He raised his eyebrows in question.

Mercedes laughed. "No, it's that damn Zumba class my girlfriend is making me take on Saturday mornings!

That's really funny, you're the second person today to ask me." She had noticed that her clothes were starting to fit a little looser, but she never thought twice about it.

He tapped her new nose with his finger. "Maybe we see more of your beauty, than you do–yourself." With that being said, he walked away to put in her order.

Mercedes finished her meal, picked up her purse, and waved goodbye to Josh. He was dealing with an unhappy looking customer, and he lifted his hand to acknowledge her departure. Mercedes felt a little disappointed. She loved coming into the deli, and always enjoyed their conversations. He was a very upfront man, with no pretense as to what surrounded him. He enjoyed people and was a constant support to his customers and the community. Josh not only contributed money to the neighborhood charities in the area, but he also donated his time to deliver food to the elderly. They both respected each other, and Mercedes always considered the little deli her 'comfort zone'. For some reason, Mercedes left questioning her choice to cut her hair. *Did my insecurities push me to change?*

T HE last two weeks had been very stressful at work, and Mercedes hardly had time to breathe. The interest rates had dropped, and the stock market was making a comeback. Every investor was calling Mercedes and demanding immediate attention. Her work hours were extended, and her workload was overwhelming. Yet, she didn't complain, because it was creating a great income, and she was putting it away, like a squirrel does with its acorns. The only thing she had a hard time managing was her social life. That became nonexistent.

Mercedes had barely walked into her kitchen and turned on the lights, when she noticed the time. It was past seven o'clock and she was exhausted. She opened the refrigerator and looked inside—nothing caught her attention, so she closed the door. Then she went to the pantry. "I guess it's chicken soup tonight," she muttered to herself as she pulled the can off the shelf.

She slipped out of her shoes and wiggled her aching toes. Then she mumbled to herself, *"Whoever invented these pointy toes with six inch heels can go straight to hell!"*

Mercedes walked over to a kitchen drawer and took out a can opener. She dumped the soup into a ceramic soup bowl, and was walking over to the microwave when the phone began to ring. The loud noise coming from the phone startled Mercedes, and she dropped the bowl on the counter. Everything in the bowl splattered everywhere. The ceramic bowl, shattered, had scattered everywhere.

She screamed at the top of her lungs, *"Damn, shit, fuck!"* as she walked over and picked up her phone. With an angry voice, she yelled into the phone. "Hello!"

"Wow...did I catch you at a bad time," Emme said softly.

Looking around the room for a towel, Mercedes barked into the phone, "There hasn't been a good time in weeks. I'm exhausted and hungry, and I just spilled my only can of soup all over the counter!"

"I could do with some Chinese food. Want me to bring you some Wonton soup from our favorite Chinese restaurant?" Emme offered, with a sincerity that calmed Mercedes down.

With her phone sandwiched between her shoulder and ear, Mercedes walked over to the refrigerator and took out the leftover macaroni and cheese, and then walked over to the cabinet to get a plate. "Nah, I just found some crappy mac n' cheese I've had for three days. What's up?"

"Just thought I would see if you wanted to go to lunch tomorrow," Emme asked.

Mercedes spooned some macaroni on the plate and popped it into the microwave. "I have a final appointment with Dr. Schwartz. He just wants to make sure everything is okay with my nose. Want to tag along, and after, we can go for a quick lunch?" Mercedes picked up the tiny pieces of ceramic, put them into the trash, and began to wipe the soup off the counter.

"Great, I'd love to. Maybe he can give me a shot or two of Botox. I can see my forehead begin to move and when it does that...it's a matter of time before my creases are back. Ugh!" Emme started to laugh.

Mercedes smiled. "Okay, Emme, I suggest you call Alisha and see if he has time. I mean, you can't just barge in there and expect him to do it."

"Why not? There is a doctor on every corner of this city dying to Botox anyone, at any time! The money whores will fit you in anytime." Emme began to laugh. "What time should I stop by?"

"I'm taking a late lunch, so does one o'clock sound okay?" Mercedes asked.

"Works for me!"

"See you tomorrow." Mercedes hung up, and pulled the dried looking macaroni out of the microwave.

Mercedes was on the phone in her office when Emme quietly sat down on the chair in front of her desk. Emme watched as Mercedes was talking to her client. Mercedes was one of those people that talked with her hands flying in all directions. It was like dodging bullets when you got into a conversation and were standing too close to her. Emme began to mimic Mercedes and her flying hands. Mercedes smiled and waved one hand at Emme to try to make her stop. Emme continued to tease her further—she began to over exaggerate the movement. Mercedes turned around in her chair, so she would not break out into laughter.

A few moments later, Mercedes hung up, looked at Emme, and rolled her eyes. "I hate when I have to mentally massage my immature and paranoid clients. Geez, you'd think the earth was coming to an end, or might fall off its axis, when the stock market takes a small dip!"

Emme laughed and shook her head. "If you really hate your job, I told you that I would take you in as a partner anytime you want. Personally, I know I could not do what you do. Too many financial extremists out in the world today. And I think a lot of them are now packing guns! Actually, it seems like everyone is carrying guns nowadays, even elementary school kids." She sat back in the chair and shook her head.

Mercedes threw her hands in the air in defeat. "First, I'd make a lousy business partner, especially when you're talking about anything to do with fashion!" She stood up and pointed her finger at herself. "I'm not exactly a person who is a fashionista. Look at me! I wouldn't know how to pick trendy fashion if my life depended on it!"

Emme stood up, and mimicked Mercedes with her pointing finger. "You're right! It's good your life doesn't depend on it, because I think you would fail miserably down at the buyer mart! So, stay where you are...you're a brilliant financial counselor!" She came around the desk and gave Mercedes a hug and a kiss on each cheek, and backed up to look into her face. "So...how much did you say the market fell?" She opened her eyes as wide as they would go. But her eyebrows didn't raise either, with all the toxins that deadened the nerves.

"Two hundred and sixty-three points!" Mercedes laughed at her own absurdity. "I would have been screaming at my advisor, also!"

Emme raised her eyebrows in agreement.

Mercedes looked at Emme's face. Then she pointed her finger at Emme's eyebrow. "You're right! Your eyebrows are moving again. You do need some more Botox!"

Emme grabbed Mercedes' hand, and in an exasperated voice said, "Get your ass moving, slowpoke!"

They both waved to Mary as they walked past her desk. She was on the phone and waved back. They walked out of the office and waited for the elevator doors to open. When they did, Michael, Zackary, and Alexi stepped out of the elevator.

As the men past the ladies, Michael turned his head and called Emme's name. She turned around to look at him. "When are you going to go out with me, Emme?"

"Tomorrow...." she replied sweetly. Mercedes rolled her eyes as she held the elevator door open. She knew what was coming. She always went through this when she hung out with her friends. It didn't matter where they were, or what they were doing. Men always tried to 'hit' on them. Even the grocery store became a challenge, with her friends. Christina, Jennifer, and Tessann loved all the attention and enjoyed the games. Games that Mercedes considered a waste of time. Emme was the only one who found the club scene claustrophobic at times. Men persistently approached her with puppy dog eyes and hands filled with her favorite drinks. But she knew the reality of the lifestyle. Most of the guys looked at her tattoos and piercings and thought her a novelty to be seen with, or they hoped she was an overnight fuck. Emme was not a stupid woman, and she could enjoy the game as good as the best. Sometimes she would surprise them with her nasty sarcasm. The same sarcasm she was about to lay on Michael.

"Really...tomorrow? What time?" Michael took a step toward her.

Quickly she blurted out, "Half past a monkey's ass, Bucko!"

Mercedes busted out into laughter, and grabbed Emme's arm, pulling her into the elevator before she could see the look on her partners' faces. "I'm in deep trouble now, Emme!" she gasped out as she continued to laugh.

Both of them were holding their stomach, as the laughter continued. "Oh my God!" They both turned around and looked at Michael's face just as the elevator door closed. He looked crushed.

Mercedes shook her head, the smile still planted on her face. "That was so mean!"

Emme lifted her eyebrows . . . .

They were waiting for Dr. Schwartz to enter the exam room. Mercedes was sitting on the chair and Emme was standing next to her. There was a slight knock on the door and the doctor entered.

"Hey there, Mercedes. How's it going?"

"Pretty good."

He looked into her nose and ran his fingers down the top. He touched a few other places, including under her eyes. "It looks great."

"Yeah, I love it." Mercedes gushed.

"Great!" He pointed to where Mercedes was sitting. Then he said, "Hop up onto the chair Emme. We're doing a little Botox and some Restylane, right?"

Mercedes got out of the chair, and immediately looked at her friend with questioning eyes.

She sat down in the chair. "Yep! I thought my upper lip was a little thin. It's been a few years now."

"Well, once I open a bottle you have to pay for the whole thing." He started touching her lips, and her lines around her mouth. "You might have a little left." He turned to Mercedes and said, "Why don't you take the little we have left and do your upper lip?"

Mercedes shook her head and politely said, "No thanks."

Emme looked at her friend and jumped out of the chair. She turned around and touched Mercedes' upper lip and said, "What a great idea, Dr. Jeff."

"It will only be a little. Actually, very little!" He looked at Mercedes, and moved his hand onto the top lip.

"No.... Thanks," Mercedes said.

"Come on, Mercedes. Your top lip is way too thin for the bottom one. Just a little filler like Restylane will make it a little fuller. Besides, if you don't like it...it dissipates in a few months." Emme nudged her friend's arm. "Come on, it's just a little. And it's my treat. I have to pay for a full bottle anyway."

Emme's eyes pleaded with Mercedes.

Dr. Schwartz pulled a hand mirror off the counter and handed it to Mercedes. "I want to stay out of it. It has to be entirely up to you, Mercedes." He leaned against the counter and crossed his arms on his chest, with a slight grin on his face.

Mercedes looked in the mirror and touched her lips with a finger. "I like my lips...." Mercedes said defensively.

"Oh, for Christ's sake, babe. Look at your thin upper lip. Don't you want it to look like those big luscious lips on television showing off the new red lipsticks? Hell, Gwen Stefani even has those big lips and so does Angelina Jolie!" Emme tried to reason with her.

"Okay.... Let me think about it when you're getting yours done. Look, there might not be anything left anyway!" Mercedes was twisting her hands together in fearful expectation.

The doctor numbed Emme's lip with a topical cream. Then, he used the hypodermic needle to inject the Botox across her forehead, and down to the crow's feet next to her eyes. Mercedes stood silent, mesmerized by the whole procedure. When he was done, he picked up the needle and injected the filler into her numbed lip line. Immediately, his fingers massaged the lip to spread the thick serum evenly.

After he was done, he held up the vile with the filler and said, "I have some left over. Do you want to do it?" Before she could answer, he said, "You probably won't want to go back to work today, because your lips might be red and a little swollen!"

"I can call the office and let them know. I don't have any afternoon appointments. I think I will give it a try, but only if you can't see a noticeable difference."

"There will be a difference, but I will make sure it's minimum." Emme stood behind Mercedes, quietly clapping her hands in approval.

That evening, as Mercedes laid in bed, she was thinking about how she was beginning to morph from a moth to a butterfly. Her upper lip was now fuller, and for some reason, it had changed her appearance. It had given her a sexier, more sensuous look, and it highlighted her beautiful green eyes. She had looked in the mirror before going to bed, and what she saw amazed her. She was actually transforming from that 'nobody' to a pretty young woman.

All during her childhood, she always felt so lonely and scared. Once her father had left when she was eight, he was nowhere to be found. He just disappeared off the face of the earth—never to be seen or heard from again. This marked the beginning of her years filled with abuse at the hands of her mother. During the first eight years, Mercedes was the *'lighthouse of her father's tumultuous storms.'* She kept him grounded during his chaotic and violent marriage. He loved her and always made her feel special, by frequently letting her know how beautiful she was. He would come home from work and immediately seek her out. They played together—they took walks together—they went to the zoo to feed the elephants and monkeys together—and some evenings, he would sit quietly and read her books. His continuous attention to Mercedes became a big conflict in the house. Her mother was jealous of their close relationship. The horrible fights, at times, became violent, and they left emotional scars on Mercedes. The verbal abuse that was slung around would leave her trembling in fear. Fear—that one day he would leave her—suffocated her; and that one day did come. Unable to take her mother's mood swings, verbal abuse, and constant anger, he packed his bags and left.

Mercedes was the spitting image of her father, and this was a constant reminder to her mother. She was a woman who was damaged, and didn't know how to connect with her daughter or husband. The day he packed up and left was a major turning point in Mercedes' life. From that day forward, her mother's anger was always directed to hurt, or maim her. Betty had no filter, and most of her words were directed to intentionally rip Mercedes apart. In her mother's eyes, Mercedes never did anything right, and was always chastised for the smallest of things. Accidently spilling a glass of milk at the dinner table was punishable by a spanking with a large paddle, and three nights without any light in her room. She didn't mind the spanking, although most of the time it left tremendous red welts. It was having no light in her room that left her panic-stricken. She was deathly afraid of the dark, and she has never been able to shake that fear—even after years of psychotherapy. Her therapist had explained that the cause of this fear could be traced to a traumatic childhood experience. When they took an in-depth look back at her childhood, there were just too many painful occurrences that could have generated the fear of darkness. Over the years, she had learned how to deal with it, and lighting candles had become her salvation. Whenever she felt this phobia begin to transcend, she would light a candle. Every night she would light a candle in her bedroom. Not only did she enjoy the fragrance, but the small flicker of light on the ceiling and walls got rid of that sense of darkness.

Her mother's mood swings were as radical as the changing weather. One day she would be happy, and the next day her anger was crushing. In those days, little was known about bipolar disorder. Bipolar disorder, also known as manic-depressive illness, is a brain disorder that causes unusual shifts in mood, energy, activity levels, and the ability to carry out day-to-day tasks. Most symptoms of bipolar disorder are severe. They are different from the normal ups and downs that everyone goes through from time to time. When Mercedes was younger, she began to recognize the triggers, and she would retreat to her room—at times for days. It wasn't until she was older that she researched it and finally could put a name to the horrible symptoms. Mercedes' psychotherapist told her that it could be genetic, then he reassured her that she had no symptoms, except for the residue of her abusive childhood.

There was never any affection or attention within her world, except for an occasional teacher who praised her for all her hard work. There were no family members—aunts or uncles, sisters or brothers. Her mother's family was nonexistent and even to this day, she never knew why. Her mother never mentioned anything about her family, or her childhood, and only once was the word 'sister' uttered from her mother's lips. Betty had never wanted children, but her father had insisted for them to have a baby. This made Mercedes feel unwanted. It also left her with tremendous guilt. A guilt that was so heavily embedded, it created these great waves of despair, especially since her father never came back into her life.

Mercedes and her mom moved around a lot, and at times they lived in shelters. Her mother had a hard time holding onto a job, but when she was working, things managed to calm down a little. Then, after a while, the chaos would start up again. The constant uproar in Mercedes' life pushed her into becoming a loner. Rarely did she have friends, and if she did, she never brought them home. It wasn't until high school that she started to form any kind of closeness or connection to others.

Emme sat down next to Mercedes one day at school during lunch. Eventually they met for lunch to discuss their classes, boys, sports, and sometimes the future. It took a while for Mercedes to open up enough to trust her. Emme's large group of socially energetic friends could be overwhelming at times. Mercedes liked her friends; however, it wasn't until her senior year that she opened up enough to accept them unconditionally.

Mercedes' world then settled down a little the last two years of high school, and it was as close to normal that she could ever recall. Her mother had held a job grooming dogs and cats at a nearby shop, and sometimes after school, Mercedes would stop in and help the owner when they got really busy. She was a brilliant student, and many of her teachers used her to tutor others. She was happy to earn the money and be able to have a small social life with her new group of friends. By her senior year, she was awarded many small scholarships that she stashed away for her continuing education. She wanted to go to college and knew that the only way she was going to get anywhere in life, was to do better than her mother had done. So she became very resourceful by saving her money wisely, and learning to invest it in the stock market. To the amazement of her Business teacher, she showed him how her shrewd business sense and free-spirited nature could succeed at what she set out to do. By the end of her senior year, she had taken a pittance, and turned it into a year's tuition to a four-year University.

The girls she hung out with didn't have any business sense, nor did they work. They came from affluent families that all loved and respected Mercedes for her ambition and educational drive. Only Emme gave her any kind of competition. She loved her friend, Mercedes, and so did her parents. They were always very generous, knowing Mercedes' circumstances, and would help her out as much as she'd let them. It was her friends, especially Emme, that made her feel important. They always included her in their parties and social affairs, and sometimes still had to push her into participating. They adored Mercedes and her humbleness, and always pushed her to 'step out of her little circle.' Mercedes loved being around them, but she always felt insecure about her looks. They were all very pretty girls that could keep up with the newest of fashion trends. They were the popular socialites that all the high school boys flocked around. Every other week, someone was going steady or breaking-up or just goggling over a silly football player—except Mercedes.

From the time she was small, her mother had repeatedly humiliated her for having inherited her father's ugly features—the high forehead, crooked, flattened boxer nose, eyes too close together, and thin lips. Without caring about any damage it might do to her daughter, her mother constantly called her *'the ugly duckling.'* This took a huge toll on Mercedes during her high school years. Her lack of confidence made her bashful, vulnerable, and she went into a reclusive place filled with depression. Having a mother who never gave her any encouragement, self-esteem, or affection was difficult to live with. There were times that Mercedes had contemplated suicide. No one knew of those thoughts except for Emme. She watched Mercedes fall into deep depressions, and witnessed the pain it caused, but there was nothing she could do.

Broken *image*

A lot of those memories always seemed to resurface during stressful times. It was the only way her body would shut down, until she learned to conquer her childhood fears, through psychotherapy. Years ago, she wasn't the person she is today. She worked hard to get to where she is now. After working hard in high school, she received a scholarship to a University nearby. Mercedes was barley eighteen when she walked out the door, never to return. It became her mission in life to survive on her own. With a graduate degree hanging on the wall, and a mountain of debt, she was able to find a respectable job. It took every bit of her energy and resilience to prove to the company that she was the best. After years of devotion, they finally recognized her value, and it skyrocketed her into a very lucrative position amongst the good ol' 'boys club.' She studied and read all she could find that dealt with economics and investments. She passed every test for her investment licenses with the highest grades in the class. It had not been an easy road to get into this elite group. But everyone in the financial circle also realized she had gotten there because of her hard work and perseverance, and not because of beautiful Barbie-doll good looks.

Her generation seemed to push out Barbie dolls by the hundreds. If you weren't one—then you could easily become one, on any corner, in any city of California. Cosmetic surgeons were a dime a dozen. They pushed out the same tiny noses, puffed-up lips, arched eyebrows, new chins and cheeks, anything. Television, movies, magazines, and advertisements showcased all of those beautifully remodeled women and men. It was a reality on the streets of Hollywood and in Beverly Hills, where young beautiful men and women came to grab that brass ring, as the carousel slowly turned. Everyone wanted to be famous, and there were those who would go to any length to get there. Plain and simple was a rarity, and Mercedes fit rightfully into that category.

Beauty was sold at a high price. It got you in the door—it got you promotions—and sometimes it got you in trouble. Beauty was a commodity that had all kinds of perks. Mercedes knew that, and it surrounded her on a daily basis. That's why she had to work harder. She didn't have that commodity to sell. She only had who she was; and over the years, she had mostly liked what she saw in the mirror. Only tonight, she could actually see all those subtle changes—and those changes were scaring her. As she laid in bed thinking about life, she slowly drifted off to sleep.

T HE alarm went off and Mercedes reached over and shut it off. She rolled onto her side and closed her eyes. Dreamland was beginning to take hold again. Then another obtrusive noise rang out. She grabbed her phone, and on the small screen she saw Emme's name.

"What are you doing, checking up on me to make sure I'm ready by eight o'clock?" Mercedes said, still sounding sleepy.

Emme's energetic voiced blurted out, "Hell no! I'm calling to tell you to bring a change of clothes, thought we might do a little shopping after Zumba."

"Are you kidding? You practically kill me in class and then you want me to shop until I drop. That's like a double dose of hate!" Mercedes rolled onto her back and smiled as she watched a spider walk across her ceiling. Immediately, she rolled off the bed in fear that it would drop onto the bed.

"Quit your complaining. You had an itsy-bitsy cold for a few days, and you haven't been to class for two weeks. Get your ass up and quit bitching. Pick you up soon." And then there was a dial tone.

Mercedes smiled until she looked up and the spider was gone. She didn't have time to deal with that now; she only had an hour to get ready.

The class was over and Mercedes and Emme were getting dressed in the locker room after their shower. Mercedes put on a pair of black leggings and a tunic top that almost went to her knees. Then she slipped on some soft leather shoes. It was a casual look, but it certainly didn't display her new curves that were beginning to take shape. She looked in the mirror, combed and spiked her hair, and put on a little blush and lipstick.

Emme quietly crept up behind Mercedes, wearing jeans and a T-shirt. "Come on kiddo, what's taking you so long?" Emme said, tapping her toe.

Mercedes turned around and glared at her friend. "It's all your fault!"

"Why am I to blame?" Emme stuffed her clothes into the gym bag, and zipped it up.

Mercedes did the same with her clothes. Then she spun around and pointed to her hair and makeup, and said, "It takes me a long time to get beautiful now! Before it was so easy...all I had to do was stick my hair into a pony tail, and I was out the door. Now, with this new haircut and makeup, I find myself in front of a mirror most of the day. Thanks to you! Grrrr...!" Mercedes growled like a mad dog.

Emme's finger tapped Mercedes on her new nose. "Tell me girl...have you really looked at yourself lately? You lost weight, fixed your nose, plumped your lips, and you look frickin' amazing. Not a bad trade off, kiddo!"

Mercedes picked up her bag and grabbed Emme's hand, "Let's get the hell out of here before I change my mind. You know how impatient I get with shopping!"

After spending the day walking around and shopping on Melrose Avenue, they finally finished in Emme's store.

Mercedes and Emme were sitting in her employee lounge sipping on a glass of wine. Both the women looked exhausted, and Mercedes had a stack of packages sitting on the floor next to her.

Leaning her head back on the couch, Mercedes closed her eyes and sighed. "I think I'm getting too old for Zumba and shopping in the same day," Mercedes complained.

"I think you did just fine! We managed to get some great new clothes for you. You look the best I've seen you in years!" Emme leaned over and kissed Mercedes' cheek. "And take that as a sincere compliment! You'd been letting yourself go for a long time."

"I don't know why I'm letting you and the girls push me into so many changes." Her body ached and she was exhausted. "I may have bought those snazzy clothes, but I'm not sure I will wear them. Some of them are just too fashionable for me. I'm a simple girl with old-fashioned tastes, and...some of my new clothes are definitely not conservative."

Emme sat forward and looked angry. Or as angry as she could with all of the Botox that took away her ability to move anything above her nose. "Missy...you *will* wear those clothes! In fact, you are going to the club with me and the girls this coming Friday."

Mercedes' eyes opened wide, but nothing else moved on her face either! "Oh, I don't think so, Emme. I have so much work to take home this weekend. I...I'm not up for it," she began to stumble over her words as fear spread through her body.

Emme's eyes looked sad. "It's a special celebration. Christina is turning thirty this weekend. You have to go. She'll be disappointed if you don't."

"Can't we just go out to dinner? Why is it always 'The Club'?" Mercedes shook her head. "You know how I hate sitting around while all of you socialize with the guys."

Emme bounced her finger on Mercedes' chest. "Fine, you call Christina and tell her you don't want to celebrate this milestone with her!"

Mercedes grabbed Emme's finger. "Fine, I'll go."

Emme stood and turned toward Mercedes. She picked up all the packages and handed them to her. "Damn right you will! And this is what you're going to wear!" She shoved one of the packages into her hand.

Mercedes dropped the package and put up her fingers into a pretend religious cross.

Both the girls started to giggle like school kids. "You are so evil sometimes. Zumba, shopping, and now a commitment to a club night! A hex on you, Emme Martex!"

Later that week, Mercedes walked into the office. Mary was sitting at her desk and her look of surprise spoke a thousand words. "Oh my! You look stunning today, dear. That is a lovely skirt, and what a beautiful sweater."

Mercedes stopped in front of Mary's desk. She blushed a bright red. "I thought this black skirt was a little tight, but my friend insisted it fit me perfect! Most of my clothes don't fit anymore." She began to tug on the length and it still stayed three inches above her knee. "I don't know what I was thinking today, when I put it on! Emme and I went shopping this past weekend. Seems I lost a little weight and everything was hanging on me."

"I don't think you have to worry about this skirt hanging. It's more like painted on! But with your weight loss it looks...nice...."

"Thanks, Mary." She rolled her eyes. Then she continued to walk down the hall to her office with a face the color of a tomato. What she didn't see was that Mary was standing there shaking her head, as Mercedes' tight skirt slipped up a few more inches.

Mercedes gazed in the floor-length window overlooking the city and saw her reflection. "I got pretty daring today with the tight skirt and green sweater that fits like a glove." She ran her hands down her hips and tried to tug her skirt down, again.

"Knock, knock!" Jarrod said out loud, as he sauntered into her office. He casually leaned against the wall and began to strip Mercedes down with his eyes.

After a slow wolf-whistle, he said, "Wow! You look like a million today. Nice...sweater...great color to match your eyes?"

Mercedes looked away. She could have sworn that his left eye slightly winked at her, but she knew better. This was probably the first time in a year that he had entered her office. For some reason, he always stood in the arc of the door and talked from there. At times, it seemed like he didn't want to get too close—just in case she had cooties. If he talked to her at all—most of the time it was done by messages from Mary, emails, or intercom conversations. He was a decent boss. He never sat over her shoulder and scrutinized her job, or how she handled her clients. He knew she was good with the clients, and they were all very loyal and supportive of her. He never over-managed her, and always gave her a great amount of space within the office. Mercedes liked that, but the past few months had changed. He was more and more in her face. When she turned around, he was always there. Lately, he would stop by her office, as he stood by the door, and created some easy chitchat.

"Thanks, Jarrod." Mercedes walked over to her desk and sat down, feeling slightly miffed. She hated when men visually stripped a woman down with their eyes. Watching them at the club really made her sick to her stomach. Her only reprieve was that they never looked at her like that—she was too unattractive for them. They also never ventured any further to see if she had a brain, or if she was an airhead like most of the beautiful women in the clubs.

He cleared his throat to get her attention. "Humm, I have this wealthy client who is so hard to deal with sometimes. He's coming in, and I thought maybe you could work with us today on his portfolio." Jarrod said, still leaning against the wall with his arms crossed over his chest. *He was more casual than ever before.* Mercedes thought to herself, as she watch him out of the corner of her eye, and pretended to be flipping through some papers on her desk.

"I have two clients coming in this afternoon." She looked up from her papers.

"What time?" he asked.

"One and three...." she countered.

"Great! He's coming in at four-thirty, so just give me a ring when you are done with your last one. I really need some help with him." He smiled.

Mercedes was feeling more confident than ever before, and her sarcasm displayed that lately. "Why don't you ask Michael or Zackary? They are really good with lopsided clients, and they've always been your 'go-to' guys!" Mercedes had been wanting to say that for the past few years. He always pulled the boys in with his new clients. He never included her, and rarely asked her to do anything except manage her own clients for the firm. The good ol' 'boys club' was always prevalent. They hung out with each other, went to lunch together, and only looked for Mercedes when they got into a tight bind.

Mercedes' mind was racing like Parnelli Jones down a straightaway. This was so out of character for Jarrod. *What was he up to?*

"This client is French, and I think you might make a great match." There was a smirk on his face, as he pulled away from the wall.

"I don't know if I'll be done with my client," Mercedes said. Then, silently to herself, she said, *Checkmate.*

Ignoring her last sentence, he said, "Just give me a call when you're done, I'll keep him busy until then. Thanks." He walked out the door without a backwards glance.

Mercedes' day was exhausting, and she really didn't want to join Jarrod and his client for another meeting. After her final client of the day had left, she took a few minutes for herself, and went down the elevator and out the front doors. In the front of the building there was a magnificent water feature that was very calming and comforting for Mercedes' intense nerves. She walked over to a bench and sat down. She took a deep breath, and tried to analyze how much had changed the last few months. The warmth of the sun felt good, and the soothing sound of the water was beginning to unwind her.

Fifteen minutes later, she was walking through the door of the suites, and down the hall to her office. She picked up her purse and went into the restroom to freshen up her makeup, apply some lipstick, and spike and spray her hair. With that done, she walked down the hall to Jarrod's office, and knocked on the door.

Jarrod opened the door and stepped aside for Mercedes to enter. There were two chairs in front of his desk. One was occupied by a handsome man who stood up at the sight of Mercedes entering the room.

Mercedes smiled at him and thought to herself, *At least he has enough manners to respect women, and stand up to acknowledge me, when I came into the room. It must be his European background. This rarely happened with spoiled, wealthy American men.*

"Mercedes, I'd like you to meet a friend and client of mine, John-Paul Lambert."

John-Paul extended his hand to Mercedes. "I've heard a lot of great things about you."

His French accent is sexy and he's a very handsome man, Mercedes thought as she extended her hand.

He stood there looking impeccable, dressed in his perfectly fitted tailored suit. Mercedes wasn't sure if it was a Brooks Brothers, Desmon Merrions, or a Fivorvanti. But whoever it was, she knew it cost more than her Honda, when it was brand new. "Pleasure is mine, Mr. Lambert." Mercedes said.

He took her hand, turned it over, and he lightly brushed his lips across the top of her wrist. Then he looked directly into her eyes with an intensity that made the hairs on her neck stand up. "Please call me John-Paul, like my friends do." He was reluctant to release her hand, and Mercedes carefully tugged it away and grinned. "John-Paul it is!"

Mercedes had seen his type before. She had heard through the office gossip that he was an extremely wealthy man whose powerful and ruthless business dealings constantly put everyone on their guard. Even Jarrod couldn't handle him, though he gave their company a lot of his business. He was one of those men that always got his way, and when he didn't, there was hell to pay. Mercedes had never met him, so she didn't know what to expect. His slightly French accent, along with kissing her hand, had thrown her off kilter. He looked to be in his late forties, with thick, wavy black hair, graying at the temples, cut to perfection. Although slightly on the longer side, it gave him a more European look, along with his soft Italian loafers with no socks. His six-foot frame was shaped and muscular. His demeanor was very casual, but it was his beautiful blue eyes that completely captivated Mercedes' attention, along with his accent.

After the meeting was over, Mercedes stood up and held out her hand again. John-Paul slowly clasped her hand and gently held on to it. Feeling a slight attraction, and an immediate frustration, Mercedes pulled it back. This was a man who knew what he wanted, and had no qualms as to how to get it. He could get any woman he wanted and rumors had him 'bedding' every actress in Hollywood, including the married ones. Mercedes was too bright to play his games, and she never mixed business with pleasure. She had seen too many people lose their jobs, and their dignity, because they were sucked into the *sinful game of lust*. Mercedes listened and watched him intently, sizing him up, as the meeting had progressed. He was smart, savvy, and untouchable.

She had run into many men of wealth, and with it, came the power. Their savoir-faire, and familiarity with their position, had sometimes increased their irrepressible egos. That wasn't always confined to the wealthy—actors, athletes, and anyone famous were part of that group too. Mercedes had clients from all walks of life, but she never had a problem with her wealthy or famous clientele. They just considered her their quiet little mouse, who worked to take good care of their accounts. She was comfortable, knowledgeable, and knew how to keep them happy. Somehow, things were beginning to change and this was throwing her entirely off balance.

"Thank you for your confidence in us, John-Paul. We will take really good care of you." After listening to what she had said, she was sure it was coming out much too aggressive for a man with his expectations.

"I will take your word on that last sentence, Mercedes. Is there any chance, seeing as I kept you later than usual, that I could take you out to dinner? You must be hungry." He lifted his eyebrows in anticipation of her answer.

Mercedes knew he was not one who got turned down very often and also didn't take rejection very well. But she didn't feel comfortable with his invitation, and her quick thinking would save them both embarrassment. "That's very kind of you, but I have plans tonight." She smiled and shrugged her shoulders.

"Maybe some other time," was all he said.

Jarrod looked surprised. He knew her constant routine was work and home. He came around his desk and shook John-Paul's hand, and he walked out the door.

Once John-Paul was gone, Jarrod turned to Mercedes, "Wow, you did a great job with John-Paul," he said, sounding somewhat stunned.

She looked at him in confusion. "I do a great job with all my clients. He's no different."

He shook his head. "I mean, you knew exactly how to handle him. What to say...how to say it...and this is the first time I've seen him so acquiescent."

"Maybe he just liked my point of view on investments. He seemed submissive enough to at least listen. Most men like him wouldn't give me the time of day. Sometimes, they think women aren't as savvy, or knowledgeable, as men in the business world."

He moved a little closer and laughed. "I think most men think beautiful women...are just 'beautiful.' They refuse to acknowledge that some are surprisingly intelligent also!"

Mercedes looked at him, confused again. "Yeah, well, I'm not beautiful, so most men figure I worked hard to be in my position; so I must have something between my ears, other than a pretty face!"

It was his turn to look confused. "You are kidding me...right?" Then he did what he did earlier in her office, and stripped her down with his eyes. And this time he whistled again. "I don't know all of what has transpired with you in the past six months, but...boy, have you changed in every possible way!"

Mercedes looked slightly miffed as she picked up her pile of papers off his desk. Then she turned toward him, and said, "I haven't changed! I lost a few pounds, bought some new clothes that fit, cut my damn hair, and put on some fucking lipstick, that's all!" Anger was pouring from each step she took, as she brushed by him and walked out the door.

She walked out without a backward glance, but she heard his raised voice, "Look in the mirror, Mercedes. You have changed!"

By the time Mercedes got back to her office, she was seething mad. As she sat down at her desk, she said to herself, *"Why is it...that when you make a few little changes...everyone thinks you've gone from the 'ugly duckling' to a 'beauty queen'! Grrrr...."* She growled.

With all this anger still brewing inside, she picked up her things and stormed out of the office. As she passed Mary's desk, she clinched her fist and held it up in frustration. Mary just gave her a sweet smile and waved.

Mercedes was driving her old beat-up car down the street, still feeling the exhaustion and resentment of the day. When her stomach began to grumble, she made a quick decision to stop at her favorite deli and have dinner. The meeting with Jarrod's client had lasted longer than she thought, and she knew that she had nothing in her refrigerator or pantry that would make her happy tonight. Feeling the fatigue in every bone in her body, all she really wanted was some homemade chicken soup, and a hot bath to wash off the day.

The parking lot wasn't crowded, so she immediately pulled into a parking spot, and got out of her car. She tugged down her black miniskirt that had raised an inch higher and showed more leg then she wanted. She smoothed out her tight sweater, and walked towards the door. When she entered the restaurant, she noticed that part of the regular dinner crowd was still there. Looking tired and moving slower than usual, her eyes scanned the room for an empty booth. She didn't feel like sitting at the counter, and she was positive that her skirt was too tight to take the stress of sitting on a stool. Suddenly out of nowhere, an arm wrapped around her waist, throwing her off balance. Suspicious of who it might be, she quickly turned around and bumped chest-to-chest into his hard body.

Trying to keep her from falling backwards, he held on tight. "Whoa...slow down, kiddo!" he said with a big smile on his face.

Mercedes' eyes opened wide, but she didn't move away from his encircled arm. After a tough day at the office, it felt good to have a friendly face and his arms encircling her. It had been years, at least, since she had felt that feeling of reassurance. "Hello, Josh. Am really glad to see a friendly face tonight. It's been one hell of a day!"

He dropped his arm, moved back a little, and scanned her body. Then he did a very low wolf-whistle for her ears only. "Well, if this is your indication of a crappy day, I'd like to be there when you've had a good one!"

Mercedes' face turned red, and she reached up and covered his staring eyes with her hand. "Stop that! Just find me a booth where I can sit down and die!"

He took hold of her hand covering his eyes, led her to a vacant booth, and carefully sat her down. "That bad, huh?"

She slipped in and leaned back against the seat. "Worse!" She closed her eyes and inhaled a deep breath, and then exhaled it slowly.

He slid in across from her. "If it's any consolation to you, I think you look great today! That's a new and very stylish outfit you have on." His eyebrows lifted in question.

She smiled, "Thank you, Josh. Yes, it is, and I'm beginning to feel out of my comfort zone lately. My friend took me shopping, and I'm not sure her taste in clothes fits who I am. All of a sudden, it's drawing a lot of attention, not only with my coworkers, but with clients."

"I would say fitting is not your problem. The way I see it...you've made some major changes, and they are all coming together. It kind of reminds me of my ex-wife." He looked away, and pursed his lips. "She pushed herself to become the perfect looking actress, and forgot about the 'down-to-earth' values that got her to where she was to begin with." With his eyes downcast, he shook his head slowly, as if he was remembering something.

Curious about his statement, she asked, "What do you mean?"

He looked up, and sat back against the seat, as sadness crossed his face. "When I first met my wife, she had simple likes, simple values, and enjoyed the simple things in life. Once she set her goals on becoming an actress, everything changed. Her goals were then based on a new self-image she wanted to achieve." He sighed. "She eventually became a person I didn't really know. Little by little, she began to change, until everything changed, including her personality and attitude. She replaced her clothing style, she altered her looks, she no longer wanted children, and she started hanging around with a different group of friends. I sat by myself trying to figure it all out as she evolved into a different person. Somebody I didn't know, and definitely somebody I didn't marry."

Mercedes looked surprised that he had actually opened up about his personal life. "Wow, I'm sorry... Josh."

Josh looked at Mercedes and said, "Don't be sorry. Learn from it, and know that life is what you make of it. God gives us what he thinks we need to survive." He stood up, looked down at Mercedes and asked, "Chicken soup and a tuna sandwich?"

Mercedes nodded her head. Then he turned away and walked toward the kitchen. For the first time, she saw him walk away with a slower gait, and with his shoulders hunched forward.

Mercedes could see his pain. She could also see how his ex-wife got caught up in the *'Hollywood scene.'* California was a tough state to live in when it came to being one of the '*beautiful people.*' Beauty became a very competitive game. Attaining fame and fortune became the prize—at any expense.

Mercedes could feel herself slipping further and further into the '*beauty game.*' And Josh sat on the sidelines watching it too . . . .

Eleven

BY Friday afternoon, Mercedes was in no mood to go to the nightclub for Christina's birthday. It had been a lousy week and everything that could go wrong—went wrong. On Tuesday morning, she woke up with a toothache. The pain was so intense; she could barely get out of bed. She took a few aspirin and hoped it would go away. When it didn't, she called Mary and said she would be in late.

After waiting for her dentist's office to open, she called to see if she could get in on an emergency basis. When she got off the phone, panic began to set in. Her dentist was on vacation and they gave her a list of dentists covering for him, but none were available until two days later. She started going through the yellow pages online, and after numerous calls and a pounding headache; she finally got an appointment with someone in the area. Hours later, she was sitting in his chair, squealing in pain, as he probed and prodded in her mouth, trying to determine her problem. It wasn't until he took a set of x-rays that he determined it was not a toothache at all, but instead, an intense sinus infection. During the next few hours, she went to the pharmacy, picked up an antibiotic, some pain medications—went home and waited for them to kick in. After cancelling two appointments with her clients, and sipping on hot tea, she was finally able to feel some relief. She went into the office and worked way into the evening, trying to play catch up.

The next morning, she went in early and saw those two clients she had cancelled. It had been a long day and finally at 7 p.m. she decided to go home. Feeling fatigued and tired, she slowly stepped out of the elevator and made it to her car. Once seated, she put the key in the ignition and turned—nothing happened. After numerous unsuccessful tries, she got out of the car, kicked the tire in anger, and went in search for the garage attendant. He too could not get the car started. Finally, she called a tow truck service and had it towed to her nearby repair shop. Mercedes slipped the key under the front mat, and decided to walk the six blocks home.

Worn out and hungry, she finally got home, and realized that she had left the garage door opener in her car. Now she had no way to open the garage to get into the house. With a low grunting sound of frustration that slipped through her lips, she tried desperately to remember where she had placed the spare key. Because of her lack of sleep from the sinus infection, and the two long days she had just endured at work, she could not remember exactly where it was. She knew she left it under a stepping stone leading down the side of her house and into the backyard. She just wasn't sure which of the seventeen stepping stones it was under. It had been many years since she had used it, and the struggle to remember was about to push her over the edge.

She remembered all too well the day Emme had said, "DO NOT hide your key in an obvious place." And she had taken that advice, without using the common sense she usually flaunted.

On that sound advice, she was now locked out of her house, and unless she wanted to camp out for the evening, she needed to dig up those stones, one-by-one, in order to get in. She walked around the side of the house where it was now pitch black. Without a light or tools to help in her predicament, she got down on her hands and knees, in her tight skirt, and began to lift up the first stone.

The first stone was really hard to get up and she needed a broken branch to help lift it. With very little light, lots of mud, slimy fungus, and creepy crawlers—her fingers began to feel for the key. Feeling horrified with what her fingers were touching, and not knowing what the slimy stuff actually was—bile began to creep up her throat. On the fifth stepping stone, her finger felt a small piece of metal. Suddenly, her heart began to beat out of her chest, as her fingers finally wrapped themselves around the key. Without even knowing it, tears of happiness started spilling out of her eyes. Carefully, she replaced the stone, stood up, and slowly walked over to the front door. When she opened the door, she bent down and put the key under the doormat, with a heavy sigh of relief.

She walked directly into the kitchen, turned on the sink faucet and let the hot water run over her hands for a long time. Three times she soaped them and cleaned out the black grunge that had lodged under her fingernails.

With hunger gnawing in her gut, she made a peanut butter and jelly sandwich, put it on a plate and went upstairs. All she wanted was for this day to finally be over.

Early the next morning, Mercedes walked the six blocks to the repair shop. The garage doors were open, and three men were bustling around the shop. When she finally found who she was looking for, she groaned in relief.

Mercedes saw Fred Zanger, the owner, under the hood of her car. "Morning, Fred. I see you've had my car up on the rack. Did you get a good look as to what is wrong?"

One hand was touching something under the hood and the other hand was clutching a work order. He didn't turn around, but his voice bellowed out, "Morning, Mercedes, I saw your note on the front seat first thing this morning when I came in. I thought I would see what was wrong, so we can order the part immediately." He turned around and walked over to where she was standing, and gave her the male 'once over' look. "Wow...you look nice."

With a scowl on her face, Mercedes ignored his comment and said, "So, what do you think it is, Fred?"

He wiped his hands on his dirty work clothes, and began writing on the work order. "Like I told you the last time—this car has so many miles, it's so old that eventually everything is going to give out. Looks like the starter is gone, and I'm not sure about the clutch. It doesn't seem to engage. We had a hard time putting it into gear to get it over in the bay...." He stopped writing and looked at her eye to eye. "I really think you should consider buying a new car. This is going to become a money pit for you."

"I know, Fred. Every time I bring it in—you say that. Maybe it's time for me to start looking around. Any suggestions?"

He smiled and said, "Yeah, something reliable. This is going to take at least few days with parts and all. I'll hold off if you're going to look for another car."

"That might be a good idea, Fred. Thank you! If your guy can drop me off at the rental place, I'd really appreciate it."

He nodded his head and yelled across the bays, "Hey, Jack, come take Mercedes to the rental place."

"Thanks again, Fred!"

"Take time to look for a new car, Mercedes. This one is not going anywhere—anytime soon!"

She turned around and began walking toward Jack. Mercedes didn't notice that Fred was eyeing her every step of the way as she crossed the parking lot and got into Jack's car, nor did she hear his low whistle.

An hour later, after all the paperwork was signed, she rented a car from an agency down the street. The only thing they had was a sporty BMW convertible. This irritated Mercedes, but there was nothing she could do. She loved her old clunky car with the cracked windshield. With no other options available, she pulled into the underground parking lot and the attendant gave her a thumbs up and smiled.

He ran over to the car and opened her door. "Nice set of wheels," he said with a whistle.

Mercedes got out of the car and bent down to look at the wheels. "Humm, I never looked at the wheels." Her confusion of the meaning of what he said made the attendant laugh.

"I meant—you got a nice car!"

"Oh...!" Mercedes exclaimed as the light bulb went off, and she got his meaning. "Don't get too excited, this is only a loaner, because mine is in the shop," she said with a smile and she began to walk toward the elevators.

"Too bad," he said as she walked away.

Mercedes was over an hour late to work, and there seemed to be a lot of chaos stirring through the office. Friday mornings were usually the winding down day of the week, time to tie up the loose ends. From some reason, the minute Mercedes stepped in the door, things got hectic, and by the late afternoon everyone's nerves were frayed. All her clients were calling, on the verge of hysterics, because of the large drop in the stock market. Others were questioning the drop in the Chinese and Japanese markets. For hours, Mercedes' phone constantly rang. By noon, Mercedes had a screaming headache. Her clients all knew, coming into the investment group, that there was always a chance of risk that involved speculation. Nothing was ever a sure thing in the market that had been volatile for years. Yet, when the market was on an upswing and everyone was making money, she never heard from them. Nor did they call to praise her for her good choices that kept their portfolios growing at a good pace. It was only when the market began to dip, did her phone ring off the hook.

Mercedes had taken a break and went downstairs to the lobby to get a snack from the concession stand. Not usually one to indulge in junk food, this morning had driven her to a chocolate bar and a small bag of potato chips. On the verge of buying a high energy drink, at the last second, she left it on the counter, afraid it would really push her over the edge.

Once seated back at her desk, she slipped out of her high heels, rubbed her sore feet, and moaned in relief. She didn't know why she had let Emme and Jennifer talk her into wearing high heels to work. She hated wobbling around the office, and she always felt like she was on the verge of falling flat on her face. To her it seemed more painful, and a big sacrifice, than its value of looking good. In the magazines, online, and on television, the fashionistas deemed it a *necessity* in the modern-day business attire for women. The fashion magazines were ruthless when it came to any kind of comfort for the working woman. It was all about the 'look' and the 'fashion statement' it created in the workplace. Emme insisted that her new fashion statement, along with her new haircut, made it mandatory to complete each new ensemble with a sexy pair of heels—her feet hated it, and the blisters were nonstop.

Mercedes was researching a portfolio on her desk when her cell phone rang.

"Hi, Emme, what's up?" Mercedes put the folder down, and leaned back in her chair. A smile crossed her face knowing what was to come. She pinched the bridge of her nose to absorb some of the pain from her ghastly headache.

Then she heard the words she was dreading with all her heart.

"Well, what time should I pick you up tonight?" Emme asked.

"Half past a monkey's ass!" Mercedes blurted out.

"I'm not letting you off the hook! What time?" Emme asked her friend.

Mercedes continued to rub her nose. "I was just playing with you, Emme."

"You can play with me 'nicely' tonight. What time?" Emme asked again.

Mercedes closed her eyes and sighed. "Do I really have to go? It's been a long time since I've been to a club, and I haven't missed it at all. Besides, I've had one of the worst weeks of my life. First, I had a toothache, which was really a sinus infection. My dentist was out of town, so I had to find a new one. Then, my car broke down and I had to have it towed to the shop. When I got home, I was on my hands and knees in the dark looking for a fucking key under a rock. Not to mention, both my knees are scraped and killing me. I had to get a rental car, and they only had this luxury one, filled with gadgets and buttons. Today the market dropped, and my ear has been plastered to the phone. Is there any way I can bow out? Don't you have any mercy on me?" She pleaded after her tirade.

Emme sighed and said, "Look, don't you think at your age, that you need some kind of social life other than work and the little deli?"

"But I like my life. You guys keep pushing to change me, and in some cases you have done that. I don't even look like me anymore when I look in the mirror. It doesn't mean I like it or I don't. It's just been overwhelming." Mercedes could feel her head pounding and was listening to her heartbeat in her ear.

"I know the past few months you've gone through some tremendous changes, and all for the good. By no means is it meant to hurt you. We just want to see you enjoy life. We don't want you going through life with regrets of missing out on anything." Emme stated.

Mercedes smiled. "So, you've become my fashionistas, my social directors, and now my incessant therapist?"

Emme laughed. "Yep! And that is the beauty of having me as a friend. I wear a dozen hats!" This time both of the friends started to laugh.

"Okay, I'll go tonight, but just for a little while to show the girls I can hang with the 'magnificent four'! And to celebrate Christina's birthday."

"Wear your new silver dress I dropped off from the shop last week! I'll pick you up at nine."

"I'll meet you there. I'm not as stupid as I used to be. I'll drive my own car so I can leave when I want.... Oh, and don't laugh incessantly when you see the car. Did I mention in my rant that the convertible top is down, and I don't know what frickin' button puts it back up?"

Emme laughed and the phone went dead.

Mercedes sat forward and laid her head on the desk; she took a deep breath and let it out slowly.

Mercedes looked in the mirror and it was like looking at a stranger. Her new haircut was very trendy and she actually liked it. It was easier to keep up and Tessann had kept it trimmed and colored for the past six months. The swelling in her nose was completely gone, and it was small and perfect. In fact, it had subtly changed the look of her face, along with the weight loss and plumper lips. Her new body was tighter than when she was a teenager, and she attributed that to Emme and the Zumba classes. The only things that were still small and nonexistent were her little boobies.

Unfortunately, the new shimmering silver dress showed off every inch of her new svelte body, including her flat chest. It was a great dress, and Emme's taste was as impeccable as all her clientele praised. It hugged Mercedes' body like a glove, and was short enough to show off her endless long legs. The scoop neckline came lower than Mercedes would have liked, but because her chest was so flat, it didn't seem to show much of anything. She spiked out her hair, used a little glitter gel that added to the dazzle, and then applied sparkling silver eye shadow to show off her green eyes. To finish it off, she used a blush that showed off her small freckles, and then painted on a soft pink lip gloss onto her new plump lips. Add on the new rhinestone stilettos, and all-in-all, she had blossomed into a striking 'club' girl.

Mercedes barely made it out the door in her new heels that added another five inches to her statuesque appearance. The menacingly thin heels were more than she could handle, and the fear of falling with each step was stressing her out. When she finally reached the BMW, you could hear her grunts as she fell into the seat behind the steering wheel. Not only was the car much lower to the ground than her plain and simple Honda, it also had way too many lights, buttons, and extras for her to absorb.

Tonight she was lucky. It had an automatic touch-start, or she would have never gotten out of her driveway looking for the ignition. And she certainly didn't want Emme to pick her up. Her plans were to stay at the club for just a little while, then go home, and back to her comfort zone.

Regrettably, the evening was beginning to fit into the rest of her awful week. When she got home from work, she must have touched a button in the car as she struggled to get out. Instantaneously, the convertible top automatically came up and over, and with perfect precision, it tucked into the trunk. Not wanting to deal with it then, she left it for later—and later was now. Her final obstacle before she left for the club was to get the convertible top back up. Although the weather didn't call for convertibles, after a half hour of pushing and hitting every button in the car, she finally gave up. Twice she had gotten out of the car and opened the hood, or popped up the trunk in search some other way to get it back up. Frustrated and angry, all she wanted to do was to get to the club, come home, and call it an evening.

As she bent down, and crawled into the driver's seat, she mumbled to herself, *"Once I get there, someone has to know how to get this frickin' convertible top back up!"*

All the girls were waiting outside for her when she pulled into the valet parking line. The valet opened her door and put out his hand to help pull her out of the front seat. It took a lot of maneuvering to get out of the car, and into an upright position. Towering over the young valet, she looked at him with pleading eyes, and handed him a twenty dollar bill. "Could you find a way to get the convertible top up? I know you can do it." She smiled sweetly.

The valet smiled and bent down into the front seat of the car. He touched a button, and the top automatically came out of the trunk, and connected itself to the top. Then the valet latched it, and turned around and smiled. "How's that?"

"Thank you...." was all Mercedes could get out of her mouth. She blew him a kiss out of gratitude, and the young valet started to blush. He pushed the money into his pocket and waved goodbye.

Mercedes walked up to the girls. Their wide eyes and dropped jaws were enough to make Mercedes instantly turn around to see if she was missing something going on behind her.

She swung her head back around and asked, "Did I miss something? You all look like you've seen a movie star."

Emme stepped forward and announced, "Holy crap! You look fab...u...lous!" The other girls stood there speechless.

Mercedes looked embarrassed. "Emme picked out the clothes. Jessann cut my hair. Alisha's doctor fixed my nose and plumped my lips. Thanks to Zumba, I'm twenty-four pounds lighter!" With a worried look on her face, she pointed a finger at Jennifer and Christina. "What terrifies me the most, is wondering what those two are planning next!"

All the girls began to laugh, and Mercedes blushed. Christina came forward and hugged Mercedes, "Thanks for making my birthday special. I appreciate it. And wow...you look fantastic!"

The girls gathered around Mercedes and began gently pushing her toward the club. There was no way that the bouncer would not let her in tonight. That 'ugly duckling' was now a 'beautiful swan.'

When they finally made it to the front of the line, the bouncer didn't recognize Mercedes. Instead, he gave her the typical male slow body scan. Then he plastered a big smile across his face and gave her a slow wink. In lieu of opening her mouth and saying something she would regret, and afraid he would not allow them in, she closed her mouth, and waited until they were almost inside the club. Then she turned around, put two fingers in her mouth and blew a high-pitched whistle to the bouncer. When his eyes met hers, a defiant look crossed Mercedes' face. She stuck her arm high in the air, and flipped him off. A look of confusion crossed his face. Before he could retaliate or kick her out of the club, Mercedes turned around and pushed her way inside with a big smile on her face. All of her friends noticed what she did and they gave her questioning looks—except for Emme. She winked at Mercedes.

You could see all the anticipation on the girls' faces as their bodies were already starting to sway to the music. The

evening was just starting and everyone was in party mode—
except for Mercedes. Christina, Jennifer, and Tessann were
leading the group to the table and drawing enormous
attention. Jennifer was flaunting 'her girls' and prancing like
a 'pageant queen.' Christina was suggestively eyeing and
smiling at all the men. They paraded past a table that
Michael and Zackary were sitting at with a group of guys.
When Mercedes saw them, she gave them a small wave.
Michael yelled out, "Hey, Mercedes, why don't you and your
friends join us?"

"Later...." was all that she said as they continued to
draw lots of attention from the male and female clubbers.

When they reached the table, Mercedes stood for fear
her dress was too short for her to sit on the tall stool. After
scanning the room, she started to feel uncomfortable and
restless. Her heart was racing and her hands began to shake.
Why am I here and when can I leave, was the silent question
she kept asking herself—over and over.

With great eagerness, Jennifer said, "This should be an
exciting evening. Especially because our favorite disc jockey
is here and our favorite band later." She paused, and then
added, "Oh...and Jake's going to be here later!"

Mercedes knew there would be no 'later', but out of
curiosity she had to ask. "Who's Jake?"

Before she could answer, the music starting blasting
across the room and everything was buzzing around them.
The tables were on the edge of the sunken dance floor and
the surrounding area was set up with couches, lounges, and
small tables, giving the club a relaxed atmosphere. Elegant
chandeliers hung above the sunken dance floor. The lighting
had been dimmed and was almost nonexistent, except for a
reddish glow that came from the middle of the chandeliers.
The two-story complex was a mixture of art-deco
sophistication and rock-star glitz. A haven for the
entertainment industry insiders that liked to mingle with
eager partygoers.

There were a few evenings that Mercedes had recognized some popular movie stars like: Paris Hilton, Lindsay Lohan, Chris Brown, and David Arquette. That didn't impress her—nor did it impress Emme, Alisha, or Tessann. They all had celebrities as clients and found most of them were pampered little twits that expected everyone to jump when they said—jump. At the office Mercedes didn't care who they were, she treated them like the rest of her clients. When they started to pull their tantrums, she would show them to the door. The smart ones would curb their attitudes, knowing that Mercedes wasn't about to take their over-inflated egos. It was a different type of thrill when Christina and Jennifer spotted a famous celebrity. They wanted to be part of the chaos, and loved feeding into their oversized egos. Most of the time, they desperately tried to fit in with all the groupies that played that 'tag-along' game.

After an hour, Mercedes just wanted to go home, take off her heels, and soak in a hot bath. All the music, the over-stimulating socializing, and the packed crowds were beyond her capacity to want to stay around. She was sitting quietly, sipping on a drink, when Emme came over and stood next to her. The table was filled with lots of strange people who were hanging around and trying to talk above the music. Groups of men surrounded the girls, and they took turns endlessly moving back and forth to the dance floor.

Emme leaned over and asked Mercedes, "Are you not having a good time?"

Mercedes stepped down off the stool and onto her wobbly heels. She turned toward Emme and said, "Not really. I find this a big game of cat and mouse. But I was hopeful that after my second drink it might look a little better. Instead I realized that most of the people here were a bunch of creeps. The women flaunt their bodies, and then men shop for the bodies that entice them the most! I don't even think that intelligence enters into the equation. Do you?" She sighed.

Emme laughed and gave Mercedes a hug. "I get it, my friend. There's only so much I can take, too!"

Suddenly, Mercedes felt a hand massage her shoulder, and without looking back, she figured it was one of her girlfriends. Only when she completely concentrated on the finger movements, did she come to the realization that it wasn't a woman's touch at all.

On the verge of panic, she spun around, and an unknown male body leaned close into hers. His voice whispered into her ear, "Where have you been all my life?"

Mercedes pulled away and turned around, to find this gorgeous man standing in front of her with big brown eyes and a dazzling smile. He was tall, muscular, with a full head of spiked hair and was dressed impeccably in club attire.

She looked at him with curious eyes, then her cynicism pushed her to say, "I've been hiding under a rock! Can't you see the scales growing on my back?" her voice was dripping with sarcasm.

He pulled back, crossed his arms over his chest, and smirked out of one side of his mouth. "Ouch...I can hear the razor tongue that goes with the scales!" he laughed and continued to smile.

Mercedes mocked his stance. "Maybe you can tell me to what I owe this presence of yours...along with the massage?" She asked sweetly.

"Let me introduce myself. My name is Jake. And when I see a beautiful woman, I'm like a magnet!"

Mercedes nodded and said, "I see you're filled with all of the 'right' clichés to impress all the 'Twinkie heads' around here!"

"Ouch...I feel like I'm being shredded by your sharp tongue, again!" He looked at her with curiosity.

She finally relaxed a little and said with an honesty that stunned Emme, who was still standing next to her. "I'm sorry, but my friends dragged me here kicking and screaming tonight. This really isn't my scene. I apologize for my rudeness."

He reached his hand across and tapped her petite nose and said, "I do not believe you are a 'Twinkie head'—quite the opposite. You are...."

Just as he was opening his mouth to say something else, Jennifer came over and wrapped her arms around him. Then she gave him a big kiss on his lips as she rubbed her 'girls' along his chest. His face turned a deep shade of red, and he put both his hands on Jennifer's shoulders and slowly disengaged her arms, pushing her away.

Jennifer then put her arm around Mercedes and said, "Mercedes...I see you met my friend, Jake."

Mercedes stepped back and unwrapped Jennifer's arm from around her. "Actually, he just showed up and I had no idea who he was...I do remember you saying that a 'Jake' was going to meet 'you' here. So, if you both will excuse me, I'm going to take a walk." She grabbed Emme's hand and began to walk away.

She heard him faintly say, "It was a pleasure meeting you, Mercedes! Hope to see you again."

They slowly walked around 'people watching' all the clubbers. Getting bored, Mercedes finally said, "Let's go to the restroom so I can take a deep breath, and have a little peace and quiet for a few minutes."

Emme nodded and they walked to the ladies room and opened the door. It was pretty packed inside, and many of the women were in all kinds of inebriated states. One girl was sprawled out on the floor, in the corner, so drunk she looked on the verge of passing out. Another was arguing with her friend at the sink area, as one girl splashed the face of her friend with water, trying to sober her up. Another girl was hanging over the trash can throwing up and crying. Two girls were waiting patiently in line for a vacant stall, when all of a sudden, the noise from the last stall became alarmingly familiar. The grunting and groaning was hitting a sexual climax. Mercedes bent down, looked slightly under the door, and confirmed there were two pairs of familiar legs—Jennifer and Jake. One pair had pants around hairy ankles, and the other had on stilettos dangling in the air. There was definitely a lot going on, and Mercedes and Emme could only shake their heads in embarrassment, as the screams got louder and louder. Done with the whole scene, Mercedes and Emme left the restroom, laughing all the way back to the table.

Once they were back at the table, Mercedes sat on the stool and Emme stood next to her. This time a nice looking young man came over, stood next to Emme, and tried to start a conversation. The girls could tell he was intoxicated and his bloodshot eyes only verified their opinions.

"I haven't seen you here before, is this your first time?" he asked. His voice was slightly slurred as the words came out.

Emme smiled and shook her head. "Nope."

He moved in closer and slid his arm around Emme and Mercedes' waist. "You beauties should come more often. Can I call my buddies over, and can we buy you two beautiful women a drink? Then maybe later, we can all go to my place and I can make you really happy!" his suggestion fell on deaf ears.

Mercedes' eyes opened wide in disbelief, as Emme turned around and gave him her best smile. Then she said sweetly, "You know what would make me so happy...?" She took her hand and slid it across his zippered pants.

He leaned in closer, as his head swayed back and forth. He whispered in her ear, "What...?"

In a loud, deep voice for all to hear, she yelled, "If you would fuckin' get off my foot, and get your fuckin' arm off my waist, and if you'd act like a bee and fuckin' buzz away!...That...would make me happy!" her loud voice was dripping with sarcasm.

All the people around them stopped to watch the scene. Just as he was starting to take his hands off Emme and Mercedes, Jake walked up and grabbed the guy by the neck of his shirt, yanking him off balance. Immediately, the guy turned to swing a fist at Jake. Mercedes jumped down off the stool and grabbed Emme's hand and headed to the other side of the table. Mercedes watched as the grown men began to scuffle, then two big bouncers came over and pulled them apart. The bouncers grabbed the drunk by both his arms and briskly began walking toward the front doors. Jake straightened up his shirt and walked back over to the group.

Mercedes and Emme were standing there, shocked, when Jake walked over to them.

He put his hand on each of the girls' shoulders and apologetically said, "I'm really sorry, ladies. Some men are the biggest jerks! Can I buy you a drink and make up for it?"

Jennifer came rushing over and put her arms around him with a big smile. "That was so exciting. Thanks for rescuing my friends." She instantly planted a big kiss on his lips.

Mercedes looked up at Jake and kindly said, "Thanks for the offer, Jake, but I think I've had just about all I can take of this place. So, I'm leaving." She looked over to Emme, "Are you coming or staying?"

"Tomorrow is Saturday and we have an eight o'clock Zumba class, so I'm leaving." Emme followed Mercedes to where all their friends were, and they said their goodbyes. Alisha had already left, Tessann was on the dance floor, and Christina had celebrated a little too much for her birthday. She was passed out on the couch next to the table.

As Emme and Mercedes walked out the door, they both had a look of relief on their faces. Emme hugged Mercedes and said, "See you in the morning."

Mercedes looked at her with sad eyes, "Do I have too? Can't I take a break?"

"Nope...." The valets pulled up with their cars, they both got in, and drove off.

When Mercedes got home, she climbed the stairs, went into the closet and put on a T-shirt and flannel bottoms. She walked into the bathroom and while she was brushing her teeth, she stared at herself in the mirror. When she was done, she walked into her bedroom, lit a small candle, crawled into bed and shut off the light.

Before she drifted off to sleep, she mumbled to herself, *"God...a man actually said I was beautiful tonight. Nobody has ever said that to me."* A tear slid down her cheek.

Twelve

MERCEDES turned over and shut off the blasting music. She crawled out of bed and shuffled into the bathroom. She turned on the light, looked in the mirror, and noticed the dark circles under her eyes. *"What do you expect when you burn the candle at both ends, missy!"* she said as she put on her gym clothes.

After she was done dressing, she went downstairs; and the smell of coffee brewing made her smile. All her friends laughed at her moderately old-fashioned coffee pot. They all had the new-age and extremely popular Keurig. Where all you had to do was pop in a little cartridge and it makes one perfect cup of coffee. Mercedes didn't care, nor did she want one. She was a creature of habit who never fed into fads or newfangled inventions. She was old-school and stuck to her principles. Rarely did she stray from the old way of doing things, just to join technology with its constant changes. Not unless she had no other alternative, in that case, the 'technology' won out.

Mercedes' phone started to ring, so she walked over to the counter and picked it up to see who it was. At that moment, she heard a knock at the front door and didn't answer the phone.

Why would Jennifer call her this early on Saturday morning?

She poured a second cup of coffee and walked to the door. Mercedes opened the door and handed Emme a cup of coffee. "Morning...did you sleep at all?"

Emme laughed. "I slept like a baby for five hours and then the stupid alarm went off!"

Mercedes held up her phone and took a sip of coffee. "Jennifer called me a few minutes ago, but I didn't answer. Wonder what she wants! I thought for sure she would still be cuddled up in bed with 'Jake the Rake'!" They both laughed at Mercedes' nickname for Jennifer's new flame.

Emme snatched Mercedes' phone. "What the hell could she possibly want? I wonder if she's okay. Maybe she got a DUI?" Emme pushed the message button.

Jennifer whiny voice said, "I'm really upset, Mercedes. How could you outrageously flirt with my boyfriend, Jake? I think you and I should have a little talk. Could you call me?"

Emme's eyes opened as wide as they could, and her jaw dropped open. *"What the fuck is this jealously crap?"* she screamed. "I was with you the whole night and you never said more than a few sarcastic words to him! Oh man, she's off her rocker! And she's barking up the wrong tree...."

Mercedes was beyond stunned. She was speechless. She snatched the phone back and redialed Jennifer's number.

"Did you want to talk with me?" Mercedes' loud, angry voice bellowed into the cell phone.

"I'm so pissed off at you, I'm about to scream."

"Well, scream as loud as you want! Oh and say 'good morning' to Emme. We're on speaker and she's standing right next to me. I'm shocked to hell with your message."

"Shocked! You...are shocked? I'm the one who is ready to strangle you!" she hissed.

"For what?" Mercedes backed her phone away, and looked at it, as though she was talking to a crazy woman.

Jennifer hiccupped and started to cry. "Because you went home with Jake! I've been seeing him for two weeks and...I thought we were in love...until last night!" Jennifer was about to break into hysterics.

Mercedes was seething. "What the fuck are you talking about? I didn't go home with Jake, and he didn't come home with me; so whoever is feeding you that pile of bullshit is doing it to ruffle your feathers!" Mercedes and Emme were looking at each other in sheer confusion.

Mercedes calmed down and softly said, "Look, when I said goodnight to you guys, I left alone. I had enough of the bar scene. I worked all day and all I wanted was to go home and get some sleep. Hell... Emme followed me out to my car, and she left too."

"Then why did Jake disappear at the same time? And when I texted him, he wrote back, 'I left with your girlfriend." Jennifer began to cry. "I really loved him...."

"What...?" Emme chimed in, "He may have left with your girlfriend, but it wasn't Mercedes or I. So I suggest you text him again and find out who." Emme was angry now, and her face was as red as a tomato.

"He won't answer my texts or calls...." She sobbed.

"He's a dickhead and I suggest you tell him to 'fuck off'! Have more respect for yourself. But, don't call screaming at Mercedes for your own insecurities and bad choices!" Emme raised her voice a few octaves.

Mercedes entered the conversation with a gentle voice, "I would never do that to you, or any of my friends. You know men aren't attracted to mousy little me. I'm so surprised that you would even consider him being attracted to me."

"Well, when he came back to the table just before he disappeared, he had said 'I think your friend is hot. How come I've never seen her before'?" she barely whispered. "Then he said to a friend, 'I'm going to find her.' So, I figured 'her' meant you!" Jennifer sighed.

Emme grabbed the phone and said abruptly, "Is that before, or after you fucked him in the ladies' room stall? Look, we have a Zumba class in a few minutes and I don't want to be late over some of your silly nonsense. Go find the 'other her' and screw up her morning!" Emme touched the off button of Mercedes' phone and handed it back to her.

Emme exploded. "For Christ's sake, what is wrong with her? Those club guys are all players and he's playing her like a fine-tuned violin! When will that girl ever learn?"

Mercedes closed the door behind them as they walked out to her loaner car and said, "She's not very bright when it comes to men. Cut her some slack, Emme."

Emme looked at Mercedes and for some reason broke out into laughter. "She's not bright when it comes to anything! I can't even imagine her thinking you would leave with a man you didn't know—a frickin' stranger. Thirty years, and you would think she would know you by now! Hmmpffff...."

Mercedes slid in behind the steering wheel of the fancy car and started the engine; she looked at Emme who was starting to calm down and said, "I want my car back!"

Emme's face turned red again. "Let's not fucking go there right now. Your car is a piece of junk that needs to be recycled into a new washing machine!"

Early Monday morning, Mercedes' hand stopped the alarm and pulled the covers back over her eyes. She wasn't ready to go to work. The weekend passed by so quickly that she didn't have time to do some of the things she had planned—like replanting her spring garden. She did get to drop off her clothes at the cleaners, and do a little grocery shopping; but she just needed one more day to finish her long list of 'things to do.' She spent part of Saturday with Emme, and Tessann. The main topic of their conversation got Emme to the boiling point, again. Even Tessann couldn't believe that Jennifer had called and accused Mercedes of playing around with Jake.

Tessann commented with a disdainful look on her face. "He's the biggest player in the club. I can't tell you how many times he's hit on me."

Emme and Mercedes immediately gave Tessann a questioning stare.

"Oh no, don't you go there! I was at the club all night, and went directly home by myself!" Tessann smiled as she watched Emme and Mercedes sigh in relief.

Mercedes turned over on her side as she continued to think about Friday night and what could have made Jennifer believe that Jake could possibly be attracted to her. She wasn't a blonde bombshell. She wasn't tall, statuesque, augmented, or beautiful. She was just plain Mercedes, amongst her friends and 'clubbers'. She could never compete with her friends when it came to beauty. She was nobody special, with the exception of being a brilliant businesswoman who could hold her own amongst any major player in her field of expertise. But, then again, the men in the clubs weren't looking for a woman with brains, they were looking for that ornament—eye candy to hang on their arms or flash to all their friends. Mercedes laid there wondering what Emme was so mad at—that wasn't like her to go ballistic over one of Jennifer's brainless rants.

Mercedes finally got out of bed and went into the bathroom, looked in the mirror and walked into her closet to get ready for work. She was going out to lunch today, with

Jarrod and John-Paul, to discuss an investment. Jarrod had sent her an email on Friday because he was out of the office all day. She sent a note back declining his invitation. During the weekend, he had responded by sending her yet another email, not requesting, but insisting she attend. Not wanting to cause any dissention with her boss, and trying to keep peace, she sent him back an email with one word, 'okay.'

Trying to keep on her tight schedule to get to work, Mercedes looked around her closet and picked a new black business suit, a red silk blouse, and a pair of red stiletto heels to go with it. The skirt was a little shorter and tighter than normal and Mercedes was constantly tugging it downward. When she was finished dressing, she looked in the mirror, and was shocked to see the fashionista she had become. With her hair spiked out, some makeup perfectly applied, and a great pair of black dangling earrings, she picked up her purse and briefcase and walked out the door. At the last moment, she decided to stop off at the deli to get a cappuccino to go. It had been a few weeks since she had stopped in the deli, and she really missed the great coffee and chaos.

Mercedes pulled into the parking lot and it was full. Deciding to pass on the coffee, she was just coming out of the driveway, when she noticed a parking spot on the street. Taking an immediate course of action, she pulled up to the curb, shut off the engine, and got out of the car. The well-worn sidewalk and her stilettos had become a dangerous accomplishment as she slowly walked toward the deli.

A few people were standing outside, waiting their turn to get a table in the deli, as they enjoyed a sunny California day. Mercedes opened the door, walked in, and carefully sauntered up to the counter. Within a few minutes, her order was taken and she stood there waiting patiently. Suddenly, an ear-piercing wolf-whistle drew the attention of many customers. Mercedes turned around to see where the whistling was coming from and to who the recipient could be. Without warning, she bumped right into Josh.

His hands came up to steady her just as she was about to fall over. "Whoaaa...pretty lady! You nearly knocked me over." Josh smiled.

Mercedes' eyes opened wide and she started to laugh. "I was just looking to see what the commotion was all about. I wanted to see who was doing all the whistling! Did I miss something or somebody famous?"

His hand came up and his index finger tapped her nose. "I whistled at you, pretty lady. Don't you look beautiful this morning." This time his whistle was for her ears only as he did the once over with his eyes. "Are you on your way to work?"

Mercedes blushed and looked down at the unexpected compliment. It had been years since an attractive man had actually given her a flattering comment. "Thank you for the nice compliment." Her eyes darted everywhere but towards him. "Yes, it's just another day in Paradise, and I have a lunch client I'm really dreading." she mumbled.

He pulled her chin up with one finger to look into her eyes and said, "Another day in Paradise would have us stranded in our swimsuits on some deserted island, not me here working the breakfast crowd, and you at the office!"

Mercedes' eyes focused on his big smile and she began to laugh. "You're right! Sun, beach, palm trees, and Pina Coladas!" Then she shook her head. "The best I can hope for today is that my work week goes fast and Friday comes around in a hurry!"

"Did you get your order in?" he asked. Mercedes nodded. "Stay here and I'll go get it." He walked quickly to the back, into the kitchen Mercedes watched every muscle in his body move as he walked away.

Five minutes later, Mercedes walked out the door with a big smile on her face and a hot cup of coffee in her hand.

Her smile immediately vanished when she looked at her windshield and noticed the parking ticket lying under the wiper. Feeling really brainless, she looked up and read the small print on the two-hour parking sign—no parking Monday mornings 6a.m. to 12p.m. for street cleaners. She snatched the ticket off the windshield and stuffed it in her purse. When she bent down to climb behind the steering wheel, she angrily muttered, *"Son of a bitch!"*

Mercedes pulled into the underground parking area and the attendant didn't raise the gate to let her pass. Instead, he walked over to her driver's window and bent down. He wasn't a very tall young man, and he was slightly overweight. His dark black hair was not short, but long enough to hang down over his dark brown eyes. Slightly agitated, Mercedes rolled down her window and gave him a look of confusion.

"Did you need me for something?" she asked with a slight terseness attached.

He bent down to eye level with her window and with a slight Persian accent, he said. "No. I just wanted to say that I like your new car. You look very pretty sitting in it, and I'm very glad you're not driving that deathtrap."

Mercedes frowned and she barked out, "My car is not a deathtrap! I've had it for ten years and I've kept it in great running condition! This is just a loaner while my car is in for minor repairs!"

His eyes looked remorseful for making her angry with his comment. "Please, I didn't mean to offend you or your car." Then he gave her a big grin and said, "You look very nice today."

"Thank you. Can you please open the gate, so I get to work; I'm running a little late." She said in a very ill-humored voice.

"Yes...yes...." He jumped up and ran to the boxy attendant station and hit the button to open the gate.

Mercedes pushed her foot down on the gas pedal and you could hear the tires screeching before she let up and drove off to find a parking spot.

Once upstairs, she said hello to Mary and walked directly into her office. Placing her purse and briefcase down on her desk, she picked up her paper cup and took a final swallow of her coffee. Feeling slightly stressed over her aggravating morning, she reached over and hit the button on her office phone to hear the messages.

"Hi, Mercedes, this is Fred Zanger at the repair shop. I've looked over everything and I think you might want to consider buying a new car. The rings are leaking and your transmission is about to go out. I'll fix it if you want, but the parts and labor are three times the value of the car; and I don't know, once it's done, if the engine will make it more than a year. It's got one-hundred-ninety-two thousand miles...well, give me a call and we'll discuss it."

Mercedes laid her head into her nestled arms on the desk, and inhaled a slow, deep breath. Just as she was going to exhale to calm her jittery nerves down, she heard a tapping on the wall. With her head still cradled in her arms, she cocked her head slightly to the side and looked to see who was invading her space at this horrible moment in time.

"Wow, you look wiped...long weekend?" Zackary asked and started to laugh. "Saw you Saturday night at the club...boy did you look hot in that shimmering silver number you were wearing! And your girlfriend with the purple hair was damn hot too! How come you didn't come over and say 'hi'?" His hand continued to lightly tap on the wall.

Before Mercedes got a single word out of her mouth, Michael also leaned his head into the open doorway and said, "What's up, Mercedes, you look really...thrashed. Are you still hungover from Friday night?" Michael began to laugh and it caused Zackary to join in.

Mercedes was silently counting to ten. She narrowed her eyes and was about to say a few choice words when Michael piped in again, "Do you want to go to lunch with Zack, Alexi, and me this afternoon? Thought we would take in that new restaurant down the street." He smiled broadly.

In a slow angry voice she said, "You guys are so amped on caffeine that you can't even see I'm having a horrible morning! Could you both get the hell out of my office before I throw something!"

At that comment, both their eyes opened wide and their jaws dropped down. "But the day has barely started...how can it be so 'crappy' already?" Zackary questioned.

"Take my word for it...it's a 'crappy' morning! I was running late, then I got a parking ticket, and now my mechanic said my car is not repairable. Wouldn't you consider that a 'crappy' morning?" She raised her head, sat straight up in her seat, and pointed her finger for them to leave.

"We'll catch you later...." Michael said, walking down the hall with Zackary.

"I don't think so, boys!" she mumbled to herself. And, as if a second thought popped into her head, she jumped out of her chair and wobbled to the door and yelled down the hall, "Don't count on me for lunch!" She wanted to add 'ever' to the end of the sentence, but thought she would be wise and not create any more commotion with those two. With a sigh of relief, and a need to get her day started, she slowly walked back to her chair and sat down.

Her mind was spinning in circles as to what she was going to do about her car. *Did she fix it, and spend a lot of money, not knowing if it would break down again?* She loved her car and had grown accustomed to all its little quirky problems. The passenger windshield wiper only went halfway across the windshield on rainy days. But it didn't bother her, because it didn't rain very often in southern

California. She had to pick open the cover to the gas cap with a small nail file she kept in the car, every time she got gas. But she didn't care about that, because it only had become a ridiculous challenge whenever she needed gas. The window on the back door wouldn't go down anymore, and the antenna had to be replaced on occasion when she parked her car on the city streets. Mercedes didn't mind any of these small grievances, she loved the used car she had purchased on her own at eighteen, and she had worked very hard for three years to pay it off.

Mercedes picked up the phone and called Emme. She needed to talk to someone who knew how she felt about her car. "Hello, Emme?"

Emme sounded out of breath. "What's up...are you okay? Why are you calling me this early?"

Mercedes was on the verge of tears and her voice was cracking, "I've had a bad morning and now I'm having to make a big decision about my car. And you, of all my friends, know how much I love my 'crappy' car."

Emme's voice softened and she said, "Hold on a sec, I just ran out of the shower to answer the phone and I need to wrap a towel around me." There was a rustling sound, and Emme came back to the phone. "Oh, babe...I know you love that little piece of junk with all your heart. And I get the history of it being your first car that you actually bought on your own. But, sometimes, you have to let things die a quiet death. In your case, you have to be happy you had it for ten years and now it's time to find another car that will be with you for another ten years."

Mercedes started to quietly weep. "I know you're right, but this is hard for me. I didn't have a normal childhood, nor did I ever have a parent who ever cared. For a long time, it was just me and my car. For a few months, I even slept in her when I was homeless."

"I know, sweetheart. Don't cry." Emme said soothingly, as she had done on many occasions when Mercedes had fallen to pieces. "I have a great idea. Let's go out this weekend and find you a new friend, Mercedes. A brand new, shiny one that will be more reliable and you can love just as much."

Mercedes hiccupped. "Okay, you're right. I need to let her go. Let's plan on Sunday."

Emme made a shivering noise. "Brrrrr...I've got to go dry off. This weekend it is! And Mercedes...?"

"Humm...?"

"She's going to be fine. She's going to junk heaven!" Emme started to laugh.

Mercedes pictured the visual and she too began to laugh. "Thanks, Emme."

Emme hung up the phone and Mercedes sat back in the chair. She took a Kleenex and wiped her face and decided to look online at new models of cars she might be interested in. As she was browsing, she thought of the cars her girlfriends had. Emme didn't spare a dime when she wanted something. Six months ago, she bought a high-end Mercedes that was the first model of its kind. Emme was like that. She liked to create the fashionable trend and not just be part of it. What Emme really wanted, but could not justify and neither could her accountant, was a new SLS-AMG Sport model. After two accidents and one stolen car, her accountant said 'no' to the two-hundred-fifty-thousand dollar overindulgence. After a month of vacillation, she finally leased a o63-AMG C-Class for close to a hundred-thousand dollars. It was something that made her happy— and something she worked hard to afford.

Christina had a smaller, cheaper version of the Mercedes C-Class. Tessann drove a new sporty Audi TTS Sport convertible and had the tickets to prove it. Jennifer was a struggling actress and worked for her daddy. Her taste in cars didn't match her pocketbook, so she settled for a used

250 IS Lexus that her mother had passed down to her. Alisha was happy with a SUV that could accommodate her growing family.

Most of their generation didn't know what it was like to drive a clunky 'old beater' that had four sad tires, lots of dents, and a missing window or two. They were spoiled and thought they deserved more. It was a pretentious generation that cared what others thought, and they became very competitive against each other. Except for Mercedes. She didn't really care what people thought of her car. After all, *"It is just a form of transportation,"* her mother would say.

Mercedes wasn't a trendsetter and she wasn't into name brands or following what others did. She just wanted a car that would get her to and from wherever she was going, without breaking down. So she continued to look on her computer for the next hour as the latest models of cars flashed across her screen. She didn't want anything too large, and she definitely didn't want anything too small or low to the ground—like her rental. Every morning it was like an obstacle course when she had to get into that car. First she had to bend down, then she had to turn to the side, and finally she had to carefully slide into the seat. It wasn't like that with her little Honda. She just yanked the door open and slid in.

She wanted something practical, economical, and just enough power to get her up and down the canyons to the beach. It didn't have to have a high-performance engine that had enough horsepower to get up to 140 mph in ten seconds. There was no purpose unless you were on a racetrack. There was no point to speed on the California freeways—they were always congested.

By noon, Mercedes was exhausted dealing with clients and worrying about what to buy. Just as she was getting ready to step out of the office for her lunch meeting, Michael and Zackary stopped outside her door, and asked, "Hey, you sure you don't want to come with us? I heard their food is really decent."

"No thanks. I promised Jarrod I would go to lunch with him and his client." Mercedes was pulling out her hand mirror and lipstick from her purse. She began to methodically put on her lipstick.

Michael popped his head inside and said, "Oh, you mean that French jerk who looks down women's tops? And since when have you become so...buddy-buddy with the boss?"

Mercedes started to laugh out loud and said, "I wonder if they heard that down the hall. I think they're sitting in Jarrod's office with the door open!"

Michael's face turned bright red and his head twisted around immediately. Suddenly his body relaxed and Mercedes listened to his heavy sigh of relief.

Mercedes began to giggle. "I was just kidding." Mercedes slipped her lipstick back into her purse. "I'm meeting Jarrod at his car in five minutes."

"Sometimes you can be such a bitch." Michael said, dripping in sarcasm.

Mercedes shook her finger back and forth. "You better be careful with your choice of words...nowadays that could be considered sexual or employee harassment in the workforce!" She stood up, waved a few fingers, and walked past them as she headed to the parking lot to find Jarrod.

Their reservation for lunch was at a famous Beverly Hills hangout for the wealthy and famous. During their lunch, Mercedes had spotted a few very famous businessmen and actors sitting around. It was a haven for those who wanted to lounge and discuss business without any bothersome public displays of harassment by the paparazzi, or overzealous fans.

Broken *image*

The proprietor only allowed a select group of people to patronize his small restaurant, and kept things very private. Usually, large groups of rowdy paparazzi hung around outside waiting for anyone famous to appear, so they could snap a picture and sell it to the tabloids. Movie stars and their children were top money makers on the list for the tabloids. Often those pictures would explode into a raging battle over privacy, and sometimes into fist fights. Unfortunately, this was a big part of the new culture of celebrity status. Nothing was sacred, and everyone was a target in the Beverly Hills area.

Mercedes didn't notice the paparazzi when she arrived at the restaurant. When lunch was almost over, she got up to use the restroom, and she knew they had to be outside in full force. Sitting in a secluded window booth was Brad Pitt and a few other gentlemen. Despite Brad being dressed casually in jeans and T-shirt, the businessmen were all dressed to the hilt in their expensive suits. Mercedes smiled, and wondered what kind of transaction was going down. *Was he looking for financing of his newest film? Was it his group of financial advisors? Or were they his associates?* Nobody looked familiar and she knew practically every financial adviser in the area, if not personally, then strictly on a professional or visual basis.

At another table was Jennifer Garner and Ben Affleck and their three young children–a very energetic group of little ones. With a slight bounce in her step, Mercedes smiled as she walked past and acknowledged the playful children who were doing exactly what children do—amusing themselves at a lunch table. When she made it back to her table, she took her seat next to John-Paul, and across from Jarrod. Their lunch was just about over and the dishes were being cleared away. It had been a very interesting conversation during lunch and Jarrod seemed quite happy with the outcome. On the other hand, all Mercedes wanted to do was go back to the office and get some of her work done.

Ready to leave, Mercedes started to say her goodbyes. "Well John-Paul, it was a pleasure doing business with you." Mercedes said, extending her hand.

John-Paul took her hand and brought it slowly up to his lips and gave it a soft kiss. "The pleasure is mine. Did I tell you that red is a very beautiful color on you? You look very striking today."

"Thank you." Mercedes was getting a little nervous. "I thought we came up with some good financial advice today. Good luck with your decisions. I think they are the wisest they can be." Suddenly, Mercedes felt a hand skim across her leg under the table. Immediately, she took her hand and pushed it away. Not to draw a lot of attention, and never having to deal with a situation like this before, she cocked her head to look directly at John-Paul with a deliberate look of reproach in her gaze.

He rose and stood behind Mercedes' chair. Then he wedged his hand between the back of her chair, touching her back. "I thought perhaps I could take you back to the office. Or better yet, The Beverly Hills Hotel for a drink. When you were in the restroom, Jarrod said he needed to run a few errands before going back to the office; so I suggested I could drop you off," his suggestive and flirty French accent became more pronounced. She smiled and leaned forward.

Jarrod looked slightly confused as to John-Paul's statement. "I did say that, didn't I?"

Mercedes knew exactly where this was going and felt very uncomfortable. As a quick thinker and a bright young woman, she countered, "I was just going to tell Jarrod that my dearest friend works down the street, and I had made plans to stop by and drop something off. So, this is a great opportunity for me to go for a short walk, catch some beautiful sunshine, and get an errand done." She smiled and stood up. "Thank you, gentlemen, for a very educational lunch. The food was excellent, as always, and the conversation was very enlightening!"

John-Paul turned to Mercedes again to plea his intentions. This time he touched one of her dangling earrings. "I'd be glad to take you to your friend's to help you drop off whatever it is you need to give her."

Jarrod immediately chimed in, looking a little guilty. "I can do errands later and take you back, Mercedes."

"See you later at the office, Jarrod. Enjoy the day, John-Paul." Mercedes placed her purse on her shoulder and started toward the entrance of the restaurant. She didn't know where the hell she was going to go, or how she was going to get back to the office, but she was so angry with Jarrod that he put her in this situation with John-Paul—all she could see was red.

Once she walked outside and into the sunshine, a little of her anxiety dissipated. When she saw a Mercedes-Benz dealership down the street, a big smile crossed her face. She would kill two birds with one stone—she would browse the new cars, and then ask to test drive one back to the office. She patted herself on the back for being a smart cookie, and very resourceful.

As Mercedes stepped off the elevator to the office, her anger began to increase. Although she did get to test drive a car she liked, she had wasted precious time away from the office. This was Jarrod's fault, and she was going to march into his office and let him know it. She stopped off at Mary's desk and picked up her mail.

"Hello, dear. Did you have a nice lunch?" Mary asked in her sweet voice.

Mary saw the anger on Mercedes' face. In a low, solid voice, Mercedes said, "Is Jarrod in? Is he alone?"

Mary could see something had happened and Mercedes' face was getting redder by the moment. "Why yes, dear, to both questions. He came in after the lunch meeting. I was wondering where you were. Didn't you go together?"

165

Mercedes started to march back to his office the best she could in her stilettos. She turned back to Mary and said, "It's a long, ugly story...."

Mercedes knocked on his closed door. She wanted to just barge in and rip his head off, but her right half the brain told her to maintain her best business decorum.

"Come on in."

Mercedes flung the door open to add some high intensity drama to her anger that he was about to witness. Then she grabbed the door and slammed it shut and turned to glare pointedly at him as he sat glued to his seat. After a few seconds of trying to compose herself a little, she spat out, "You...fucking lunatic. Who do you think you're dealing with—a thoughtless tramp? Don't you ever...and I mean ever...set me up like that again! I did you a favor by joining you for lunch to help with that asshole. And what is my payback...I have to find a ride back to the office or be pawed to death by that testosterone smitten French dickhead! Why...."

Jarrod stood up and leaned forward on his desk with both hands. His face was red and sweat was dripping off his forehead. "Calm down, Mercedes."

"Calm down! I'm wearing fucking stilettos," she points down to her shoes, "and I have to walk back or find a ride to the office...are you kidding me! How condescending to want me to calm down! You fucking walk in these shoes!" *Figuratively as well as literally, jackass!*

Jarrod's eyes opened wide and he was at a loss for words. Mercedes felt the hair on her neck raise and she spun around and flung open the door. Standing in front of her, with shocked faces, was the entire office staff. Mary took in the anger on Mercedes' face. She immediately turned around and walked back down the hall, giving Mercedes some space. Mercedes took one step forward and said with squinted eyes, "All of you go back to your offices. This is none of your damn business!"

From behind her, Jarrod stepped forward and pointed to each person who was still standing there. "Back to your offices, and close your doors. This avenue of entertainment is over for you!" Then he looked at Mercedes and said, "Can we go back into my office, talk about this calmly, or would you prefer to leave the office and discuss...this?"

Mercedes looked at him with narrowed eyes, "Leaving with you once was enough for me today. I will be glad to talk calmly about this absurd afternoon." Mercedes turned around and went to the seat in front of his desk and sat down. Jarrod stood there until all the doors were closed. He inhaled a deep breath and let it out slowly, as he closed the door, and walked behind the desk to sit down.

Mercedes just stared at him and could see his discomfort. Finally, he said, "I'm really sorry about what went down at lunch. I had no part of it and actually was quite surprised when he brought me into it."

Mercedes shook her head and said, "I don't believe you! If that's the case, why didn't you stand up for me?"

He leaned back in his chair. "I never told him I had errands to run. He made that up. He was playing both of us. I swear." His nervous hands went up and pulled the knot down and loosened his tie.

"I go to the bathroom and come back and he has his hand on my leg, under the table, and suggests we go to the Beverly Hills Hotel for a drink! Are you kidding me?" Mercedes sat forward in the chair and crossed her hands on the desk. "I don't socialize with my clients or anyone else's except for pre-organized social events. And I didn't appreciate his forward, arrogant behavior. Totally unacceptable to me. I will not work with him again. He's all yours, and I don't really give a damn how or what you tell him."

Mercedes stood up, walked to the door, and put her hand on the doorknob. Jarrod stood up and said, "I'm really sorry, Mercedes. He did say when you were in the restroom he thought you were very attractive. I had no idea.... I'm just glad you went to visit your friend."

Mercedes turned around to look at Jarrod. This was the first time they had ever had an argument that centered on a client. "I had to find a ride back to the office. I had no plans with a friend; I made that up so I wouldn't wind up embarrassing you or him—and to keep you from losing him as your client. You owe me big time!" Mercedes walked out of Jarrod's office and closed the door. She walked down the hall and into her office and slammed the door shut.

She hit the button on the intercom and waited for Mary to answer. "Mary, could you do me a big favor and please bring me a cup of coffee, and if you have any aspirin hanging around, I would love a couple."

"Sure, dear. Black or with cream and sugar? I'm never sure what you want. It always depends on your mood and I would guess, 'black' right now."

"Yes, please."

Mary came into the office holding a tall cup of hot coffee. "Here you go, sweetheart. I'm so sorry your day didn't go well. Care to talk about it—if not—let me know what else I can do." Mary sweetly smiled and turned to leave the room.

When Mary called her 'sweetheart,' it melted Mercedes. It was never done in a patronizing way, but more motherly. Mary had a kind soul that Mercedes adored. When she used words of endearment, it always made her feel comforted. At this moment in time, Mercedes needed those kind words and someone who cared.

Mercedes whispered, "Please don't go, Mary. I need to talk."

Thirteen

"I'VE never been so mad in my whole entire life! How dare he put his hand on my knee and start moving upward...." Mercedes turned to Emme and took off her sunglasses to show her big, beautiful green eyes with extraordinarily long dark lashes. "Who the hell does he think he is?"

Emme kept her eyes on the traffic, but began to laugh. "A red-blooded Frenchman who was smitten by a beautiful woman! That's who!" She shook her head and a sad expression crossed her face. "Sometimes I wonder how deep your pain really is, Mercedes."

Mercedes was silent for a moment, thinking about what Emme said.

Emme quietly asked, "How does it feel to have a nice looking man attracted to you? I don't think you've had that kind of attention from a man in a very long time. Not since you were in high school and hormones were raging." Emme pulled up to the red light and stopped. "How does it feel to be adored, admired, and sexually desired?" Emme turned her head towards Mercedes to see her face.

Mercedes turned her head away and the pain was beginning to flood her thoughts. Tears were gathering and her shoulders slumped forward.

Emme curled her lips, and slowly spit out these angry words. "Your mother was pathetic. She never showed you what it was like to be wanted, or cared about, or even loved; and...you never really had a father-to make you feel like his princess. You had nothing...absolutely nothing." Done with the anger, her voiced soften and she said, "So, now when a man shows you a little attention, you just don't know how to handle it. Sometimes I don't even think you get it, when a man is flirting or interested in you. If you do, then you just ignore it. You feel undeserving and of no value. Well, you are valuable...and you are beautiful...and you are the brightest star I know." Emme kissed her fingertips and brushed Mercedes' face with them. Then she turned back and started to drive down the street.

Mercedes had a tear spill down her cheek. In a soft voice she said, "I was so scared and surprised, I didn't know what to do, other than brush his hand away." Mercedes twisted in the tiny seat with sad eyes. "I guess what triggered my anger was he had the audacity to wink, when I looked him straight in the eyes!"

Emme sighed. "Oh brother! That is what we call 'flirting.' Now that you've morphed into this beautiful butterfly, you don't know how to spread those wings. The girls and I are going to have a slumber party and explain to you the rules of engagement!" Emme smiled. "He winked at you, to let you know that he was attracted to you." Emme pulled into the parking lot of a car dealership and parked the car. She shut off the engine, turned her head toward Mercedes and said, "Look, my naïve friend, you had better get used to all this male attention—have you looked in the mirror lately? You are drop-dead gorgeous!"

"I look in the mirror every morning. Too much is changing too quickly. I don't want the attention. I just want to be who I was before." Mercedes said.

"Well, take a good long look. You lost over twenty-five pounds and have one of the tightest and firmest bodies of all your friends—including Ms. Liposuction! The Zumba classes have worked miracles. You straightened out your nose, added some beautiful plump lips, and an awesome haircut that shows off those green eyes of yours." She looked at Mercedes and said, "And I'm not in the least surprised Jennifer called you like a maniac a few weeks ago. She's very jealous! It took her a lifetime to attain beauty. It only took you six months!"

Mercedes looked confused. "But that's not what I see when I look in the mirror. I see a sad little girl who still thinks she's an ugly duckling."

Emme whipped open the door and said, "Get over it! And get used to the new you! Come on, let's buy you a new 'baby.'"

After spending the entire Sunday shopping for cars, it came down to two models. One was a foreign economical car that got great gas mileage, but came with few or no extras. Mercedes liked the price tag and didn't mind not having a lot of extra options. She would have been happy with roll-up windows. She didn't need the backup camera, the high-tech electronics, or a zillion different buttons. It was frustrating enough when she couldn't find that damn button to close the convertible top of her loaner car. What would she do when her front panel of the new car looked like an airplane dashboard filled with bright orange lights, flashing buttons, and a large GPS screen that rotated like a roasting chicken.

Emme's face showed her frustration. "Why not treat yourself to the best? You're doing really well, you spend a lot of time in the car—close your eyes and picture yourself in a sporty little car. You deserve it!"

Emme and she were sitting in a car on the showroom floor. "I know, but it's so expensive and that scares me." Mercedes said, looking around the fancy car with every possible upgrade. The inside was filled with a dark brown leather interior, an open sunroof, and soft music crooned out of the twelve speakers.

"Why?" Emme looked perplexed. "It's not like you have anyone to leave your hard earned money to, or a sibling, or a child to spend it on." Then she pointed her finger at Mercedes and shook it around. "And don't you dare think of leaving anything to your mother! If that were the case, I'd beat the crap out of you!"

"Really?" Mercedes wrinkled her new nose.

Emme tapped her wrinkled nose. "I want you to spend it on you! Spoil yourself a little, just once. You are the hardest worker bee I know, and you deserve to treat yourself to things that you can enjoy."

"I don't know what it's like to treat myself to extravagant things or to be pampered and spoiled."

Emme looked very devilish when she said, "Oh boy, I bet 'Frenchie' would have spoiled you rotten with vacations, jewelry, flowers, and God knows what! Maybe you should have gone to the Beverly Hills Hotel, even if it was for only a little tryst in bed!"

Mercedes gasped and looked at Emme with big eyes. "I can't do one night stands or take advantage of someone! I wouldn't even know what to do."

"It's easy. Especially if it's someone so filthy rich they're willing to buy you clothes, shoes, and jewelry to keep you around!" Emme shook her head. "Oh brother, you need some real lessons in life if you want to live in the fast lane of beauty! Rich old men will give anything, spend anything, to have a beautiful woman draped on their arm. How the hell did you think Jennifer got that beautiful diamond necklace?"

When Mercedes walked in the door of her home, she was beyond exhaustion. Every bone in her body ached from test driving new cars and finally negotiating with the salespeople. She turned around to take a final look at her new car parked in her garage. It was a shiny white Mercedes-Benz CLA C-Class with dark brown leather interior. It was very expensive, and the most extravagant gift Mercedes had ever splurged on herself, other than her home. And right at this moment, she was feeling guilty.

"Welcome to the real world, Mercedes." Emme said when they were sitting in her new car on the ride home. She touched a button and said, "Call Emme." And suddenly, Emme's phone rang. "Look at all these wonderful hands-free features. I'm going to teach you how to use them, so you can enjoy them. You're not in that 'clunker' anymore; and you have a built in Bluetooth instead of sneaking your phone to your ear, in fear of getting a ticket.

Mercedes' face turned red. "I know...I get it, Emme. I just have a hard time looking at all the things I've done without, and still don't find that need for them. When I was growing up, we didn't have two sticks to rub together and luxuries were unheard of. I learned not to need them."

"Well, you can afford them now. It's not the 'needing' of them—it the 'enjoying' them!" Then she leaned over and gave Mercedes a big wet kiss on her cheek. "I'm so fucking proud of you—my friend. Today was a major milestone in your life. A life so devoid of any pleasure, that you just didn't know what it was like, not to punish yourself! Those days are gone. You've grown up. Now, God damn it, enjoy life a little!"

"Thanks, Emme. You are my dearest friend."

Emme had an excited look on her face. "I can't wait until the girls see your new sporty wheels. They're going to be so jealous. Especially Jennifer. She feels insecure, as it is, driving her mother's old pink Lexus." Emme started to laugh.

Mercedes felt a frown cross her brow. "I don't want anyone to be jealous of me, especially Jennifer."

Emme gave a very devilish growl. "I like to see the pot stirred up a little.... Everyone is going to be very envious, I know I am. So, get over it!"

Mercedes picked up Emme and drove down the street to the shopping center. The girls were going to hang around together and do some shopping. It had been awhile since they could all get their schedules synchronized to do what they loved most—shop. Emme left her manager in charge of her busy store and decided to sneak away for a few hours and enjoy time with the girls.

Mercedes parked the car and Emme gave all the girls a call on her cell. "Meet us on the third floor of the parking structure. I want you to see Mercedes' new car. We're in the row next to the elevators."

Mercedes rolled her eyes and sighed. "Why did you do that? I don't feel comfortable with showing them my new car. It's like bragging. That is so not me!"

"Well, of course it's not like you to get a swelled head. I have one for you!" Emme laughed.

Mercedes sighed. "A car is not a big deal."

"The girls brag all the time. Come on, Mercedes. Lighten up a little. They will be excited for you." Emme opened the car door and saw the girls walking toward them. She raised her hands and waved to them.

Christina ran over to Mercedes who had just got out of the car and shut the door. "Oh, wow! Look at this beauty...wow, wow, wow...Oh my God...!" Christina hugged

Mercedes and was jumping up and down. "Open the door, let me see the inside."

Tessann was grabbing the handle of the passenger door and opening it with uncontrolled excitement. "My God, what an awesome car! You fucking lucky bitch!" She screamed. "I love my car, but this one is next on my list!" She nestled her ass in the seat and said, "I bet you're having a blast driving around town in this."

Emme stood next to Mercedes and watched the uncomfortable look cross her face. She rubbed her arm and said to the girls, "Mercedes is having a hard time getting used to treating herself to something so extravagant. Isn't she silly? It was really hard for her to let go of her little Honda!"

Jennifer walked over to Mercedes and smiled. "I hate my pink piece of shit my mom gave me. I want a new car like this one. But, of all my friends, you deserve it. You've waited a long time, and you've gone through a lot with your old crappy one. I'm happy you finally spent the money and got this for yourself...."

Tears welled in Mercedes' eyes. These feelings were so new to her. Having people actually be happy that she did something for herself, instead of begrudging her something nice. For the next half hour, Mercedes had to open every door, and explain all the wonderful features of her car. Emme watched from a distance, and acknowledged that slight change in Mercedes, as she embraced the acceptance of her friend's happiness.

The rest of the day was spent browsing through the stores. When they were finished, they decided to have an early dinner at the outdoor Farmers Market on Fairfax Avenue. It was a typical sunny California day and summer was just around the corner. Christina, Tessann, and Jennifer had plans to go clubbing later that evening, and Emme actually had a date with an old boyfriend.

The girls were sitting around a large round plastic table, with matching chairs, in the courtyard of this collection of outdoor restaurants that served every kind of ethnic food. Emme was just about to put her chopsticks filled with noodles into her mouth, when Mercedes asked, "Why are you going out with 'Mumbles' tonight? I thought you quit seeing him last year?"

Emme put down her chopsticks and started to laugh. "He called yesterday and said there is a great concert at the Forum tonight and he had some tickets. His date flaked out on him at the last minute, and I thought...what the hell!"

Christina leaned over and whispered in Emme's ear and they both started laughing.

"What's so funny, guys?" Mercedes asked, feeling a little left out.

"Nothing, I just told Emme that there was nothing wrong with a great dinner, concert, and for dessert a great fuck!" Christina giggled.

"I guess I must be really backwards. I just don't get it. Is the 'fuck' really meaningful or is it just another way to stroke your ego?" Mercedes questioned.

The girls looked surprised at that comment.

Tessann smiled at Mercedes and her impeding look of innocence. "It's all about life, Mercedes! Having fun and just enjoying 'each moment' in time! Nothing is forever or permanent. Not your job, not your friends, not your surroundings, or your life. You could be here one day, and gone the next, so why not take every day and live it to the fullest!"

Emme watched Mercedes' face and the gathering cynicism. "Our grandparents and parents struggled with living the 'ideal' life, constantly pursuing their dreams, and always trying to be perfect. But many times those dreams were crushed. I remember twice in my lifetime, the economy crashed and took my parents' home, their jobs, their planned retirement, and everything they worked hard for. Those were life changing moments for me to have to watch them start over. By then, their health was beginning to fail, they didn't have that youthful stamina, and soon they became helpless. In the end, it really wasn't about living the perfect life, abiding by the golden rules, or 'putting away for a rainy day.' What was the point? If you're middle-class and struggling on a daily basis, we all wind up in the same place at the end. Their generation was about reaching for that brass ring...ours is about living each day. That was the big learning lesson for our generation. Don't you think? Isn't that why they call us the 'all about me' generation?"

"I don't know. I came from such a different background. We never had anything, and life was a constant struggle to just have a roof over our heads, and food in the fridge. I've been so busy working hard to get ahead in life...I guess I missed that point."

"Exactly! Somewhere down your yellow brick road you became a traditionalist, and unadventurous about life, and it has held you back. Although lately, I can see these little changes taking place that make me smile." Emme leaned over and hugged her confused friend. "Look...I'm just going out with Mumbles to have a fun evening, nothing more, and nothing less."

Mercedes didn't understand the concept of going on a date with someone you had previously dated, and then quit seeing for over a year. She never had a long-term relationship, and didn't know much about the dating world. In fact, she really didn't know much about life at all. It had been years since Mercedes had been on a 'real' date or was attracted to anyone special.

The only things she did learn about relationships was through her friends, who never seemed to get it right either—with the exception of Alisha. Christina, Jennifer, Tessann, and Emme always seemed to have a revolving door of suitors. It was a flaw in their society that led to the disintegration of morals. It sunk to a new level, with a casual, careless cycle of bedmates; with little or no comprehension of a lasting or meaningful relationship. Many of them put little credence into finding that one special person, settling down, and having a family. Life was a game to them, and they were just here to have a good time—all the time. They could jump on to their phones, tablets, or computers and find social sites that offered millions of potential suitors. Sometimes their relationships started and ended with just the touch of their fingertips on a keyboard. When it came down to social skills, their generation was damaged, and they didn't even care, nor did they notice.

Except for Mercedes. She was different from her friends. She had watched her mother travel through life being miserable, lonely, and always trying to catch that elusive *happiness* she craved. Men frequently floated in and out of her mother's life, leaving Mercedes confused and distrustful. Mercedes wanted more than a life filled with that rotating door. She wanted a monogamous relationship with someone special that she could love and trust. Someone who gave her that infinite security her mother never had. She knew what she wanted, but with the lack of experience, and little knowledge, she definitely didn't know how, or where, she was going to find her knight in shining armor. She just knew that she was not going to find him in a club filled with narcissistic and worldly men.

Emme bumped Mercedes' shoulder with her hand to get her attention. "Did you just hear what I said?"

"No. My mind was drifting somewhere else."

"I just plan on having a great evening out, without any strings attached."

"Well, I hope you have a great time." Mercedes said, trying to wrap her head around the thought of a meaningless one-night stand.

Christina turned to Mercedes and asked, "Why don't you come out with us to the club tonight?"

Mercedes shook her head, and put a bite of her seafood salad into her mouth.

Jennifer chimed in and said, "Yeah, come out with us tonight. We aren't going to make it a long night. I have a lunch shift at the restaurant tomorrow, so I can't sleep in."

"I'll think about it, but I really would like to go home and pick up that great book I've been trying to read for weeks. In fact, I brought home some brochures from my travel agent the other day and thought I would look through them. I was thinking of taking a short vacation."

Christina screamed in an excited voice. "Wow, what a great idea! Why don't you find a great place in Mexico along the beach and let's all go on a vacation together!" High fives were floating around the table at a speed Mercedes could not keep up with.

Mercedes' eyes opened wide and panic began to set in. She knew where this excitement was leaning towards, and she wasn't sure if she could handle a vacation with all the girls. Wild drunken parties, insane excursion tours, loads of men coming in and out of the room, and not one ounce of relaxation. She had already been there a few times, and it was utterly exhausting. She was looking into a quiet spa in Arizona, or a short trip to Washington D.C. to visit the magnificent monuments she had never had a chance to see—except for on television. She wanted something comforting and peaceful.

Jennifer spoke up in an energized voice, "Oh, that sounds so awesome. I don't know about you guys, but I need a break!"

Mercedes looked at the girls' faces and knew she had said the wrong thing, and was deep in trouble now. She asked, "How about Hawaii? They have lots of quiet beautiful beaches. Some are really private and tranquil. We could all have a quiet time in the small town of Lahaina on Maui. I've even seen these small catamarans that sail into the sunset!"

Jennifer leaned forward, brimming with excitement, and burst out laughing. "Are you kidding me? Mexico is the place to be! It's the party heaven of the world. They have some of the most amazing clubs, and a nightlife that doesn't stop. I've been to Hawaii and that's for the old folks or families. I was so totally bored to death that all I wanted to do was scream. Mexico it is! Let's take a vote!"

Mercedes looked at the girls and had no idea how to get out of this spinning circle of excitement.

Tessann added, "I agree! Mexico is close, cheap, and their nightlife never stops!"

Emme looked at Mercedes, who was now quiet. "We haven't been on a vacation together as a group for a few years. Mercedes, you've got this new beautiful body, so let's go and show it off in Cancun!" She nudged Mercedes shoulder, and said, "When should we go? When can you guys get off work?"

"Two months," Tessann said, "it will give us all enough time to get organized and let our employers know."

Mercedes grinned the best she could. "I'll stop by my travel agency near the deli and see what's available. Then I'll let you know." Mercedes stated with a little enthusiasm, which mostly bordered on fear.

The next hour was endless chatting about the vacation and all of the fun they were going to have. It was nonstop discussion about the clothes, shoes, and skimpy bikinis they were going to pack.

fourteen

ON the way home from the shopping center, Mercedes could still feel the frenzy of excitement the girls were spinning about the upcoming vacation. Mercedes pulled into the parking lot where the travel agency was located. The only spot open was right in front of the deli, and as soon as she shut off her engine, there was a loud knock on her window. She looked up in surprise and gave Josh a big smile.

Josh opened the door and Mercedes slipped out of the car. He walked halfway around the car and came back with eyes as big saucers. "Whoa...what happened to your 'beater car'?"

A frown crossed Mercedes' face. "I had to put her to rest! Unfortunately, my repairman said there was no hope—she was terminal."

Now a big frown crossed his face. "Sorry to hear that. I know how much you loved that car." He looked at her car and dipped his head inside to take a better look at the innovative dashboard filled with buttons and gadgets, the soft leather interior, and a stereo system that was beyond his imagination. Then he gave a long, slow whistle. "You did well. This is an amazing hunk of metal and damn beautiful set of wheels. I bet this set you back a pretty penny!"

Mercedes looked down at the ground and shifted her feet back and forth. When she finally looked up, she said in a quiet voice, "Emme talked me into this. I would have been happy with a small little clunker or more of an economical car. In fact, I would have kept my old car if it was at all possible. This just seems so...so...not me."

He patted her on the shoulder and smiled. "I know how hard you work and you deserve the best...but why do you let your friends talk you into *their* dreams? Why don't you do what makes *you* happy?" he asked, drawing his eyebrows together.

Mercedes looked away again. The meaning of his question hit her deep in the gut. She felt this need to defend her actions, but instead she simply said, "Does that mean you don't like my car?"

He slung his arm around her shoulder. "Of course I do! I think she is a stunner!" he said quickly.

"What made you call it a 'she'?" Mercedes slightly grinned.

"Because if it was a 'he'...I might get very jealous!" He started to laugh.

Mercedes smiled and her mood brightened up.

He grabbed her hand and started walking toward the deli door. Mercedes stopped and said, "Save me a table. I'll be right back. I promised the girls I would pick up brochures at the travel agency, and I want to do it before they close."

He reluctantly let go of her hand and she jogged down a few shops to the agency. Ten minutes later, she walked into the deli. She looked around the room and when she saw him, he pointed toward an empty table. Sitting on the table was a cup of steaming black coffee.

Mercedes slid in the booth and put her purse down. She placed the brochures on the table and picked up her coffee cup, taking a sip of the hot brew. As she was flipping through the pages of the booklets, Josh came over and sat down across from her. "Thanks for the coffee," she said.

His hand went to the booklets and picked one up. "Wow...are you planning a vacation?"

Mercedes nodded. "Yes. It's in the beginning stages of planning. As you can see, it's just a handful of brochures filled with beaches, hotels, and exotic surroundings." She picked them up and waved them around.

He snatched them from her hands and started to go through one. A loud whistle came through his puckered lips and then he said, "Which one of these places do you want to go to?"

Mercedes looked at the brochures he was holding and pursed her lips. Finally, she said, "None." She clasped her hands together and sighed. "I want to go to a secluded island where there is nothing, and nobody, to disturb you. Someplace where you can walk along the beach collecting sea glass and not see a person for miles!"

He looked at the brochures again and said, "Then why these party towns in Mexico?" he questioned. His eyes never left hers as he waited for an answer.

"Because my girlfriends want to go have 'fun' and this is where the 'fun' is. So, I guess I was outnumbered and my vote didn't count." The big pout on her face said it all.

He gave her a frown as he watched the disappointment cross her face. "Well, I like your idea better! That would be my choice, too. I guess your friends just don't get the true meaning of vacations. And unfortunately, like you said, *'your vote didn't count'!*"

She tried to grin. "Next time I won't say anything to the girls. I'll just quietly book it, and go by myself!"

"Sounds like a great idea...next time just make it—all about you!" They both bumped knuckles and started to laugh.

"I'm so sweaty and tired. She worked us to death today in class! Do we have to do this now?" Mercedes complained.

They were walking through the door of Emme's store. "Our trip is just a few weeks away and I just received all the summer wear from my buyers, so before I put it out, I thought you'd have first choice to pick out a bathing suit or two!"

Mercedes frowned. "Do I need a bathing suit? I haven't worn one since that pool party three years ago at Christina's." Mercedes' face turned red. "I can't believe my top floated up and I didn't know it."

"Well, it's not like you have a great set of jugs to hold it in place. For God's sake, you have the tiniest poached eggs I've ever seen!" Emme laughed.

Mercedes looked mortified. "That was really 'mean' to say."

"It's hard to hear the truth, isn't it?" Emme took her hand and dragged her to the back room of the store. "Get over it. Your boobies are smaller than ever, since you lost all that weight. Now with your new body, we need to find something to balance the bottom."

Mercedes' eyes opened wide. "Toilet paper or socks...like when we were kids?"

Emme walked over to the table in the back room. It was filled with swimsuits, and lots of summer clothes she had picked out the night before, hoping Mercedes would come to the store and shop. In one hand, she picked up the package of size 'D' foam falsies for bathing suit tops. In the other hand, she picked up a bathing suit top. "Here, put the top on and let's see how this works."

With a look of humiliation, she said indignantly, "I am not wearing those falsies!"

Emme gave her a dark look. "They are not falsies; they are called breast enhancers now!"

Angry and stubborn, Mercedes said, "What the hell is the difference, all the fashion assholes did was change the name!"

Emme grinned and said, "Changing the name to 'enhancers' increased the cost to fucking thirty dollars! Give the geniuses a little credit!"

Mercedes put on the top and she had no boobies to hold it up. Not even a little cleavage. It nearly brought her to tears a few times, dealing with trying on the swimsuits and adding the enhancers. But Emme was patient and caring, and would not let her down that dark road.

An hour later, Tessann showed up, and for the next two hours, they all tried on summer wear for their impending trip. When they were almost done, Tessann was helping Mercedes adjust the top of her swimsuit. She helped her put the enhancer in and said, "Have you ever thought of a small augmentation? It would even your top and hips out and give you a perfect hourglass figure. It would fill your bathing suit top!"

Mercedes shook her head. "No! I know Christina, Jennifer and you have had it done, but it really isn't something I would consider."

Tessann showed off the skimpy summer dress she was wearing and how it fit her to perfection. "Look, I didn't go really big. I kept them proportioned to my size." She took down the top to show Mercedes. "Jennifer is just plain nuts to have them the size of Dolly Parton. She always feels this tremendous need for attention. Between you and me—that is really sick. Then we have to look at her mother that was her role model."

Emme walked over with another summer dress and handed it to Mercedes. "Clothes would fit you a hell of a lot better and you would never have to stuff your summer clothes."

Mercedes shook her head again in frustration. "No. I'm okay with the way I am."

Tessann hugged Mercedes and said, "If you ever want to reconsider it, let me know. I have the best doctor who will only give you what your body will look good in."

Mercedes smiled. "Thanks...."

When the girls were done at Emme's store, they went down the street and shopped a little more. With enough bags to fill her suitcases, Mercedes headed home to rest and relax.

"What...? I don't know if I heard you right." Mercedes yelled into the phone.

"We are meeting over at the spa at one." Jennifer said.

"Who is 'we'?" Mercedes asked.

With frustration in her voice, Jennifer said, "All of us."

"Well, I'm not going to be there. I don't need to have my body sprayed with a tan just to make me look good. What the hell happened to getting a tan naturally on your vacation? Isn't that the normal way?" Mercedes' exasperation was beginning to reach a peak.

"What rock were you born under? In order to look good sitting on the beach in a skimpy bikini, you need to have a tan. Seeing as summer hasn't started yet, the only way to do that is to have it sprayed on before you go on vacation." Jennifer's annoyance was very evident.

"Well, count me out!" Mercedes hissed.

"Okay...the three of us will be laying on the beach with these beautiful tans and you will be next to us looking like Casper the ghost! How's that for a fucking visual?" Jennifer laughed.

There was silence and finally Mercedes said, "I'll think about it."

"Well, don't think too hard, or too long; we leave on Saturday for Cancun. And the appointment is tomorrow. I'll catch you later...." Jennifer hung up.

Mercedes was angry and in the heat of the moment, she dialed Emme's shop. An unfamiliar voice answered and Mercedes blurted into the phone, "Hello, is Ms. Martex there?"

"Sure, hold on a sec."

"Hello, this is Ms. Martex, can I help you?"

"Oh, hell yes, Emme! What the hell is all this stuff about a spray tan?"

"Hey, calm down, Mercedes. The rest of us decided last minute to do it because we are still wearing 'winter white' skin and we're going to a beach were everyone is tanned." There was silence, so Emme continued, "You have a choice. You can join us or you can pass on the tan. That is entirely up to you!"

Mercedes inhaled and exhaled slowly, ending in a sigh. "How do I have a choice when I'm going to be sitting next to my tan friends on the beach?"

Softly Emme spoke into the phone. "It's only a spray that washes off within a few days. It just gives us a day or two to get our own."

"But I've heard it's not good for you and there's a chemical called DHA that can damage your lungs!"

"Oh, Mercedes, for God's sake, you're not using it on a day-to-day basis. You're using it once! Look...do what you want. We're meeting there at lunch on Thursday. If you want to, fine, if not...no biggie! I have to go, I have a client here right now. Chin up, love ya!" Emme hung up.

Mercedes sat there looking at the dead phone. She sat back and closed her eyes and the first thing that came to mind was three beautifully tanned bodies and one chalk-white ghost!

Thursday had rolled around and Mercedes walked out of her office at noon with a small bag filled with a pair of clean underwear, a bra, T-shirt, and athletic pants. As she was walking down the hall, she noticed a very sexy blonde sitting on a chair in front of Michael's desk. Mercedes popped her head through the open door to get Michael's attention, but he was too absorbed in the blonde.

"Excuse me...Michael," Mercedes said in a louder voice. "I'm leaving the office for an hour or so and I need a favor."

Mercedes watched as the blonde stood up and turned around. Tall, statuesque, all legs, tan, and beautiful is how Mercedes would describe her. Mercedes felt this quick flash of envy surface.

"What do you need, Mercedes?" Michael stood up and introduced the woman. "This is my new client, Suzanne Martin."

Mercedes smiled. "Sorry to interrupt you, Suzanne." She looked at Michael and said, "Michael, I'm expecting a client to come in and pick up this envelope. So, if I'm not back in time, could you give it to him?"

"Sure...anything else?" Michael looked irritated for some reason.

"No. I'll let Mary know." She turned to the blonde and smiled. "Nice to meet you, Suzanne."

Suzanne nodded and sat down. Michael sat down and went back to ogling the blonde, as Mercedes continued down the hall. Then she muttered to herself, *"He must be frustrated that she is his client and not his bedmate!"*

Mercedes stopped at Mary's desk and waited until she hung up the phone. "If Ralph stops by to pick up the envelope, I left it with Michael and his blonde bombshell!" Mercedes laughed and so did Mary.

Mary stood up and patted Mercedes' hand. "Okay, dear. I bet you're excited to leave Saturday morning."

"Yes, I'm going nuts getting ready." Mercedes admitted.

"Are you all ready?" Mary asked softly.

"My desk is all cleaned up. But that only means I'll come back to a big mess. Oh well...I'm glad I took off tomorrow too, so I can pack and get organized at home." Mercedes smiled and the excitement showed on her face.

Mary leaned over and gave Mercedes a hug and said, "Have fun and send me a postcard!"

"You mean, you don't want a sombrero for your hubby?" Mercedes laughed.

"No. His sombrero days are over. Now, they are golf caps!" Mary patted Mercedes' back and smiled.

"I'll be back in an hour or so...please hold down the fort."

"Oh...I thought you were leaving to go home. Last minute shopping? Anything I could do to help?"

Mercedes started to giggle. "No, I'm meeting my friends for a spray tan in a few minutes. Pray I don't come back looking like an orange alien from Mars!" Mercedes held up her crossed fingers.

Mary looked puzzled. "Spray tan? I thought you lay on the beach for a tan?"

Mercedes rolled her eyes. "My friends believe in the spray tan first, vacation next. Crazy, isn't it?"

Mary started to laugh. "I'm so glad I'm not in your generation...such foolishness...."

"I agree...." Mercedes smiled.

"Well, dear, I hope you have a great, relaxing time. I can't think of anyone who deserves it more. You're a very bright young lady with a tremendous future, and I've always respected your work ethics. You're not like most of the women in your generation. You're solid, strong, and predictable." Mary said in a humbling tone.

"Thank you, Mary. Your kind words mean a lot to me." Mercedes gave Mary another hug.

Two hours later when Mercedes walked in, she could hardly recognize herself in the mirrored wall facing the elevator in her office building. She was wearing a pair of tight athletic pants, beach thongs, a skimpy wife-beater T-shirt, and a perfect faux sun-kissed tan. When she opened the door, Alexi was standing at Mary's desk and they were talking. Alexi looked up and whistled. "You look frickin' amazing. Great tan! For a minute, I thought you just got back from Mexico instead of leaving Saturday." He turned around and yelled down the hall toward Michael and Zackary's offices, "Hey, you guys, come take a look at our vacation girl!"

Mercedes turned all different shades of red under her tan. "Oh please, don't make a big deal out of this. I just did it to appease my friends; and so I didn't standout on the beach, looking like Casper the ghost!"

Michael and Zackary sauntered down the hall and into the room. With eyes open wide and jaws dropped down to their chests, they stopped dead in their tracks. "Holy cow!" Michael exclaimed, with his head shaking in disbelief.

Zackary was standing next to Mary and his fingers began to tap on her desk. "You can say that again.... Holy cow, you look incredible!"

Mercedes was blushing and speechless. "Thanks, I can't wait until my vacation on Saturday." Filled with embarrassment, she quickly turned and walked down the hall to her office.

"Boy, I wish I was going with that party group! Damn, damn, damn!" Michael said loud enough to make Mercedes turn around and purse her lips in disgust. She walked into her office and slammed the door.

"Hey, Mercedes. I just want to be a fly on the wall. Is that okay?" Zackary blurted down the hall.

Mercedes opened the door, stuck her hand out and flipped them both off.

"Party pooper!" Michael yelled.

She walked over and sat down at her desk. Shaking her head in confusion, she said to herself, "I just don't see the big deal. I just got a little tan and the men in the office go berserk! Hmmpff...."

Fifteen

FROM the moment they got off the plane, the party began in full swing. Emme and Mercedes doubled up in one room, and Christina, Jennifer, and Tessann were housed in a suite. The rooms were vividly decorated with a strong Mexican heritage influence. Heavily textured white walls flowed to ten-foot ceilings that had dark wood beams going across from end to end. The heavy, dark wooden furniture brought a richness to the room that only hand-carved tables, chairs, and chest of drawers could do. The distressed Mexican pavers covered the floors and area rugs were scattered around. Each room had a balcony that overlooked the perfectly maintained, lush tropical grounds filled with trees, flowering bushes, and assorted local flora. The vast pool was sculptured to fit into the landscape. Included were wooden bridges and patios filled with lounges all along the poolside. The large thatched umbrellas, called Palapas, were constructed of palm leaves and made to withstand the sun, the rain, and gale force winds, which could occur at any given hour of the day or evening.

The pool had two large bars in the center, with underwater barstools circled around them. People were sitting in the water drinking their Mai Tais in scooped out pineapples, and Pina Coladas in hard-shelled coconuts. They were listening to music, as the upbeat rhythm blared out of the hidden speakers made to look like large rocks. Sounds of the steel drums brought the spirit of the tropics to life, in-a variety of tropical music styles including reggae, calypso, Latin, and pop.

Past the pool was the vast expanse of ocean and clear azure blue skies. Palapas, lounges, Adirondack chairs, and wandering vendors selling their wares dotted the crystal-fine sand along the beautiful beach. Boats pulled people high in the sky, as they parasailed across the ocean's clear blue water.

Mercedes stood on the patio and inhaled a big breath of ocean air. Slowly, she exhaled and said, "This is the most beautiful hotel I've ever been in. The rooms are amazing, and the grounds look like a great place to explore."

Emme started to laugh out loud. Her finger pointed to the distant bar by the pool. "Looks like our girls are already exploring the scenery, tasting the tropics, and cuddling up to the native hunks. All while wearing their skimpiest bikinis!"

"Oh my God, you're right! Look at those hussies surrounded by half the guys at the pool!" Mercedes shook her head in amazement.

"Get used to it for the next five days."

Mercedes continued to stare at the girls. "I wonder if they bothered to unpack?"

"My guess...their luggage is still in the lobby!"

An hour later, Emme and Mercedes walked down to the pool in their new bathing suits. Mercedes felt uncomfortable with her hidden 'enhancements,' so she wore a cover-up top. The rest of the girls left little to the crowd's imagination. Including Emme, her full display of body art and piercings attracted lots of attention.

Mercedes was sitting on the side of the pool with her legs dangling in the refreshing water. The girls were laying on the lounges right next to the edge. A handful of hopeful suitors were splashing in the water and teasing the girls.

Mercedes took a sip of her sparkling water and asked, "Jennifer, why don't you jump into the water and give these poor young men a thrill!"

Jennifer gave her biggest smile and giggled. "Are you kidding? I want to keep my tan for a few days!"

Emme laughed and jumped into the water, when she came up for air she said, "Are you serious, Jennifer? You're worried about that orange tan! For God's sake, you're here to have fun in the sun. Not to preserve a spray-on tan!"

Looking embarrassed, Jennifer slowly sat down on the edge of the pool and slid in. Emme suddenly had this devilish look cross her face and she pushed a big splash of water at Jennifer. Then Emme turned to the guys and encouraged them to join in. "Come on, you group of pansies, get her wet!"

Jennifer put her hands up to protect her hair. "No, stop! Don't get my hair wet!" Jennifer screamed, but nobody listened to her.

Christina, Tessann, Mercedes, and Emme laughed hysterically as Jennifer got her full initiation into the Mexican Riviera.

Mercedes mumbled to herself, *"You wanted 'fun'...you got fun!"*

That night, they walked along the beach to a popular restaurant that was filled to capacity, with music blasting and young people everywhere. Mercedes and her friends had just finished dinner and they were sitting at a big table with young men that kept the girls' drinks continuously flowing. It was starting to get late. It had been a long day of traveling and sunbathing. Mercedes looked stunning with her spiked, streaked blonde hair, minuscule shimmering silver dress, made of lamé fabric, which showed off her new body. All the girls looked eye-catching, and the crowd, filled with testosterone and alcohol, acknowledged that.

Mercedes was tired and ready to retire to her room. She watched her friends as they displayed their vibrant personalities. The group had broken into smaller groups. Mercedes watched from a distance as her friends flirted and teased the men. Jennifer was sitting in the lap of a handsome, stylish man whose hands were floating across her entire body. She squirmed and wiggled and continued to tease him. Mercedes just shook her head in amazement. Then she stood up to walk to the restroom, she was so bored. After she was done, she looked in the mirror and put on some lipstick. When she walked out, she bumped into a man. The area was dark and he steadied her with his strong arms. She looked up into his smiling face. It was the same man that Jennifer had been giving the lap dance.

"Hey there, beautiful lady," he whispered near her ear, with his hand holding her steady on her heels.

"Sorry. With the darkness in this hall, I didn't see you. My apologies." Mercedes pulled away from his grip and turned to walk away.

He slipped his hand around her elbow to stop her from leaving. "Don't go.... I've been waiting for you. While your friend was trying to get my attention, my eyes were watching you. I followed you here." He pulled her against him.

Mercedes backed up, feeling like she needed some space. "I'm not interested, thank you." Mercedes smiled sweetly.

He pulled her close again. "I won't bite. But, I sure as hell know, I can make you feel good."

Mercedes peeled his fingers off her arm. "No thanks."

He touched her face with one finger. "You are the most beautiful woman in the room. You know that!"

Mercedes had enough. "Look, get your damn paws off me, you asshole! Find someone else who might be interested, because I'm not!"

He smiled and baited her, "Oh...I get it. You're into women, not men."

SMACK! Mercedes slapped his face as hard as she could and walked off. She had never slapped anyone in her entire life. At times, she wanted to slap her mother, but it took great control to refrain from any physical violence. Tonight, he deserved what he got. She had never experienced a confrontation like this. He had no respect for her; nor did he care that he was treating women like whores. This was beyond Mercedes' comprehension. Her friends may like this treatment, but she demanded more respect.

Mercedes walked into the room and back to the table. She angrily whispered into Emme's ear, "I'm going back to the hotel."

Emme looked at Mercedes' angry face, "What happened? Are you okay?" She watched as tears accumulated in Mercedes' eyes. "Come on, let's go. I'll gather the girls. It's better if we go back to the hotel, so if they get tipsy, we can take them to the room. Good idea!"

Mercedes hugged Emme. "Thanks."

The trip was crazy and fun, with lots of water, sightseeing, booze, and men. They had a tremendous playground filled with everything a young adult could ever want. Even Jennifer acknowledged there was much more than just hunky, delicious men. So Mercedes did what she always did when the girls went on vacation—she booked interesting and fun excursions during the day, and at night the girls played in the clubs. Mercedes took great pleasure in the loud tropical music and exotic atmosphere, while she sat and quietly watched the girls play 'musical chairs' amongst all the drunk and obnoxious guys. They stayed close to the hotel during the evenings, and usually frequented their hotel's nightclub, or the one next door.

She enjoyed sipping her sparkling water, and on many occasions you could find her out in the pool area, listening to the steel drum music, and absorbing the warm balmy breeze. The loud, crowded clubs were not her partiality, nor did the first evening make her want a repeat of that egotistical buffoon's performance. That apologetic man showed up a few times, expressing tremendous regret for his drunken behavior. And although he was sorry, Mercedes refused to acknowledge his presence after that first evening. Many times she blew off interested men, preferring to go back to her room to watch a good movie, or reading about their new adventures she had planned for the following day.

Mercedes was impressed with Cancun and its centuries of historical background. She was in awe of the pyramids of Kukulcan in Chichen Itza. Only Emme and Tessann went because Christina and Jennifer were too hungover to take that beat-up old school bus two hours to the site that was located on the Yucatan Peninsula, about one hundred and seventeen miles west of Cancun. Mercedes was impressed that it was named as one of the 'New Seven Wonders of the World', and she was excited to explore it, along with the old ancient artifacts that the brochures had promised. Mercedes and the girls were surprised at its size, symmetry, and astrological importance and thought it was an amazing testament to the Mayan civilization and Mexican heritage.

All the girls went to Tulum and a few male followers joined in. It was a full day of zip-lining, cave snorkeling, and appreciating the ancient ruins of Tulum. It was considered by many as the most beautiful of the Mayan ruins. It wasn't a large expanse of area, but the girls thought it was exquisitely poised on the twelve meter cliffs above the azure waters of the Caribbean Sea. Mercedes loved the peaceful feeling, and for a while she sat on the cliff's edge overlooking the ocean, enjoying the solitude.

During the free days, the girls split up into groups and enjoyed the pool, the local attractions, and the beach. Mercedes, Emme, and Tessann spent a full day of shopping at an out of town open marketplace one morning, and enjoyed the warm Mexican culture, along with authentic Mexican cuisine. In the more rural communities, Mercedes loved the simplicity of the people, their hospitality, and their openness. That same day, they also flagged down a cab and went to the shopping center that reminded the girls of Rodeo Drive in Beverly Hills. It was international, high-end multinational businesses, as well as American brand stores that screamed of opulence. Mercedes didn't expect that and she felt it took away from the natural Mexican environment and its distinct ambiance.

The girls were waiting for the plane to board. Jennifer was sleeping across two chairs; and Christina was on her cell phone, tucked in a seat near the wall. Mercedes, Emme, and Tessann walked back to the boarding area with a fresh cup on Starbucks in their hands. They sat down in the chairs facing the window that viewed the planes taking off on the runways.

"What a great vacation." Tessann said. "Lots of good times to remember."

Emme took a sip of coffee and said, "It's always a great vacation when no one gets arrested, winds up missing-in-action, or gets into a fight over some dude!"

"I would definitely come back here again; and I loved learning all about the Mayan civilization. It was a very interesting place, with lots to do and keep us all busy. Hell, Jennifer and Christina had the odds stacked in their favor! There were four guys for each of them. They were in 'male heaven'!" Mercedes started to laugh.

Tessann giggled and said, "I don't know...she was a little miffed at you, Mercedes. On that first night, she had her eyes on that one guy. Remember? The one she was doing lap dances on."

Mercedes looked at Tessann with questioning eyes. "She never said anything to me. I never looked at him, flirted with him, or gave him any attention! That little bastard followed me to the bathroom, and I wound up slapping him across the face for his arrogant and belligerent attitude. Why the hell would she want a drunk idiot like him, anyway?"

Emme rolled her eyes. "Those are her favorite kinds of guys—bad boys! It must have killed her to see you get some attention."

"He was drunker than a skunk! What's there to be jealous of?" Mercedes was beginning to get irritated.

Emme turned around and looked over at Jennifer sleeping peacefully on the chairs. Then she shook her head and said, "Personally, I would think she would be happy for you. For years, you sat in our shadow all by yourself. You never complained. You were never envious, and you never showed any form of resentment. Now...you finally look the best I've ever seen you look in twenty years, and you literally deserve all the attention you're getting."

Tessann smiled and patted Mercedes' shoulder. "I completely agree."

Mercedes' eyes narrowed and she questioned, "Did she say something? She never said anything to me. I wasn't even around Christina and her much when they went clubbing. " Mercedes was still trying to process the whole idea of 'jealousy.'

"You could just tell in her face, when the guys were gathered around you in the pool. Or, especially, when we all went to the Tulum ruins and that hunky tour guy would not leave your side. She tried a few times to enter into your circle with him, but he just ignored her."

Mercedes was unaware of what the girls were saying. "Oh my God, Jose is just a tour guide during the summer and studies law in Mexico City." Mercedes shook her head. "He was just teaching me about his heritage and the Mayan civilization. He was very interesting to talk to because he knew so much."

Emme started to laugh. "Well, then he definitely wasn't her type. She doesn't like someone with anything between their ears!" Emme pointed a finger at Mercedes and shook it. "Don't you dare tell her that I said that!" Mercedes and Tessann nodded their heads.

Suddenly, over the PA system the call to board their flight was announced. The girls stood up and gathered their luggage.

"Thank God they have a whole day to get all that alcohol out of their bloodstream before the work week begins!" Tessann shook her head, pointing to Jennifer's sleeping form. "Let's head back to reality."

Mercedes held up her Starbucks cup and said, "Let's make a toast to a great vacation." The girls clicked their cups together.

Emme whispered, "Well, there was one small mishap."

Tessann and Mercedes looked at Emme—puzzled and confused.

"That was when Mercedes' 'enhancement' went floating across the pool, and some asshole found it and held it up to see who it belonged to."

The girls started to giggle. But inside, Mercedes felt the embarrassment and pain of that moment.

Sixteen

MERCEDES pulled up to the gate of the underground parking. Amed ran over and opened her door and said, "Let me park this for you, Miss."

Mercedes looked at him and shook her head. "No, thank you. I've been parking my own car for so long, why do you want to park it now?" she asked. "Besides, this is my new baby and I don't let anyone drive it. Not even my best friend."

He shut the door and frowned. "I just wanted to make it easy for you, and park it over there in the corner where it will be protected."

Mercedes didn't want any favors. She learned years ago that 'favors' came attached with paybacks. "I appreciate your thoughtfulness, but no thanks," she said.

Mercedes didn't know why he was being so attentive and bending over backwards to be so nice. She'd been parking underground for as long as she had been with the company, and she could count on one hand how many times they had spoken.

Mercedes walked out of the elevator and looked in the mirror. She looked fabulous in her white summer pantsuit and turquoise tank top that dropped a little lower than she felt comfortable with—but she had worn it anyway. She didn't have any appointments because it was her first day back, so being a little risqué was acceptable. Besides, she had a great vacation and she wanted to look her best her first day back in the office. Her hair was cut to perfection, her makeup and blue eye shadow complimented her top, and her pedicure she got in Mexico showed off her manicured toes in her new summer sandals. There was no mistaking that she had been on vacation. Her golden tan highlighted her soft skin and the smile she wore verified her rested state of mind.

She opened the door to the office and Mary was looking through the mail at her desk, while sipping a cup of coffee.

Mary looked up and her eyes scanned Mercedes from the big smile across her face, to the bottom of her painted toes. "Lordy, dear girl, you look very...very...beautiful!" She stood up walked around her desk, and gave Mercedes a hug. "We certainly did miss you, darling."

Mercedes looked at Mary's kind eyes that wrinkled in the corners, and said, "Thank you, Mary. I'm sure you speak for yourself, because for years the guys didn't even know when I was gone."

"Oh, I know they missed you this trip." Mary chuckled.

"I always dread coming back. I'm sure my desk is piled high with enough stuff to keep me busy for months!"

Mary winked. "I think you will be quite surprised. I can feel it in these old bones."

Mercedes took her purse, briefcase, and large bag with her as she walked down the hall, dreading what she was going to find on her desk. She always kicked in and helped when Michael, Zackary, or Alexi went on vacation. Rarely did they lift a finger to do anything for her, or her clients, except leave a zillion post-its across her desk and computer, and stacks and stacks of work. It had been that way for years, and she refused to let it spoil her return today. She opened the door to her office and walked in. Immediately, she noticed her desk. There wasn't a thing on it, except a few pieces of mail in the wire basket that she usually had stacked with things to do.

She opened her eyes wide and spun around the room looking to see where they stacked her messages. There were no boxes, no bags, and nothing that symbolized any kind of charts or paperwork she needed to go through. She placed her things down on the empty desk and opened the drawers.

"Well, my drawers are how I left them. Nobody has emptied the desk, so I guess I still work here," she mumbled to herself. *"What the hell is going on?"* she questioned herself. *"Oh, I get it. There must be such a lot of stuff that Mary has it up at the front."* She exhaled, thinking she had figured it out.

Mercedes sighed and walked out of her office. She went down the hall to the kitchenette to pour herself a cup of coffee. She took a long, slow sip and walked out of the room and down the hall, back to Mary's desk. When she reached the front, the staff was standing around Mary's desk. When they saw her coming, all the men stood there with surprised expressions on their faces. Mercedes was speechless as to why everyone was watching her, and wondered if it was some kind of a staff meeting.

Mary was the first to talk. "Welcome back, Mercedes." She pointed to Jarrod and said, "I told you she didn't look like the same Mercedes we used to know. Isn't she beautiful in turquoise and that deep tan?"

"Holy cow, Mercedes. You look really..." he paused, "rested!" Jarrod blurted out.

Alexi and Zackary nodded their heads quickly and remained silent. Suddenly, the door opened and Michael walked in. He looked directly at Mercedes and smiled widely. "Welcome back. Well, I can see you had a great time with the girls. Damn, I wish I was there!"

Alexi and Zackary chimed in at the same time, "Me, too!"

Jarrod cleared his throat to draw everyone's attention.

Mercedes looked confused and cried out, "Can someone please tell me what's going on? Why are we gathered at Mary's desk? Are we having a meeting?" She put both her hands up and said, "Can someone tell me why...all of a sudden I feel like I'm in a *Twilight Zone* movie?"

"Oh dear!" Mary said and the men just laughed.

Mercedes looked at her coworkers. "Okay, I get the joke. Where is the mess that belongs on my desk?"

Mary came around her desk and put her arm around Mercedes' waist. "Well, I'm really happy to say that all your coworkers chipped in this week!" Mary displayed her sweet, endearing smile.

Mercedes looked shocked and shouted. *"What...?"*

"I said—"

Mercedes interrupted Mary. "I heard what you said, I'm just standing here trying to absorb it!"

Jarrod suddenly found his voice, "We just thought all of us could pitch in and take care of what had to be done, could be done, and needed to be done. I think there are a few things you need to take care of and I have a few notes to give you, but other than that, the boys did a great job. Don't you think?"

Mercedes looked at her coworkers and was speechless.

Michael broke the silence. "Well, how was your trip to Mexico? Did you bring back some pictures on your phone that you care to share? I bet your friends looked great in their bikinis."

Zackary piped in, "Yeah, care to share some bikini photos!" The men in the room started to laugh, but when they saw the angry look on Mary's face, they immediately stopped.

Mercedes finally spoke. "Thank you all for helping me out while I was gone. I sincerely appreciate it. I never expected it, nor had you ever done this before."

Alexi moved forward. "You are always chipping in and helping us, and I thought it was time we pay it forward."

Mercedes walked over and hugged Alexi. "Thank you."

Mary stepped in and took Mercedes' hand, "You don't have to hug this group of 'idiots,' young lady. All you needed to do was thank them."

Zackary frowned, "Nothing wrong with a hug."

"All of you scoot and get back to work." Mary pointed to their offices down the hall.

The crowd broke up and Mercedes stood there watching them as they walked away.

"Finally you got what you deserved. Why it took those imbeciles so long is beyond me. You help them all the time."

Mercedes hugged Mary and said, "Thank you so much."

It was past seven and Mercedes was exhausted. She had lots of work to do in spite of the help. Clients were calling all day knowing it was her first day back from her vacation. *"Why do they call the day I get back, can't they wait a few days, sheesh!"* She mumbled as she left the empty office. Everyone was long gone and it was nice to work in peace and quiet. Jarrod had gone to lunch and brought Mercedes back a sandwich, so she could work through her lunch. Now it was getting late and she thought she would stop by the deli and have a small dinner. She stepped into the bathroom and freshened up her makeup and added some lip gloss.

She pulled into the parking lot and parked the car. Exhausted, she walked to the door, opened it, and stepped inside. She looked around as her eyes adjusted to the bright lights. She noticed a small empty table next to the window looking out into the parking lot. She slowly walked over and sat down. Out of nowhere the waitress came over. She recognized the older woman and smiled. "Hello, Stella."

"Nice to see you, Mercedes, must be a long day for you? Haven't seen you in a while."

"Yes, first day back from vacation and I need another one! I'm so hungry right now I think I could eat a whole cow!" Mercedes chuckled. "But a half a turkey sandwich and fresh fruit would work just fine. Thanks, Stella."

Stella scribbled it down on a piece of paper and turned to Mercedes, and asked, "Some hot coffee or a glass of wine?"

"How about a hot bubble bath and right into bed?" Mercedes teased.

"I'm right there with you...."She turned and walked into the kitchen.

Mercedes got up and went to the restroom. She had been holding it in for hours, unable to leave her desk, answering endless phone calls. And now her bladder had reached its limit and it was about to burst. When she came out of the restroom, she was walking by the door to the kitchen when it swung open. Instantly, she was nearly knocked off her feet. If it hadn't been for a strong set of hands that gripped her waist, she would have fallen flat on her face. "Hey there...." Josh said.

Mercedes swung around after hearing his voice and he was standing only inches from her, his hands still gripped her waist. "Look what the Gulf winds blew in. A beautiful Mayan maiden from Cancun!" He backed up and did a scan from top to bottom and whistled. "Turquoise is a great color on you."

"Nope, not a maiden, just an old, tired Mercedes." Mercedes sighed. "I wore the turquoise because it reminded me of the color of the ocean in Mexico. It also made me want to go back after my long day." She smiled.

"We missed your face around here." He put his hand on the small of her back and began to walk her towards her table. He pulled out the chair and Mercedes sat down. Then he took the seat across from her. Her dinner was waiting and while she was eating, she showed him lots of photos in her phone and gave him a complete rendition of her vacation. Including the 'slap.'

Josh frowned. "Good for you, I'd slap that drunk asshole too!"

Mercedes was so hungry, she ate everything on her plate. She leaned back in the chair and her body began to relax. She picked up her knife and began to tap it on the table and laughed. "I think he was kind of sorry he messed with me!"

Josh stood and picked up her empty plates. "Well, I'm glad you had a great time. Those photos said it all. Man...you look great in a bathing suit. Hell, I've never seen you with a tan before."

Mercedes thought of the floating 'enhancement' and smiled to herself. "Thanks. It's those Zumba classes and no more french fries! The tan is part of the 'Cancun experience!'"

"Whatever it is...you look great!"

The next few weeks went by in a blur. Mercedes came home late each night and barely made it up to her bed, she was so exhausted. Emme came over one Monday night and brought a small giftwrapped box with her. Mercedes made them a seafood salad filled with shrimp, avocado, tomatoes, asparagus tips, and finished it with a lemon vinaigrette. She really didn't make the salad; she picked it up from Bristol Farms. However, she did put it on the plate, garnished it with a few croutons, and made it look better than the clear plastic container it came in. They were sitting on the barstools next to the counter in Mercedes' kitchen. Mercedes was pouring them each a glass of wine and they were laughing and having a great time.

"So, are you coming with us on Saturday?" Emme asked.

Suddenly, Mercedes' mood changed. She took a sip of wine and looked like she was thinking about that question. "I'm not sure. Who all is going?" she replied back.

"Well, let's see. Alisha and David. Her mother is going to watch the baby. Tessann has to work. Christina is coming, but she has to leave early. Jennifer has a date. And of course, me. I love to water ski, and it's almost the end of summer, and I've only been once this year. So, I'm thrilled Alisha and David invited us on their ski boat."

"I don't know. You know I hate crowds and Alisha said, 'David invited a few friends.' Drinking all day in the sun is really not my thing." Mercedes looked down as she pushed her salad around the plate with her fork.

"Come on, Mercedes. Don't be a stick in the mud! Come out and play!" Emme nudged her with an elbow. "Your mother is not here to say 'no' anymore. We can have a fun day like we used to when we were younger and with Alisha's parents. Come on, say 'yes.' Besides, you still have that great tan!"

"I don't know...." A grimace crossed her face.

Emme jumped off her stool and went to her purse. She took something out and then came back and slid back onto the stool. "Okay...heads or tails," she demanded as she held up the new copper penny. "Come on...heads you go, tails you get to choose."

"How is that fair? That is almost a win-win for you!"

"No, it's not! If you have tails you can just say 'no.'" Emme laughed.

Mercedes tried to snatch the coin, but Emme's reflexes were too quick. "I want to see if that's a double-headed coin!"

Emme looked surprised. "You're questioning my integrity...."

"Yes! I remember, in school, all those cheat sheets and answers you wrote on your fingers, hands, and arms! You expect me to trust you now! Hell, no!"

Emme flipped the coin high in the air and it bounced on the countertop, rolled a little and fell on its side. Both girls jumped up and bumped heads as they both tried to look at it.

Emme started doing the Leprechaun jig as she danced around the kitchen laughing and yelling, "Heads...heads...heads...!"

"Okay, you win." Mercedes said, not looking so happy.

"I'll pick you up at 8 a.m. on Saturday morning. Lake attire only!" Emme teased.

Mercedes sat there staring at the coin. Finally, Emme came over and took her arm. "Let's go watch our favorite show."

"Do we have to? We already know the 'Bachelor' is going to find his wife amongst the twenty-five beautiful women! So what is the point watching?"

"You are so silly. It's not about who he picks...it's about all the drama these women spin on television!" Emme began to giggle.

EMME looked surprised. "Are you kidding? You're wearing a T-shirt and a bra instead of a bathing suit top."

Mercedes looked bewildered at her friend's face. "What's the problem? I have don't plan on going in the water and I feel more comfortable this way."

"But it's ridiculous when you're going out on a ski boat. Where's your bathing suit top? Go put it on!"

Mercedes crossed her arms on her chest and stood there waiting for the fight. "No!"

Emme got into her face and raised her voice, "Why?"

Mercedes dropped her arms and looked at Emme and sighed. "Because I was so embarrassed in Cancun when my 'enhancement' came out; and I don't want to go through that again."

Emme leaned over and hugged her friend. "Okay, I get your point. Just put your bathing suit top on and put the T-shirt over it. You don't have to take the T-shirt off, but at least if you get wet by the waves, then you'll have on a suit and not a damn bra."

"Thanks for understanding. I'm very self-conscious of my flat boobies when everyone has these big, beautiful breasts to show off."

"Well...you have the power to change that—just like your friends."

"I know.... "Mercedes walked over to the stairs. "I'll go put it on."

As she was walking up the stairs, Emme yelled out, "Let's talk to Alisha today and see what she thinks and what her doctor can do."

Mercedes didn't say a word, she just continued up the stairs.

Emme, Tessann, and Mercedes got out of the car. Mercedes took a deep breath and let it out slowly. *Why did she feel like she was Anne Boleyn and she was walking to the guillotine?* The three women walked through the large glass doors of a large high-rise in Beverly Hills. They strolled directly to the elevators. Mercedes felt like the massive lobby, filled with twenty-foot walls and floors of polished granite, was closing in on her. *Why was she doing this and what was her motive?* Mercedes asked herself. *She didn't have to ask that question twice.*

Two weeks earlier she was having fun on the boat with Alisha, Christina, and Emme. The group was sitting on top of the boat as each took a turn riding the waves on one set of skis. Mercedes took her turn and was having so much fun that she went out again and again. She kept the T-shirt on and felt comfortable, until she heard a comment.

The boat was pulling Brad on the ski and the other two men were excitedly cheering him on as they steered across the lake. The ladies were all gathered on the front of the boat, enjoying the spray of water as the waves hit the port. They were all taking turns with the water skis and drinking their cold beers. David had invited two of his single buddies, Adam and Brad. Both were successful and extremely attractive. The girls were teasing Mercedes all day about hooking up with one of David's friends.

The roar of the engine made it almost impossible to talk without screaming. When the engine suddenly stopped, Adam's unkind comment could be heard across the whole boat. "She's really a dynamite-looking girl, but she's so flat, it would be like hugging my brother," he said louder than he meant to, probably because he had been drinking.

Everything stopped. The girls quit talking, and they looked at Adam with anger in their eyes, then they turned to Mercedes with compassion on their faces. Mercedes knew exactly who he was talking about, and her face turned bright red.

Adam looked up sheepishly and said, "Sorry, ladies, that was stupid of me. I'm quite embarrassed."

Alisha stepped forward. "You should be, Adam. How would you like me to say to my friends, 'he's a nice guy but his 'dick' is too small'?" she said, in response to his hurtful comment that wounded her friend.

"I deserved that. My apologies, Mercedes."

While Brad was treading water in the middle of the lake waving his arms for help, everyone on the boat was filled with an uneasy feeling of tension.

The remainder of the day was uncomfortable for Mercedes. Emme tried to talk to her on the way home, but she had become unresponsive. That night when Mercedes crawled into bed, she began to cry. It had been a long time and the pain was unbearable.

The girls reached the bank of elevators and waited for one to open. Mercedes' eyes were closed and her hands were shaking.

Emme stepped next to her and whispered in her ear, "Nobody said you have to do this. It's your life. If you like who you are, turn around and we'll leave."

Mercedes was silent, but she could hear her heart beating deeply in her ears. She could still feel the sting of that comment Adam had carelessly made. It had opened up a whole can of worms that evening. It had reached deep into her childhood and extracted all those spiteful and unforgiving comments her mother had constantly repeated. What had she done to deserve a mother that carried nothing but anger and hatred? She was an innocent, vulnerable child who had nowhere to turn. The past ten, twenty years, she had worked so hard at creating a life that had meaning. She stood up to those demons. Yet, sometimes a trigger set off those crushing thoughts that made her feel insignificant again. Adam's comment was that trigger.

Why did the size of a woman's breast define who she was? Why did her generation judge one another based on nothing more than insignificant body parts? She asked herself silently for the final time, *Why am I doing this?*

Mercedes laid her head on Emme's shoulder and whispered back, "What have I got to lose?"

The defeated look on her face made Emme grab her shoulders and ask again, "Are you sure you want to do this? Look at me..." she demanded.

The elevator door opened and Emme looked into Mercedes' eyes, waiting for a sign as to what she wanted to do. Mercedes took Emme and Tessann's hands and walked into the elevator.

The doors closed and they pushed the button to Dr. Schwartz's office.

It was early in the morning, and the full staff had not appeared yet. Today was her surgery day and she knew she was at least putting her life in the hands of a respected doctor. The week before, she had come to his office without letting anyone know. Alisha had set up an appointment after-hours, so Mercedes could privately talk with Dr. Jeff. He was very concerned that she was doing something she really didn't want to do. He understood peer pressure. He never agreed to that kind of influence and suggested she go home and really think about it. They talked for a long time, and he assured her that he wasn't going to make her look like Jennifer.

He had augmented Tessann, and he was adamant that her body was balanced and not top heavy. Because Tessann has small hips and a tiny stature, as an Asian, he didn't make her real big. He just proportioned her with a 'C' cup and they looked very natural. Mercedes didn't want to be one of those lopsided women that stood out in a crowd with showy breasts. She didn't want men to gawk over her because of that. She just wanted to be 'proportioned.' Unfortunately, since she had lost weight and was working out, her long beautiful legs and her now tiny waist would carry a 'D' cup. Still sitting on the side of conservation, she made Dr. Jeff commit to a 'C' cup. She wanted just enough to give her a little cleavage and to fit comfortably into a bathing suit.

The door opened and Alisha walked up to the girls. "I see you brought Emme and Tessann for support. I'm glad you told them."

"I was in shock. She never said a word until a few days ago." Emme smiled.

Alisha took Mercedes' hand and tugged. "Nobody knew. She just wanted to come in for a consultation without any pressure. When she left last week, Dr. Jeff told her she should think long and hard about this change."

"Just be glad you never had to make a major decision like this. You were blessed with a beautiful body, including great boobies!" Mercedes tapped her nose.

"Yeah, we'll see who's blessed in ten years when my 'great boobies' are hanging to the ground and yours are still perfectly symmetrical." All the girls laughed.

"Okay ladies...find something to do. This might be an all-day thing with surgery and recovery. Give our little girl a hug and then scoot! I don't want you hanging around the office like a bunch of pecking hens! You'll have Saturday, Sunday and Monday to nurse her!" Mercedes and Alisha walked through the door.

Mercedes felt like she was in a deep fog. The pain in her chest was overwhelming and she was confused as to what was going on. She didn't want to open her eyes to the blinding lights. All she wanted to do was grab onto something, and hold tight, instead of falling back into the deep dark abyss. She could hear the distant voices of people talking and thought someone was calling her name. Slowly she slipped back into darkness.

"Let her sleep a little longer," Dr. Jeff said. "The next few days are going to be a big adjustment and she'll need plenty of rest. Don't be surprised by her mood swings for a few weeks. It's very common. I'll want to see her in a few days to take off the gauze bandages and put her into a special bra. I know she's going back to work on Tuesday, so make sure she doesn't lift anything and keeps herself hydrated. That is very crucial in her recovery."

"Okay," Emme said. "How about pain medications."

"I'll give you a prescription you can fill," he said. "We'll wake her up in a few minutes and you can take her home."

Monday afternoon was a pivotal change in Mercedes' recovery. For three days, she had laid in bed, and all she wanted to do was sleep. In her early years, sleep had become her only means of protecting herself from the harsh realities of her life. It was like hiding in a cave and not exposing herself to any more pain. The girls didn't know what brought on this depression, or how to deal with it. They only knew that letting her sleep was the best way for her body to heal—the other would come later.

The first day, the pain was unbearable, and yet, she never said anything. The grimace on her face when she moved or got up to go to the bathroom let the girls know she was hurting. Whenever Emme or Christina offered her a pain pill, she declined. *Instead, she chose to dwell in her own misery, as though she deserved it by compromising the principles she had lived with for the past twenty years. Was she punishing herself like her mother used to do to her? Or was she just disappointed that she allowed herself to fall into the trap of putting more value on external beauty—than the beauty that laid within her soul.*

Emme walked into the bedroom with a tray filled with boxes from her favorite Chinese restaurant. "Look what I have for you, sunshine!" Emme said with a big smile. She placed the tray on the dresser and walked over to the window and started to pull up the blinds to get some light in the room.

Mercedes covered her eyes and said softly, "Please leave them closed."

Immediately, Emme let go of the blinds and walked over to the bed. She sat down next to Mercedes and swept the hair off her face with gentle fingers. "Why don't you tell me what is going on in that spinning little head of yours?"

Mercedes turned her head away, for fear that Emme would read into her eyes. It was hard for Mercedes to articulate, to anyone, how or what she was feeling. Her mother was a great teacher, and Mercedes had learned some hard lessons. To expose yourself to others left you vulnerable and open to more pain. So, for all these years, she just held everything deep inside.

Emme looked very serious when she said, "Let's talk about this. We've been friends for too long for me to let you wallow in all this self-pity crap!"

"I'm not 'wallowing' in it...I'm lying in it." Mercedes whispered.

"Why?" Emme asked.

"Why not?" Mercedes countered.

Emme carefully placed her hand over Mercedes' heart. "Where is this pain coming from? I know it's not your chest. It goes deeper than that."

"I feel like I sold my soul to the devil." She laid back on her pillow.

"What?" Emme looked confused.

The weight of her statement showed in her deep sigh. *I did the one thing I swore I would never do. I gave into the conflict between my spirit and beauty. I feel like lately I've been chasing this elusive feeling of becoming something I was not born to be. Do you know what I mean? Most of me has now morphed into this beautiful butterfly, who really was happy with being that moth wrapped in a cocoon."*

"Yes, I get that. But I don't quite understand it."

"I feel like altering my body to become more socially acceptable has compromised who I strived hard to become over the years. I almost feel like I've given into the image-obsessed society that says, 'if you're not beautiful, you are nobody.' And yet, I'm afraid to look in the mirror to justify it."

Emme took Mercedes' hand and placed it in hers. "You are too much into your head. You need to let all that crappy childhood stuff go. So you tweaked yourself a little to look better. We all need to feel good about ourselves."

Mercedes sighed. "Don't you see what I'm telling you? I don't feel good about what I did. I wish I hadn't."

Emme kissed Mercedes on her forehead. "Let it go, Mercedes. You are my beautiful little butterfly." Emme got up and brought the tray over to the bed. "Come on, I had them deliver a whole shitload of food. Let's eat and watch television in bed like we used to."

"I get to pick the show." Mercedes grinned for the first time in days.

"Oh brother! As long as it's not Dr. Phil!" Emme reached over and grabbed a box and a pair of chopsticks.

Dr. Jeff stood back and let Mercedes stand in front of the mirror. "Well, don't they look beautiful?"

Mercedes stood there staring, as her eyes scanned her body up and down. "They look so natural. They aren't these big bowling balls or grapefruits sitting on my chest bone." Mercedes grinned and turned to Emme and Alisha. "So, what do you think?"

Emme smiled with pleasure. "I think we should celebrate by going out and buying a new bathing suit and throwing away those damn enhancements!"

Alisha hugged her friend from behind and looked at their reflections in the mirror. "One of the best pair of ladies I've seen in a while. They fit your body perfectly!"

"Okay, Mercedes, hop back onto the chair and let me look at the stitches, put some special cream on them, and then I'm sending you out into the world to buy some new clothes. Nothing you have is going to fit now!" He laughed out loud.

"Can I go back to work tomorrow? Is there anything I have to do or can't do?" Mercedes placed each of her hands on her new breast. "It feels really numb right now. It also feels really strange to have something sticking off my breast bone."

Dr. Jeff laughed and said, "I hear that all the time. Listen, there is going to be some discomfort and you will feel numb around your nipples for a while. It's very normal. The feeling will most likely come back. No lifting your arms over your head or doing anything strenuous for now. I want to see you in two weeks just to make sure you're healing. If you have any questions, don't hesitate to call."

Mercedes looked down and clasped her hands together. "I do have a question, Dr. Jeff. Why am I so depressed lately? It almost feels like I resent my new boobies." Mercedes looked up.

"It's rare...but sometimes it's a normal reaction. The patient will feel like she lost her best friends—her old breasts. You've lived with them for thirty years and have learned to accept their size. Sometimes the change can be overwhelming. If you need an antidepressant to get you by for a few weeks, let me know. Don't take life so serious, Mercedes. I have this gut feeling this has more to do with your birthday just around the corner, than about your big changes recently."

"You're probably right. Thank you, Dr. Jeff." Mercedes extended her hand.

He shook Mercedes' hand and said, "Thank you, ladies. Now get out of my office and go get Mercedes a new bathing suit! Smile, Mercedes, you're going to be fine!" Without another glance, he left the room chuckling.

Emme threw Mercedes' sweater at her and started to laugh. "I bet it doesn't fit."

Mercedes slid her arms into the sweater and pulled it down. "This bra is so damn ugly. I feel like an old grandmother!"

Emme nudged Alisha and said, "Listen to her, already she is moaning about ugly bras. This time last year, she was complaining they didn't make her itsy-bitsy size anymore. Half the time she went braless!"

Mercedes finished dressing and said, "Let's go to lunch...." She put her hand on her breasts. "These 'new girls' are treating!" She finally smiled.

Alisha, Emme, and Mercedes walked out of the high-rise building. They handed the valet the ticket and he immediately ran to go get the car.

Alisha smiled as she walked around the car and whistled. "Holy smokes, she...is beautiful! Well, there have been a lot of major changes in your life this past year. New kitchen, new nose, new car, new boobies, and maybe we can all look forward to a new boyfriend?" Alisha looked hopeful.

Emme's eyes opened wide and she sang out, "Amen!"

A sadness washed over Mercedes' face. "I don't think you guys really get it. All of these changes have been extremely difficult for me. I was raised with nothing, and I have exceeded any expectations I placed on myself. There's this heart-stopping fear that drives me crazy sometimes when I overindulge and spend on myself. It's a 'fear' of losing all that I worked hard for and having nothing to fall back on. You guys wouldn't know about that. You had normal childhoods with loving families, who pushed you to succeed and gave into every one of your whims. My mother was betting against me. I just don't want her to win!"

Emme softly said, "Be damn proud of yourself."

"Easier said, than done, Emme. Sometimes I wish I could go back to high school where life was easier and I didn't live with any pressure."

Emme spoke up before she slid into the passenger seat. "Look at you...you've gone from 'ugly duckling' to beautiful...and from rags to riches. You've got it all going now!"

Mercedes grabbed her steering wheel and slid into her driver's seat. Under her breath, she said, *"Funny, I thought I had it all going before I made any of these big changes."*

eighteen

THE alarm didn't go off, and Mercedes immediately sat up in bed. Her heart began to race as panic set in. Instantly she looked at the clock, took in a deep breath, and prayed she had not forgotten to set it. There on the small alarm clock, in bold black letters was the word, 'Saturday.' With a sigh of relief, she laid back down, and thought about what she was going to do with her day. Today was her day, and she could lay in bed all day if she wanted. She didn't have to go to Zumba, didn't have to go to work, and for once, didn't really have any solid plans for the day—except for the evening. And those didn't even sound the least bit tempting. *Today was her day*—indeed to do as she pleased.

Mercedes laid in bed for the next hour thinking about all the changes in her life. For some reason, she had been depressed for the past few weeks—as her thirtieth birthday approached. *Was it turning thirty that had her nerves jumbled or was it all the physical changes she had gone through in the last year?* She wasn't sure; but whatever it was created this overwhelming depression that had been a major distraction for weeks. It always started in the morning when she looked in the mirror and hardly recognized herself. Although the changes had been quick to esthetically transform her into a butterfly, she missed being wrapped in that comfortable cocoon, away from all the prying eyes. *She liked being plain and simple, and had a difficult time dealing with drama, like her friends constantly did. She liked being reclusive in a world that judged others unfairly. She liked closing herself off from unwarranted ridicule. Lately she felt like someone had stripped her naked, and her beauty was now sitting in judgment. She was angry and confused, and was trying to process it all with the least amount of anxiety as possible.* But it was hard to do, when you were competing with your friends, and a media that was relentless when it came to beauty.

Magazines, television, and movies glorified the perfection of women and their faultless bodies and flawless skin. The magazine racks in the stores were filled with the do's and don'ts of what society deemed acceptable. The images were geared toward a generation of pencil thin and emaciated looking models who indelibly left a younger generation striving for the same strenuous perfection.

Her friends tried their best to bring some light into her darkness—she refused to accept it. It was almost like she was blaming them for her decisions. It was easier to blame others. She knew that. Her mother had blamed her for everything that had gone wrong in her life. In a past filled with such hurt and dejection, all the attention was overwhelming.

Just as Mercedes began to fall into that deep, dark hole, her cell phone rang and it was Emme. She wasn't sure she wanted to pick it up. Lately there had been a price to pay for answering the phone. Dinner with Christina; lunch with Jennifer and Alisha; a haircut with Tessann; and constant nagging by Emme.

"Happy Birthday to you. Happy Birthday to you...." Emme sang into the phone.

"Thanks for reminding me!" she growled.

"Hey, knock it off! It's your day and you can do whatever you want. Tonight the girls and I want to celebrate with you. You are the last one to turn thirty, and you're being such a big baby!"

Barely above a whisper, Mercedes said, "Do I really have to go tonight?"

"One, two, three...." Emme continued.

"What are you doing?" Mercedes asked. "Counting all the candles on my birthday cake?"

Emme smiled at her comment. "I'm counting to ten. Then I'm going to come over and kick your ass."

Mercedes started to laugh. "I don't think so. I have bigger biceps than you now!"

"What are you doing today?" Emme asked again.

"I'm going to sit in the house and pray that I get so sick, I won't be able to celebrate my birthday tonight." There was a silent pause. "It's really no biggie. I never had birthdays when I was younger, so why have them now?" Mercedes said.

Emme gasped and said with great enthusiasm, "I just had this great idea! I'm picking you up in an hour. That should be plenty of time to slap on a pair of jeans and a T-shirt, and a light-weight jacket."

"Why the light jacket?" Mercedes laughed. "It's going to be warm and beautiful out."

"In case I have to stuff something in your mouth to keep you from screaming."

"Why would I scream?" Mercedes paused to think. "I am...NOT getting a tattoo! AND...that just sealed it. I'm not going with you today!" Mercedes said firmly. "I feel too vulnerable today, and you have me at a disadvantage!"

Emme had been wanting Mercedes to get a tattoo for years. She didn't expect her to get piercings, but she constantly nudged her about a tattoo. Mercedes knew she was not going to give in to Emme's whim, not today, not ever! She decided to draw the line in the sand.

Emme giggled. "Would I do that? I swear on my next boyfriend, it is 'NOT' a tattoo."

"Swear on your mother's life it is *NOT* a piercing!" Mercedes cracked a slight grin.

"Just be ready in an hour." The phone went dead.

Mercedes was sitting on the curb outside her home waiting for Emme. She looked up into the blue sky without a cloud in sight. The sun was shining on her face and she felt the warmth as it spread across her cheeks. Mercedes smiled, she could not imagine what they were going to do today. Emme always surprised her with the craziest things. Whatever it was, Mercedes knew Emme would never do anything intentionally to hurt her, in any way. They had been best friends for years, and Emme had always watched over Mercedes, giving her love and support. Especially when she sank into these dark depressing holes.

Mercedes heard Emme's car coming down the street. She pulled up next to Mercedes, stopped the car, and rolled down the window. Instantaneously, Mercedes burst into laughter. Just as suddenly, she began to weep.

Emme was sitting in the driver's side wearing a pair of Minnie Mouse ears, and a big smile.

"Now...what is your problem? Get in this car!" Emme pushed open the passenger door. "I thought we would go have fun at the happiest place on earth...."

Mercedes finished Emme's sentence as she stood to get in the car. "...we're going to Disneyland!" Mercedes felt the tear slide down her cheek as she looked at her dear friend.

Broken *image*

◈

Mercedes drove up to the dinner club and into valet parking. She drove her own car, just in case she wanted to leave her birthday party early. She could never understand why the girls always planned these elaborate celebrations when it came to someone's birthday. It was strange to her, but she always managed to go along with the plans.

The valet opened the car door and watched as Mercedes slid around and stepped out of the car. Her beautiful long legs were now tight, slightly muscular, and showed off her five-inch silver heels with a thin strap that tied around her ankles. Her slim body fit into the black sheath mini-dress that had an extremely low-cut neckline showing off her new chest. Short brown hair streaked with blonde hung down over one eye—giving her a very sensual look. Minimal makeup showcased her natural beauty, and her big luscious lips were touched up with a shiny lip gloss. One year had made a big change in the person she was looking at in the reflection of the car window. The valet handed her a ticket, and she turned toward the entrance of the club. For some reason the hairs on the back of her neck stood up. With a quick flick of her head, she turned around and smiled. Three men and the valet were unashamedly staring at her with gawking eyes.

"Have a great evening, boys!" she mumbled as she continued to walk toward the crowd. She had never been to this club before and she was beginning to feel a little self-conscious. She tried to look over the crowd to see if she could find any of her friends. A sigh crossed her lips when she finally noticed Emme and Tessann standing next to the bouncer at the door. Mercedes waved and quickly sprinted towards them. When she reached the bouncer, he gave her a big smile and said to Emme and Tessann, "Why didn't you

tell me that the birthday girl was knockout gorgeous?" He didn't open the rope immediately.

Mercedes leaned over it and kissed the girls on the cheek. "You both look lovely tonight." She intentionally ignored the brawny bouncer.

All of a sudden, he bent over Mercedes so she could feel his entire body mold over hers and he put his hand on her ass. Then he softly whispered in her ear, "I've never seen you here before." He moaned and moved his hand slowly on her ass. "Do you know what I would love to do to you...?"

Mercedes went stiff and turned around to face him. "In all honesty...I don't know and I definitely don't care. So, if you would be so kind as to take your fucking hands off my ass and pull up the rope, and let me step by—this birthday girl promises not to vomit all over you!" Mercedes said in a syrupy sweet voice.

He moved back and grimaced, then he lifted the rope.

Emme and Tessann each took a hand and they walked into the club. "That was so cool. Man-oh-man, that was better than kneeing him in his balls." Emme said.

"He was a pig," Mercedes frowned.

"Not all men are pigs, only some!" Tessann added.

Mercedes could tell that the party had already started without her. Christina and Jennifer were at the table with a group of men surrounding them. Alisha and David walked over and hugged Mercedes.

Alisha frowned. "The baby is sick, but we came out to say, 'happy birthday,' but now we have to get home. Wish we could stay longer."

"No. Go take care of your sweet baby. It's my fault. I'm an hour late. I was into a great movie and never realized what time it was." Mercedes gave Alisha another hug and the couple quickly walked toward the exit.

Mercedes turned around and then walked over to the crowd. Jennifer was busy rubbing up against a handsome man. In the twenty minutes Mercedes had been in the club, Jennifer had been too busy to even notice she was there.

Mercedes walked over to Jennifer. "Surprise...the birthday girl is here!"

Jennifer turned toward Mercedes and jumped up and down against the male body next to her. Then she screamed, "Look everyone...the birthday girl is here!"

Everyone at the table looked at Mercedes. Some more so than others. All the men at the table were scanning Mercedes and smiling—one even blew her a kiss. She had become the complete center of attention. Feeling uncomfortable, she said, "Excuse me, I'll be right back." Her eyes scanned the room for the restroom sign.

The guy Jennifer had her arm around swiftly lunged and grabbed Mercedes' arm. "Hey, where are you going? Want some company?" He looked directly at her with puppy dog eyes.

Mercedes jerked her arm away. "No, thank you. I think you have more than you can handle right now!" Abruptly, she walked toward the sign.

Emme saw her discomfort and followed her to the restroom.

Mercedes walked in and there was a row of chairs along the wall. She sat down and leaned her head back and closed her eyes.

"Are you okay?" Emme whispered.

The voice next to her ear stunned Mercedes, but she didn't move her head, or open her eyes. She whispered, "I'm not used to all the attention and sexual innuendos. Putting their hands all over my body, grabbing me, groping me, and whispering ridiculous stuff in my ears.... I've never had to deal with crappy disrespect before. I always had respect from the decent men I deal with. These 'pissy little punks' think they are God's gift to women, and treat us like sex objects!"

Emme whispered. "I know. All of a sudden you are the belle of the ball and all those 'little boys' want to get into your panties!"

Mercedes turned her head toward Emme with a tear sliding down her cheek. "I just want to be the 'old me' again...I'm not so sure I can deal with all the crap that goes with the 'new me.'"

Emme brushed the hair off her face. "Be proud of who you are...don't let them get to you. Come on... it's your evening."

Mercedes stood up and grabbed Emme's hand. "I'm going home, Emme. Tell everyone I'm not feeling well."

Emme hugged her friend, and watched her leave.

Mercedes felt like her arms were going to fall off, she was carrying so much. Briefcase, laptop, jacket, flat shoes, leftovers from dinner, and her purse. She barely made it to the elevator when Amed came running over.

"Please, please...let me help you!" he begged.

The elevator door opened. Mercedes smiled and said, "That's very kind to ask, but I'm fine. It's not that far." Her arms were beginning to feel numb. She only prayed she didn't drop the stuff before the elevator doors closed. She didn't need Amed's help, nor did she want to encourage him any more than necessary. As it was, he acted like a school kid chasing the little girl in the sandbox.

Mercedes walked out of the elevator and looked at her reflection in the mirror and smiled. Her black pencil skirt and sage green turtleneck sweater gave her the image of a put together business woman. Her new style of attire also made her look curvaceous and sexy. There was no hiding her new curves that were so alluringly present. Her jacket was in her hand, and she was desperately trying to balance her load as her fingertips barely turned the doorknob and her foot kicked the door open. Standing at Mary's desk in a conversation were Alexi, Michael, and Jarrod. Upon seeing Mercedes, they tripped over each other in a rush to go help her with her heavy burden.

"Go ahead and let go, Mercedes." Michael said.

"Yeah, Mercedes, I have your computer case...." Alexi added in.

Jarrod took the briefcase out of her hand and Mercedes was left with her jacket, purse, and leftovers for lunch. "Thanks, guys, I appreciate the help. It was killer getting up here this morning with all this stuff."

Mary watched as the 'little puppies' followed behind her as she walked down the hall to her office. Their eyes were glued to her short skirt, long legs, and swaying ass. Mary shook her head in amusement when they all entered her office.

Mary heard Michael say, "Next time, just call on your cell and we'll come down and help."

"Thanks, guys!" Mercedes said as she started to slip on her jacket. Sliding one arm into a sleeve, and then the other, caused her new breasts to protrude even more in her tight sweater, making every movement look sexy and sensual. All three men stared with their eyes wide open. Mercedes looked up and blushed from embarrassment as the men just stood there following every move. "Okay...you can leave now," she said, dismissively. Immediately they scattered like a group of scared mice.

Later that morning, Mercedes went to the kitchenette to eat her leftovers. She took the bag out of the refrigerator, placed it on the table, and had a seat. She had spent the morning on the phone and she had an afternoon filled with appointments. Mary walked in while Mercedes was sitting at the small table. She was texting on her phone and didn't notice Mary until she sat down next to her.

"Well, darling, I can see you've been busy. I haven't seen you for hours!" A sweet looking smile crossed her face.

Mercedes sighed at Mary's comment. "I feel like everyone is coming at me from all directions and demanding more of my time—including Jarrod. He never used to engage me with any of his top clients. Now, all of a sudden, I'm constantly sitting in his meetings, lunches, and outside activities. I want to be left alone. I have my own clients, and after seven years of struggling, I don't give a crap about his!"

"Well, it seems like since the 'new you' has appeared, they've been taking advantage. You need to put your foot down and let them know." Mary patted her hand.

"Even the boys are constantly hanging around my office and asking me to go to lunch with them. It's like, after all these years, they want me to be part of the 'good ol' boys club.'" Mercedes frowned.

Mary sat for a few seconds—thinking. "Well, men are very visual creatures, no matter what environment they are in. You've stimulated their visual senses and they are acting like a group of immature school boys! I actually find it very amusing at times. The other times, I feel like I want to box their ears!"

"I don't get it. Why I was practically ignored for years. Wasn't my business savvy enough?"

"Humm...maybe they were just intimidated because you were a strong and aggressive businesswoman. You didn't have that sexy, fun-looking side men love to chase after."

"I'm the same person!" Mercedes hissed.

"No...you've changed! You have opened up a new, sexy part of you that generates more attention, and men crave that in women. For some reason, our society puts a lot of credibility on beauty rather than on the worth of each individual. Beauty is a rite of passage. Actors, models, and handsome people base their value on beauty and it opens those doors. Rarely are the plain or interesting people invited in." She looked at Mercedes' downcast eyes. "Your changes opened that door to a double edged sword—acceptability and vulnerability."

Mercedes looked up and said, "Who I always have been hasn't changed—I'm just a little tanner, a little thinner, larger boobs, stylish haircut, and more trendy clothes. Why am I suddenly being judged on those changes?"

"Because it is the evil of our society that forces us to be judged. Beauty becomes a currency. The media splashes it across our televisions, movies, magazines and billboards and expects these younger generations not to accept who they are, but what they can be with cosmetic surgery. My generation didn't place that pressure on ourselves. Marilyn Monroe wasn't paper thin. Ernest Borgnine wasn't a strikingly handsome man, nor did he have a manly physique. Our standards were more relaxed. We embraced what God had given us and accepted that—not everyone is perfect. We certainly didn't set ourselves up for failure."

"Why are these younger generations so fixated on beauty?" Mercedes questioned.

"Because they have technology to push them in every direction at the touch of their fingertips. They have plastic surgeons on every corner peddling beauty." Mary sighed and shook her head. "You know, we were not taught to aspire to have physiques of super models, and men to have the sculpted bodies of professional athletes. Those were ideals that few of us could ever achieve. We had better self-esteem. We attained acceptability through hard work."

"Growing up—my mother gave me the overwhelming message that I was unattractive and undesirable. My self-esteem plummeted; and I constantly had this feeling of having no value and being worthless. She constantly perpetuated negative messages—and my peers were not at all hesitant to inform me of all the ways I fell short. It became obvious to me that attractiveness was determined by a very narrow set of parameters—that was the entry fee for participating in an active social life. It was the key to deserving a chance to be loved. It wasn't until I was older that I realized the only way I was ever going to succeed—I had to be strong, and to be the best at what I did. I pushed hard through college, and sucked up all the knowledge I could. I strived to be in the top two-percent of my class, and I worked hard at becoming shrewd. It gave me the edge without having beauty to rely on." Mercedes sighed. "Now, with these changes, the door has burst open and I hate it."

Mary smiled with compassion in her eyes. "I'm so sorry, Mercedes. But now that you've made these changes, you have to set boundaries and not allow anyone to step over them. Especially with men. They love weak women; and for the first time in your life, your beauty has made you very vulnerable."

Mercedes looked miserable. "I hate the attention; I hate the aggressive behavior of men; I hate being treated like a sex object; and most of all, I'm beginning to regret my decisions. I really liked who I was...."

"Dear me. What is—is! It will all change in time." Mary stood up. "On a positive note...you look wonderful in that color green; and I think you should put a big smile on your face and let this be a big lesson."

"What am I supposed to learn...?" Mercedes looked sad.

"Believe in who you are. Look in the mirror and like who you are. Surround yourself with friends who like who you are. And most importantly, never let your friends manipulate or influence you—be your own person!"

Mercedes stood up and turned around and gave Mary a big hug. "Thanks for listening. I wish I could turn back the clock to last year. Your advice would have saved me all this grief."

Mary gave Mercedes a guilty smile and said, "Forget your leftovers. Let's sneak out for a quick lunch at that new little Bristol they opened a few weeks ago. I heard their onion fondue is to die for!"

Mercedes walked over and threw her bag in the trash, and said, "I love onion fondue!"

nineteen

FOR the past few weeks, Mercedes had been dealing with fits of depression—overwhelming emotional feelings that had been plaguing her for years. She hadn't heard from her mother in over two years and lately she had been questioning herself—why? After all, she was the only relative she had in this world, and even they had lost contact. She felt bitterly alone, and there was this sense of isolation that constantly nagged at her lately. Her friends could sense it; and they continually kept her busy, hoping that she would shake this overpowering feeling of darkness and come back out into the light again. This seemed to be a pattern of hers over the years. Only this time, nothing was the same, and she seemed more and more unpredictable.

The week before, she had gone to The Club with Christina, Tessann, and Jennifer. Emme couldn't go because she had to prepare for a vintage fashion show she was putting on for a charity. For days, Mercedes had gone to her store in the evenings. She was helping her get organized and get ready for the big community event. Emme chaired this event every year for the local aid organizations in the area that helped feed the poor and homeless. Mercedes loved helping and personally gathered a lot of donations from her own clients. Some contributed money, while others gave raffle gifts—anything; donations were appreciated and helped feed the hungry children in the area. This was Emme's way of giving back to a community that had continuously supported her store.

Emme pleaded with Mercedes to go to the club with the girls. "Look, I appreciate the help you've given me. Go do something for yourself. Go put on one of the new dresses we picked out and stay for a few hours. It's Friday night, and the girls will be so happy to see you there," she begged.

That evening, Mercedes was the talk of the night amongst her friends. She looked absolutely stunning in a very clingy short dress that Emme had picked out—displaying her rounded, sexy cleavage. She could have been a picture right out of the pages of Vogue Magazine. The young men couldn't take their eyes off her, nor would they leave her alone. They were constantly buying her drinks, showering her with attention, and hanging onto every word she spoke. All the attention was more than she could handle. As the evening continued, the young men became more and more aggressive—trying to get noticed. Her girlfriends joked and laughed at all the fuss—except for Jennifer. Mercedes could see that Jennifer was sitting alone, at the end of the table—pouting. She was used to being the center of attention and she had been drinking more than her normal. Feeling very guilty, Mercedes walked over to where she was sitting.

She sat down and put her arm around Jennifer. She could feel Jennifer stiffen her shoulders. "Are you okay?" Mercedes asked, genuinely concerned.

Jennifer didn't answer at first. She sat there staring straight ahead and continued to pout. Mercedes asked again,

"Tell me why you're upset? Was it something I did? If it was, you know I would never do anything to hurt you."

Jennifer exploded. "You never mean to hurt anyone! YOU...are 'Miss Perfect'! Perfect body, perfect hair, perfect smile, perfect clothes, perfect fucking boobs! Everything is perfect now! I wish you would go back to the 'old Mercedes'!" Jennifer stood up, and was ready to march away, when Mercedes impulsively grabbed her elbow and swung her around.

With hurt and anger dripping in her voice, she looked deep into Jennifer's eyes. "I'm sorry you feel that way. Wasn't it YOU who kept pushing me to change! Wasn't it YOU who told me I needed Botox, bigger lips, thinner thighs, a stylish haircut, and fucking bigger boobs? Wasn't it YOU that made fun of my enhancements that floated away in the pool in Cancun? Why didn't you think about that when you were making fun of all of my 'less than perfect' attributes?" Mercedes squeezed her elbow harder and spewed out, "I wish I could get the 'old Mercedes' back...so fuck YOU, you plastic bitch!" Mercedes released her elbow, grabbed her purse off the table, and starting pushing her way through the crowd towards the exit. Tears were streaming down her face as the valet handed her the keys. She got in her car and burned a long stream of rubber down the street as she left— not caring about the tears blinding her vision.

Once she walked in the door of her house, she shut down her cell phone that had been constantly ringing. She didn't want to talk to anyone. She just wanted to be left alone to suffer in her own self-pity. Slowly she walked up the stairs, blinded by her tears. Then suddenly, this overpowering fear began to take hold of her and she began to sob. Unconsciously, she stripped off her clothes, lit a candle on her dresser, and curled up under her comforter. Finally tucked into her cocoon, she wasn't going to let nothing or nobody hurt her. Late into the night, you could still hear her sobs—sobs that had, over the years, left her feeling alone and broken.

Sunday morning, Mercedes was still in bed. She had only gotten out of bed twice in two days to eat something. She wanted to stay in her bed and to be left alone—forever. She didn't want to talk to anyone or deal with her crushing melancholy. The quiet allowed her to think a lot about a past that had nearly destroyed her as a child. It also made her think about what she had said to Jennifer, *"I wish I could get the 'old Mercedes' back, too."* She didn't like the 'new' Mercedes, and she definitely didn't mean to alienate her friends because of it. Her beauty was now an ugly sword that had drawn a line in the sand with her friends. She wouldn't answer their calls. Twice she thought she heard someone knocking at the door. She needed some space to evaluate her life.

She never yelled at any of her friends before, but for some reason, Jennifer had pushed a button that made her explode. Jennifer, and her jealous 'pity party', was blaming Mercedes for something that was out of her control.

Suddenly, there was a pounding on the front door. "Open up!" Emme yelled. "I know you're in there. If you don't let me in, I'm going to break every window in this fucking house...do you hear me? I hope your neighbors hear me too, because I'm going to keep screaming until you answer this damn door!"

Mercedes slipped out of bed and into a robe. Agilely, she flew down the stairs and flung open the door. She blocked the harsh sun from her eyes that had been in darkness for days. "What do you want? Don't you know when a person doesn't answer their phone; they want to be left alone!"

Emme was flipping a good-sized rock up and down in her hand. "You're damn lucky you answered this door. Believe me, it would have been worth breaking your windows one by one!"

Emme pushed past Mercedes and went into the kitchen. Mercedes shut the door and turned to follow.

Mercedes stopped and in a harsh voice, said. "What do you want?"

Emme turned around and looked at her friend. "You look like crap! What the hell have you been doing for two days?"

Mercedes sighed. "Laying in bed, thinking."

"Oh brother...that is a dangerous thing for you to do!" Emme sat on a barstool and barked, "Make me some coffee. I haven't slept in days, worrying about you. Next time, please answer your stupid phone."

Mercedes took a good look at Emme and could see the black rings forming under her eyes. Usually she got those from lack of sleep. "Sorry, Emme. I just needed to be alone."

Emme got off the seat and walked over to Mercedes and slowly slipped her arms around her. "I get that!" she whispered in her ear. "But I still worried, along with the girls."

Mercedes began to sob, and Emme held on for dear life. After most of her tears were spent, they each made a cup of coffee and went upstairs to sit on Mercedes' bed and talk. For hours they sat there, discussing all of the anxiety that had begun to suck the life out of her. Emme explained that Jennifer felt horrible for what she had said, and the girls were appalled at her behavior.

But was Jennifer's action so bad that it sent Mercedes into a tailspin? Or was there an underlying deep depression that was triggered that night? Most of it had to do with the multiple issues that had been weighing Mercedes down for a long time, and then it was compounded by her changes. With her changes happening so rapidly and a past that was finally catching up with her—she was on the verge of a nervous breakdown.

Out of nowhere, and making a final decision, Mercedes looked at Emme and asked, "Will you go with me to find my mother?"

Emme looked surprised. "What...?"

"I want to find her," Mercedes said.

Emme looked her straight in the eyes. "Why...?"

Mercedes stared back. "Because I need to ask her a few questions."

Emme's voice softened. "Do you even know where she is? How long has it been, two years?"

Tears welled in Mercedes' eyes, "Yes. I just feel like many things in my life were left unsaid and I need some closure."

Emme took her hand and held it tight. "What is the point?"

Tears were rolling down Mercedes' face. "I just want to show her that I'm not that 'ugly duckling,' anymore."

Emme held her friend close and whispered in her ear. "Tell me you did not make those changes because of her...."

Mercedes remained silent.

Emme's angry voice was piercing Mercedes' stability. "You don't have to prove anything to her, my friend. She never deserved you. YOU were always beautiful...you just didn't see it!"

Mercedes looked at Emme with sad eyes that had cried plenty of tears in her youth.

Emme nodded her head. "Okay. I will go help you find her. But only if you make an appointment with a therapist once we do. That child in you needs to let go of what you couldn't change."

Emme slipped into the front seat of Mercedes' car. She put her purse on the floor, and looked over at Mercedes. "Hey, how are you doing?"

Mercedes started to drive off. "I'm okay...."

Emme placed her hand on top of Mercedes' and softly said, "If you fall apart, or if for any reason you can't handle the situation, then I'm going to take control and turn this car around. Do you hear me, Mercedes? I will not allow you to disintegrate into pieces after how far you've come."

"I get that, Emme. I've thought about this for days, since I asked you to come with me. I just need my own little piece of closure. I want to tell her I made it without her."

Emme patted her hand. "You still don't get it, Mercedes. She doesn't care, one way or the other, what happened to you. Those eighteen years she raised you were meaningless to her. You were just her punching bag. She was fucking bipolar, we know that! Can't you just let it be?"

A tear slid down Mercedes' face. "No...."

Emme sighed. "What did you find out? Did you get an address?"

"She lives about three hours from here. Somewhere in the Desert. That was her last known address. I tried to call, but her phone is disconnected. It was probably turned off for non-payment. That is her way of life—something was being turned off every week—then it was turned back on."

Emme looked out her window and the reflection on her face showed her doubt.

They drove hours to get to Palm Desert. Once they got there—hungry and filled with apprehension, they stopped to have lunch at a small trendy restaurant. Mercedes and Emme ordered a glass of wine, trying to curb the rising anxiety. When they were finally done with their meal, they got back into the car and posted the address in the GPS.

Within a few miles, Mercedes turned into an old and neglected looking neighborhood. After driving a few more blocks, they found their destination. She pulled up in front of a small deserted-looking house. The paint was peeling off the siding, and the roof looked beyond repair. The cement walk up to the front door was cracked and uneven. It had very few shrubs or trees that landscaped the large dirt-filled front yard. Mercedes noticed all the houses were poorly maintained in the cul-de-sac, not just her mother's. It was the trashy part of town, where rents were cheap and money was scarce. She closed her eyes and pictured all those rundown houses she shared with her mother. They constantly moved and each house was worse than the last. Each one dilapidated and filthy, and infested with rats or cock roaches. She hated those memories; a childhood that was so meaningless. All those years, the repulsive memories, flashed back as she sat and stared at the house before turning off her engine. Emme sat quietly, and let her friend take in the surroundings.

Emme finally broke the silence. "Do you want me to go up to the door with you, or stay in the car?"

Mercedes' voice cracked barely above a whisper, "Go with me...."

They both opened their doors to the car and got out. Mercedes came around and Emme took her hand as they walked up the broken walkway. They both stepped onto the cracked cement stoop and Mercedes knocked on the door. At first, just lightly. Then, much harder as they continued to wait for someone to answer the door.

Suddenly, a deep male voice came from nowhere. "Nobody lives there anymore. She's gone."

Startled to hear a male voice, Mercedes and Emme turned around and tried to figure out where it had come from. Nobody was in sight as they both looked around the uninhabited street filled with broken-down homes.

The male voice boomed again—even louder. This time, they realized someone was lying under an old car on the cement driveway next door. "Like I said already, 'the bitch left over a year ago.'" This time his legs started to appear from beneath the car that was sitting on cinder blocks, instead of tires. The creeper board slid out from under the car. He was lying down on the board while his heavy boots pushed him out further. Emme and Mercedes stood there speechless and completely mesmerized. When he was finally out from under the car, he stood up. His big husky body with a large bloated belly was dripping in sweat. He took a red rag from his back pants pocket, and wiped his dirty and perspiring face. Leisurely, as Mercedes and Emme watched, he meandered over to the stoop. Wearing an old pair of jeans, a stained white T-shirt, and heavy work boots, he made his way to within a foot of the ladies. Both stared in disbelief as the pungent smell of his body odor filled the air.

Emme broke the silence. "Do you know where we can find her?"

His eyes drifted away and he seemed to be thinking. "Don't think so. She was here one day, and gone the next."

Mercedes sounded annoyed. "Well, someone must know where she went. How about the owner of this property?"

He laughed out loud, his voice echoing throughout the peaceful cul-de-sac. "The bank owns this place now. I don't know why...it's almost worthless, except for the land."

Emme stood there with pinched brows, then she asked quietly, "Was there any mail left behind? Was there any kind of forwarding address? Was she friends with anyone on this street?"

His face perked up and he cracked a slight grin. "That mean bitch didn't have friends. But you know what...I think I might have a piece of mail sitting in the house. Let me go see."

Mercedes and Emme watched as he made his way back to the house and entered through a ripped screen door.

Within seconds he back outside walking toward the ladies. He was unfolding the envelope when he handed it to Emme.

"Sorry about the creases. I was using it as a doorstop for my kitchen door. That damn door is so unbalanced that I folded this last year and shoved it under to keep the damn door open."

Emme held the envelope and could see a forwarding address that was practically worn off. It gave a street address in a small town just down the highway. "Thank you so much."

He looked up at Emme with curious eyes, "Why ya looking for her?"

Mercedes spoke softly, "She's my mother, and I haven't seen her in years."

The man nodded his head slightly and said, "You look too nice to have a mean son-of-a-bitch mother like her. She loved her booze, but hated people. Put a pint of whiskey in her, and she screamed like a stuck pig...."

They heard more than they needed too. Mercedes turned around, and started to walk toward the car. Emme said in a loud voice, "Sorry to bother you. Thanks for the address...." Then under her breath, she said, "...*you miserable bastard!*"

Mercedes and Emme got into the car and typed the address into the GPS. The new address wasn't far away. It was just seventeen miles south of where they were, but a lot more rural. With mellow music filling the car, they drove those miles in silence. Emme could see the confliction on Mercedes' face, but she never said a word.

Mercedes finally broke the silence. "I wonder why he called my mother a bitch."

Emme turned to look at Mercedes and said with conviction, "Because...she was a bitch. Your whole life she treated you—everyone very viciously. I don't think I can ever remember her being nice, kind, or caring to anyone. Something was really wrong with your mother."

"That was because she hated being a mother. I was her burden in life, she hated me, and ridiculed me every chance she could. After a while, I just became numb."

Emme looked puzzled. "Do you truly think it was really about you? Or is it becoming obvious that she really hated life—period! She hated the world and everything in it. Didn't you ever wonder why she had absolutely no family?"

"I wondered my whole life as to why she didn't have parents, siblings, or any relatives. We were so alone in the world. I mean, it was just her and me. When I was a young girl, I would sit for hours and try to guess 'why.'" Mercedes sighed. "Did they all die in a plane crash or automobile accident, except her? Was she raised in an orphanage? Did she witness her family being murdered? Or did she run away and never look back?"

Emme asked, "Did you ever ask her?"

"Of course I did. But I always got the same answer, 'it's none of my business.'" Mercedes mimicked her mother's voice with the last sentence.

"Well, maybe this time when we find her, she will answer a few of your questions." Emme reassured her friend.

"I doubt it."

Mercedes got off the freeway off-ramp and followed the instructions of the GPS. After driving through the small town, they came to a very old, rundown motel complex at the very end of the main street. The sign read—Starlight Motel. It was a small motel with only six attached units. In front of the office was a sign that was filled with big gaping holes—'no-vacancy' was flashing off and on. There was only one car parked in front of one of the rooms.

Mercedes pulled off the road onto the worn gravel driveway. The car began to bounce as the tires dipped into the big potholes that covered the entire surface. The building was painted a turquoise blue with white trim, but most of the paint had chipped off from years of wild winds and sand storms that regularly passed through the desert communities. Mercedes could remember when she was a little girl and they lived in Arizona. The strong, dry winds blowing over the desert carried along clouds of sand or dust often so dense, it obscured the sun. Sand storms like that always scared Mercedes, and she would hide under her bed until they passed.

The small office in the front of the long oblong building looked uninhabited, with the exception of a ceiling fan that was spinning around. Mercedes pulled into a parking spot in front of the office. They both sat in the car staring at the dirty window.

Quietly Emme asked, "You sure you want to do this?"

"Yes."

Emme opened her door first, then Mercedes followed. They got out of the car and walked, hand in hand, into the office. Behind the wall-to-wall counter, an old woman was sitting at a desk watching a tiny television. If she noticed them, she didn't say a word or look their way—she just continued to watch the television.

Mercedes tapped on the counter, and slowly the lady looked up. For a minute, Mercedes caught her breath, and thought it was her mother. But it wasn't. "Hello, I'm looking for someone. Her previous neighbor said she moved here. I was wondering if you could tell me what room she is in?" Mercedes could barely swallow. She knew that there were privacy laws that forbid releasing any names of customers without their permission—with the exception of law enforcement. She just didn't know to what extent this woman would go to protect her customer.

She looked directly at Mercedes and said in a deep voice, "You the police?"

Mercedes shook her head and softly said, "No. I'm her daughter."

The woman stood up. Her straw-like gray hair hung around her shoulders in complete disarray. Her baggie polyester green pants had stains all over them, and her floral sleeveless tank top was frayed along the neckline. She put both her arms on the high countertop and leaned forward. Mercedes glanced at all her missing teeth.

"Who you looking for?" she said in a deep, husky voice.

Mercedes could smell the alcohol on her breath. "Betty Simon, or at least, that was her name years ago."

The old woman stood straight up and looked surprised. "How do I know you're her daughter? You could be lying to me. It wouldn't be the first time someone tried to pull the wool over my eyes!" she hissed out loud.

Emme tapped Mercedes and said, "Give her your driver's license."

The old woman started to laugh. "That don't mean nothing to me. You can buy those a dime a dozen anywhere!"

Mercedes reached into her purse and brought out her wallet. Her first thought was to give the lady a twenty dollar bill. Instinct told her not to antagonize her. She took out her license and a few credit cards, and handed them to her.

The old woman looked at them and inhaled a big breath and let it out slowly. "She never told anyone she had a kid! We figured some pretty bad stuff had happened in her life because she was 'off her rocker'...you know what I mean?" she said. She pointed a finger to her head, and then spun it in circles.

Mercedes nodded. "I had a pretty tough childhood and I left when I was barely eighteen. We didn't talk or see each other much over the years."

The woman turned and sat down in her chair. Her face took on a sad appearance. "I hate to tell you this, but your mother died eight months ago. She had cancer of the stomach and just whittled away in front of our eyes. She was all alone and didn't want any help. Lucky for her, it only took a few months, and then she died."

Mercedes sucked in her breath and her world started to spin in front of her eyes. She whispered, "Lucky for her...she's dead?"

The old lady nodded.

"Are you sure it was my mother? Are you sure we're talking about the same person?" The panic in her voice started showed.

Emme put her arms around Mercedes to steady her. She spoke up in a firm voice to the old woman. "Do you have anything that we can identify her by? Did she have any personal things she left behind?"

The woman opened a drawer and pulled out a picture. "I took this picture of her in front of her new car. Well, it really wasn't new—it was twelve years old. A friend of mine sold it to her for eight hundred bucks!" She handed Mercedes the picture.

Fearing the worst, Mercedes looked down at the picture. Then Emme looked at it also. Mercedes suddenly began to cry.

Through her tears, Mercedes frantically asked, *"Didn't she talk about me? Didn't she tell you she had a daughter? Anything...?"* Mercedes began to sob.

"Look, she never mentioned a daughter or family. She was a mean, angry old woman when she came here, and mean when she left. If she were a dog, we would have put her out of her misery years ago—that's how mean she was. She stayed to herself and had no friends. If you're looking to see if she left anything to you, all she had were the clothes on her back and that was it! I found very little in her room, and nothing of value—except her alcohol and this." She opened a drawer in the desk and took out a shiny object and handed it to Mercedes. It was a small, tarnished Saint Christopher medal. Mercedes stared at it as the tears were sliding down her cheeks. "My mother never believed in God or religion. One day when I was fourteen, I came home from a carnival with this medal. I was so excited...it came with a chain and I was wearing it around my neck. I got it with all the winner tickets I saved and I thought it was so special. When I walked in the house, she got really angry and ripped it off my neck. I never saw it again." Mercedes put it in her pocket and began to cry.

Emme placed the picture in Mercedes' wallet, and put it back into her purse. She thanked the old lady and walked her friend out to the car. She opened the door and sat her sobbing friend into the passenger seat. Then she walked around the other side of the car and slid into the driver's seat. For a while Emme sat listening to her friend as she sobbed over a lifetime of pain.

"Let's go home." Emme said as she started the car.

"Thank you, Emme." Mercedes said as she drifted off to sleep in the front seat.

Twenty

MERCEDES called the office and told them she had caught a horrible cold and would not be in for a few days. She was never one to call in sick, but it had been a difficult weekend and she needed some time off to sort things out. Depression had set in, and she was having a hard time concentrating and making any decisions, other than staying in bed and crying. Her feelings of hopelessness and guilt weighed heavily on her, creating a fatigue even her body couldn't fight. She didn't want to see anyone, or talk to anyone. Her need to heal her spirit had forced isolation and she became thinner and thinner. Her loss of weight and her sleeplessness worried Emme.

Emme knocked on the door and got no answer. This time, she opened her purse, and took out the key to Mercedes' house. Mercedes had finally relented and had an extra key made. Then, with a lot of coaxing, she gave it to Emme. She knew she could trust Emme, but it was herself she was doubting. Her depression was sucking the life out of her and she didn't know how to deal with it. The loss of her mother had been the final straw that had crushed her stability she had desperately built over the years. And although she had always felt alone in life, with the finality of her mother's lonely death, she was now the lone survivor of a family she knew nothing about. She had searched for relatives on a few of those online websites, but she always came up empty. Either her mother's name was not her given name, or the State she was allegedly born in was not accurate. It was a constant frustration to Mercedes when she hit a block wall in her search, and after dozens of tries, she had finally given up.

Emme walked in and called Mercedes' name. When she didn't get an answer, panic set in and she ran up the stairs. As she entered the empty bedroom, an eerie feeling crept up her spine. The candle on the dresser was lit, the bed was unmade, and Mercedes was nowhere to be found. Emme started to scream Mercedes' name over and over, then she ran out the bedroom door and collided into Mercedes.

"Hey, slow down...you nearly knocked me over!" Mercedes grabbed Emme's shoulders to keep her from falling.

Emme looked at her friend with panic still written all over her face. She let out a deep sigh. "I got scared. I called and called and you didn't answer."

Mercedes looked confused and sad. "Scared of what, Emme?"

Emme's face turned red and she said, "Something had happened to you."

"I'm right here and ready to go. I appreciate you taking me to the therapist," Mercedes said.

"I'm concerned about you. The last time I saw you this distraught was when you were seventeen and you attempted to commit suicide." Emme looked miserable. "Do you remember that night? You had a whole bottle of your mom's pills you wanted to take. I had to talk you out of it."

Mercedes nodded. "I'm not quite there yet, I'm just sitting on the edge. I'll be okay. I'm just dealing with a lot of crap right now. It's not just about my mother. I regret not having enough self-esteem...to like who I was. I hate that I changed who I was—into what I am now."

Emme looked at her mystified. "Why...?"

"That night with Jennifer, I had a major epiphany when she said, 'she wished I had never changed my looks to become beautiful.' To her, it was about jealousy and competition. To me, it was about how I was being valued on my beauty instead of who I was, deep inside. All of a sudden, my colleagues treated me differently; men gawked and manhandled me relentlessly; and then my friends were turning on me. *Over what?* The ugly duckling turning into a beautiful swan. You know what the killer is, Emme—that night, I wanted my old self back too. It had taken me so long to finally like myself, and suddenly, I was trying to be what my mother would have liked me to be. I went through those changes to see if finally she would accept me...and she was fucking dead!"

Emme looked at her and nodded. "I'm so sorry, my dear friend."

Mercedes stared at the wall. "I thought being beautiful would finally make my mom stand up and notice me." She exhaled a deep breath. "She should have given me up for adoption, or put me in foster care if I was such a burden. My life was hell, and she owed me a big apology. I needed to hear her say, 'she was sorry.' I wanted her to see I had survived." Mercedes sighed. "Only, she was dead. You know, she knew she was dying and she never called to say 'I'm sorry...go to hell...or fuck you!' Even on her death bed, she cheated me out of my childhood." Mercedes laughed maliciously.

Emme took her hand and slowly they walked down the stairs. "Come on, my friend, I need to get you to the therapist."

Weeks had passed, and even though Mercedes was back to work and continuing where she had left off, she couldn't shake the melancholy deep within. Every time she looked in the mirror, she didn't see herself anymore. She saw her mother and felt this emptiness. She became more and more reclusive as she mechanically moved through life. A feeling of separation always seemed to loom over her head, and yet, she had isolated herself from most of her friends. Emme would get angry and that still didn't push her away from the edge she was balancing on. The therapist had given her psychotropic medications and she was hoping to alter the chemical levels in her brain, to help with her mood swings and behavior—but she didn't take them. It was almost like Mercedes was on a collision course of self-destruction. She wanted the pain—it had become her form of punishment.

One Saturday Emme had showed up at the house in the afternoon. Mercedes was still sleeping in her dark bedroom. Emme opened the door with her key, instead of knocking. She walked into Mercedes' bedroom, opened the blinds, and let the sun pour into the room. "Get your lazy ass up, girl!" Emme said, as she jumped onto the bed.

Mercedes pulled the comforter over her head and groaned. Then she mumbled, "Why? What torture do you have for me this weekend?"

"Well, whatever it is, I'm not going to let you dwell in self-pity! You've done enough of that since we found out your mother died. I'm not going to watch you die, just like her—a miserable old woman. You deserve better, and if I have to come over here every day and kick your ass...then so be it!"

Mercedes groaned again. "Why don't you go to one of the other girls to mother?"

She smacked the lump under the covers. "Because I want your sorry ass!" Emme got off the bed and went into her closet. A minute later, she came out with a pair of jeans, a T-shirt, and a pair of sandals. "Okay, get up. I've got your clothes picked out, and I want you to get dressed."

"Why, where are we going...to hell, together?"

Emme's laugh was sadistic. "Does it matter; you're living in hell already! Get up!" Emme pulled the covers off Mercedes.

"Okay...." Mercedes conceded to getting dressed. She stepped out of bed and walked in the bathroom. She didn't look in the mirror anymore. Instead, she went directly to the shower and turned it on.

An hour later, Emme was parking at Venice Beach. "Let's go. We're late for our appointment."

Mercedes looked a little puzzled. "Appointment? For what?"

Once the car was parked, Emme turned and looked at Mercedes. With tears in her eyes, she said, "You are my dearest friend. I would give my life for you. I know you have been swept away by this awful loneliness since we found out about your mother. It's like you are standing by yourself in the middle of a big ocean. Everyone around you has a family they belong to—you have nobody. Not a soul—I get that! After today—you will belong to me—forever and ever and ever!"

Tears were running down Mercedes' face. "You're right. I feel like—it's me against the world. At least when my mother was alive, I silently knew that there was at least one person who had my blood. Now I have nobody."

Emme wiped Mercedes' eyes and solemnly said, "Not anymore! It's you and me babe! Get your ass out of the car!"

Emme took her hand and they began to run. As they ran down the boardwalk, people watched the two crazy ladies. For the first time in weeks, Mercedes was laughing, until Emme took her inside a tattoo parlor. Mercedes began to shake her head venomously. "No...! How many times do I have to tell you, no!" she yelled.

Emme looked at her and said, her sad eyes welling with tears, "I want to do a matching tattoo with you. Just you and me, and a little tattoo that will be ours, forever. Like being blood brothers...."

Mercedes looked down and said, "I've maimed my body enough. No more, Emme. I hate myself enough for what I've done already."

"One tiny star on the inside of your wrist will link us together forever. You will *belong* with me." She picked up Mercedes' hand and turned it over and touched the spot. "Right here...we will always have this to remember our kinship."

Mercedes slowly nodded. "Forever...?"

Two hours later, Mercedes and Emme were sitting and sipping a glass of wine outside on the Venice walkway. Both of their wrists were bandaged and taped. Emme smiled and touched the bandage that covered Mercedes' smooth white skin. "This makes us part of the universe. Two stars of the thousands that shine in the sky."

Mercedes groaned. "That frickin' hurt!"

"That's because you're a big baby! Look at my body. You want to know what 'frickin' hurt' feels like? How about my mermaid tattoo on my back!"

Mercedes looked curious and asked a serious question. "Why did you do all those tattoos?"

"We all carry pain around, Mercedes, some more than others—but all very differently. These tattoos make me happy when I look at them. Each one represents something meaningful in my life. Like this one." She pointed to her shoulder. "The howling coyote reminds me of when I was really young. Almost every night, I could hear the coyotes howling in the woods behind my home. Sometimes I couldn't wait to go to bed just so I could lay there and listen to the synchronized howling of the pack. There were usually four, and it took me years to learn that each one had a special howl and each howl told its own story. My body is like one of those 'life' boards. You know, where you pin up all your favorite memories."

Mercedes looked down and circled the rim of her wine glass with one finger. "You're very lucky to have great memories like that."

"Today is another great memory for me. I have a new tattoo that tells its own story." Emme smiled as she laid her wrist on top of Mercedes'.

"I only have one...." Mercedes mouthed silently to herself.

It was Friday and it had been a long exhausting week at work. Mercedes left the office and was too tired to go home and make herself dinner, so she decided to stop at her favorite deli. It had been a few weeks since she had been there. The last time she was disappointed because Josh was not around. She missed his smiling face and their interesting conversations, and tonight she felt her heart beating faster at the possibility of seeing him again. He always made her feel comfortable, and no matter what kind of mood she was in, he had a way of bringing a smile to her face. It had been years since a man had stimulated her adventurous side and she wasn't sure how to approach him. Mercedes decided that tonight she would let him know she was interested in more than just a casual friendship. She was finally going to let her wall down and take a leap. Feeling giddy, and on a mission to do something she should have done months ago, made her heart skip a beat.

She got out of her car and walked toward the deli. After the past few months, it felt good to experience this twinge of excitement. She opened the door and walked in. Immediately, she scanned the room and found Josh sitting at a table, talking to a young woman and holding her hand. Mercedes watched him laugh as he playfully teased her. With a spark of jealously, and her emotions quickly deflating, she turned away and began looking for an empty table. She walked over to a vacant table in the corner and had a seat. Within seconds, Stella came over and took her order.

She took out her iPad and turned it on. It was her only means of distraction as her emotions began to spin out of control and the fear of losing it crept up like the bile in her throat.

Suddenly, she looked up and Josh had slipped into the seat in front of her. "Hey there! Long time, no see," he said, noticing her sad face. "Catching up on some work?"

Mercedes looked at Josh and nodded. She was afraid to say anything because her nerves were all jumbled.

"Cat got your tongue? Are you okay?" he asked in a soft voice.

"I'm okay. I've just had a rocky few weeks. I found out my mom died, and I've been going through a lot of changes and emotions." She forced herself to grin.

A sad look crossed his face. "I'm sorry to hear that. I hope things get better for you."

"How have you been?" She looked down at her laced fingers and said, "I saw you sitting with that customer a few minutes ago and I wanted to say 'hello,' but I didn't want to disturb your party," she said politely.

He leaned forward and pulled her chin up with his finger so he could look into her eyes. "There was a time I envisioned us together. I gave you lots of messages and hints that I was interested in you. I thought you were beautiful the first day you walked into my restaurant. Your smile lit up the room and I would have kissed that crooked nose in a blink!" He sat back, and continued, "But you ignored them, and I didn't know what more to do. Hell, I just figured you weren't interested in me. For the past year, I watched you go through so many changes, trying to be someone you really didn't want to be. I heard it in your voice and watched it on your face, and at times I just wanted to shake you to make you listen. I tried to let you know, many times, that your beauty was so much more than skin deep. I wanted to warn you that one day you would wake up hating yourself, for not believing in who you are. When you backed off, and stopped coming in frequently, I thought you might have found someone special. At that point, I knew it was time for me to let go of my infatuation. I've been dating that young lady for a few months...."

Mercedes was silent for a moment, then she said in a choked voice, "I'm not versed in the ways of dating, nor in men. That was a class I missed years ago. I'm sorry I missed your hints...." With a tear sliding down her face, she picked up her iPad and purse and stood up. "Second chances are not something God gives me...I wish you happiness, Josh...." She turned and walked toward the exit without looking back. What Josh didn't see was the pain that was written all over her face. Neither did he feel her wrenching agony that felt like knives were plunging into her heart.

Twenty-one

MERCEDES could barely catch her breath, she was sobbing so hard. Her vision was blurred and she had to keep wiping her eyes to see where she was driving. All she wanted to do was go home and tuck herself into a dark corner of her house and stay there forever. Nothing in her life had prepared her for this pain she was feeling. In her mind, she kept going over and over what Josh had said. She was oblivious to his hints and messages, and now she had destroyed the only thing that gave her hope, in her world of rejection. Life wasn't fair and it never came with second chances. She knew that first hand, because her mother relentlessly told her—'there are no second chances!'

She parked her car in the garage, opened the door, and walked into the kitchen. Feeling lost and detached from her world of reality, she took a bottle of wine off her counter, opened it, and poured herself a glass. Once she had consumed one glass, she then poured another. With the glass in one hand and her phone in the other, she went upstairs. She changed into a pair of sweats and laid down on her bed. Reflecting on every negative moment in her life, and she continued to weep. She wept for that young girl who never knew a mother's love; she wept for her insecurities and a beauty that was only skin deep; she wept the inability to see what was there in front of her face. She wept...and wept...and wept....

After several hours, nothing seemed to make any sense anymore, or have any meaning. She felt the weight of the world crushing her shoulders and she couldn't stop it. All Mercedes wanted to do was stop the horrific pain that was tightening her chest. She remembered this pain from her childhood and the night she wanted to commit suicide. If Emme hadn't been there—she needed to call Emme.

With no one else to go to except for Emme, she got out of bed to get her phone. Instead of getting her phone, she went into the bathroom and opened the drawer. Slowly, her hand wrapped around a bottle of pills. With her head pounding and her disorientated thoughts streaming in all directions, she walked down the stairs, grabbed her purse, and got into her car.

She drove around and around, watching her city that was so full of life—and yet she felt dead. There were flashing lights everywhere, people walking the streets, cars coming and going, and all she wanted was to stop the ache. Something had snapped and she just wanted to go into a safe dark space where no one could ever touch her ever again.

When she finally realized where she was, her hands began to shake and some form of awareness set into place. She had driven up to the top of Cheseboro Road, to a lookout point over the city. Occasionally, she would come up here when she needed to talk to God or reflect on life. Looking down over the city made her feel at peace, but not tonight. She looked at the view and then turned her head toward the passenger seat. On the seat was a bottle of pills and a half bottle of wine. She picked up the bottle of wine, uncorked it, and took a swig. Her other hand reached over and picked up the pills.

Flipping the pill bottle in the air and catching it with one hand, she mumbled over and over, "Do I...or don't I?"

Gradually, a calmness came over Mercedes. Her attention was drawn to her new tattoo and she held it close to her chest, "Please don't hate me, Emme. I tried so hard to be strong. I want the 'old' Mercedes back, and I can't have her. What do I do, please tell me, my friend?"

Afraid of her thoughts and scared, she tried to hang on. Not quite to the point of jumping off the edge, she made a decision. "Emme would flip a coin."

She reached into her glove box and took out a shiny penny she had found in a parking lot at the store.

With peace starting to bring her back to reality, Mercedes remembered her last coin toss. "Emme picked heads the last time and won, so I'm going to pick heads this time. Heads, I take the pills—tails, Emme wins again!" She looked at her star tattoo and closed her eyes. "Since when does life balance on a coin toss?" she asked.

Taking a deep breath, she flipped the coin into the air and it fell on the passenger seat. With her heart beating out of her chest and her fingers shaking, she turned on the overhead light. "You made a promise, Mercedes. Don't be that sniveling little baby." She could hear her mother saying.

She leaned toward the dash and wrapped her hand around the bottle.

Slowly, Mercedes bent down to look. With another wave of anger, she began to cry. "Fuck you, tails! Why does Emme always win?"

Mercedes sat for a while, sipped the rest of the wine, and let her nerves calm down. She turned on the car, put it into drive, and knew it was time to head home. She had gotten lucky, and she had given life or death a fair shot. With a lot more clarity as each minute passed, she also knew she needed to see her therapist tomorrow. She needed to cleanse herself and start moving forward. She knew she needed help and maybe, just maybe, she could find her way out of this dark abyss.

Mercedes pulled into the garage and shut off the engine. She put the pills in her pants pocket, grabbed the empty wine bottle, and walked into the house. Completely exhausted and depleted, she went upstairs, stripped down, and changed into her favorite motorcycle T-shirt, pink flannel pants, and brushed her teeth. Knowing she needed to get a good night's sleep, she took the bottle of pills out of her pants pocket. She took one pill out of the full bottle, and looked at it. Instead of cutting it in half, she slipped the whole one into her mouth and downed it with a sip of faucet water. She lit a candle, crawled into bed, and shut off the light. Within minutes she was into a deep—deep sleep.

Twenty-Two

MERCEDES curled up as she snuggled deeper into her comforter. It was starting to get cold in the mornings now that October had arrived. The house was chilled, so the thought of getting out of bed did not interest her in the least. What really did draw her immediate attention was that hot cup of freshly brewed coffee she could smell coming from her kitchen. Thanks to technology, she didn't have to get out of bed to turn on the coffeemaker. Patting herself on the back, she was thankful she had remembered to pour in the water, fill the coffee bean tray, and set the timer to 'on' the night before. Most of the weekdays, she made a desperate effort to set the timer. But, sometimes her mind was filled with so many other things, she would just forget. Today was one of those lucky days she hadn't. And thank God, because she was addicted to coffee and needed her fix.

Why was she so groggy and she could barely kept her eyes open? She felt like she had slept for years, reminiscent of Rip Van Winkle, one of her favorite childhood fairy tales. She laid in bed trying to shake the cobwebs. *Why was it so difficult to think this morning?* She tried to remember yesterday, but that was nearly impossible. She looked at the clock and gasped. The pill had caused her to sleep three hours longer than she normally did. Then she smiled, and said, *"Boy, I'm never taking a whole pill again. The doctor was right when she said 'cut them in half or you will be like a zombie for days'!"*

A smile crossed her face when she finally remembered it was Sunday morning. Sundays were her day of rest from Zumba, work, and occasionally, Emme. Today, she just wanted to lay in bed all day, and try to shake the bitterness that had consumed her last night. After laying there for a few minutes, she decided a hot cup of coffee with a shot of espresso would definitely clear the fog she was in, and a bagel was the best way to appease the hunger she was feeling. Having two glasses of wine and not having dinner the night before had left a hunger gnawing in her tummy.

Mercedes slipped her legs over the side of the bed, stretched her arms up above her head, and twisted from side-to-side. She leaned over and turned on the light. Dressed in only a T-shirt and underwear, she stepped down onto the hardwood floor, then walked into the bathroom. Her morning routine had just begun. Mercedes always thought it was interesting how every person instinctively developed their own routines in life. From almost the moment of birth, everyone's repetitive behaviors usually began. Then eventually, these behaviors became the comfort zones that fit into their individual lifestyles. When you threw in a few 'likes,' 'dislikes,' and mix in some 'idiosyncrasies'—*everyone traveled through life as creatures of habit.* Only everyone's routines were slightly different, no two people were ever the same.

She placed her towel by the shower and walked over to the sink. When she leaned over to look in the mirror, a big smile crossed her face. She leaned forward and touched her crooked nose. She loved her nose, and she wasn't going to let anyone, not even her girlfriends tell her it needed to be corrected. She liked who she was, and any changes were going to be thought out before she leaped into anything headfirst! That was the biggest learning lesson from her horrible dream. That dream had really frightened her and she could still feel the night sweat on the back of her T-shirt.

Mercedes started to laugh as bits and pieces of her dream began to surface. Remembering the dream was more real than the night before, when she was sitting at the club with the girls watching them get all the attention, and letting her insecurities and emotions spin her into circles. She bent down and slipped out of her flannel pants.

Then she said to herself, *"Thank God, that was only a dream last night! Watching myself change and become so weak and pathetic was very scary. Thinking that beauty would solve my problems doesn't make sense anymore."* She stood there, then with confidence in her voice, she said, *"I've learned my biggest lesson in life. I feel like Dorothy in the Wizard of Oz. We both learned our lessons...."* She mumbled as she flipped off her T-shirt, and smiled at her tiny boobs. *"Well, I think... it wasn't enough just to be successful, respected, and loved by my friends and peers. And...if I ever go looking to be beautiful and desired again, I won't look any further than my own mirror...because if God didn't give it to me...then I never really needed it to begin with. Beauty is in your heart, and who you are as a person. It's not about a crooked nose, tiny boobs, or a great body...it's about liking who you are!"*

Mercedes brushed the single tear off her face. "That dream had me so upset, my pillow was wet from all those tears this morning! Oh Lordy—and the message at the end of the dream with Josh—was loud and clear!" She turned on the shower and waited for it to heat. "I need to become more aware of my surroundings and the messages people are sending me. I'm going to the deli for coffee and a bagel and to see Josh!"

As she slipped under the hot water, she began to laugh. "Man-oh-man, I can't wait to tell Emme about my dream...."

Mercedes' morning routine had just begun. . . .

*If you've finished reading this book,
please leave a review on Amazon,
Thank you so very much!*

About the Author

I love to garden, try new recipes, take lots of pictures and occasionally I enjoy a glass of wine with dear friends. I've never jumped out of a plane, climbed Mt. Everest, or seen the Northern Lights of Alaska. But, I have danced in the rain, sent a message in a bottle and I've rode my motorcycle down the Pacific Coast Highway on sunny California days!

My passion of writing has led me on the most amazing journey. I thrive on developing strong storylines that showcase today's contemporary lifestyles. Rags to riches, Robin Hood, and surviving the odds, seems to be my one common denominator that showcases my fascinating and diverse characters.

Also by Rene D. Schultz

Searching4Mr.Rightcom

Dorothy was befriended by a brilliant scarecrow, a warmhearted tin-man and a shy cowardly lion to enjoy her journey. Not me! I had a penny-pinching Leprechaun, an Elvis impersonator, TheYoungin, SweetBabyJames, an obsessive-compulsive Deputy Dawg, a hard-core biker, a bullshit artist, a pill-popping Viagraman, and Houdini who I wished could have disappeared. Dorothy feared the Wicked Witch of the West who nearly brought her down—I had the Predator and learned to fight back . . . .

Divorced after a long marriage, and after years of isolation, I found myself taking off my blinders and crashing head-on into a world I knew nothing about. With a demented sense of humor, a wild hunger for living on the edge, and an unexplainable need to find my 'soul mate,' I plunged into the world of online dating. Now, after years of dating and stories that brought my friends to fits of laughter, I decided to chronicle my experiences . . . .

Done Deal

Done Deal is an inspiring book about a woman who doesn't understand why the pharmaceuticals are holding back 'orphan' drugs that can save lives. Why insurance companies won't pay to keep people alive. And why the government is closing its 'blind eyes.' Cissy goes on a quest to find these answers and what she discovers is shocking. With an anger that leaves her cynical, and with time running out, she sets out to 'right a wrong.' She forfeits her integrity and leaves a legacy that will crush the greedy pharmaceuticals and the corrupt insurance companies!

With the new age of technology, hackers become a reality and new Robin Hoods emerge.

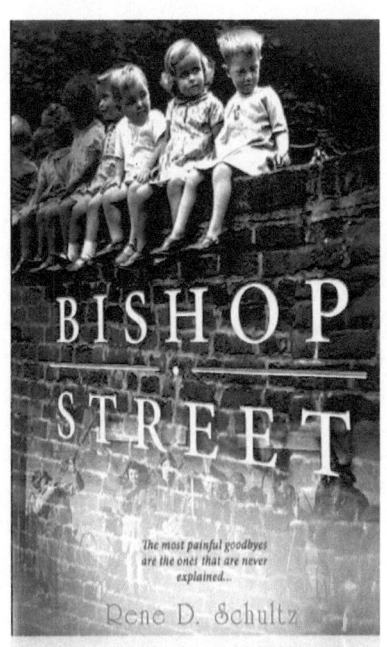

The most painful goodbyes
are the ones that are never
explained...

Rene D. Schultz

Bishop Street

Bishop Street is an emotional, gut-wrenching journey of survival, friendship, and second chances... After twenty years, Maggie makes a life changing decision to find her three best friends from the orphanage. From the small towns in North Dakota, across the exotic beaches in Mexico, and searching the streets of homeless shelters in Los Angeles... will she find more than just her friends?

Coming Soon

The much anticipated sequel to Bishop Street
will be available by the end of 2014!
Margaret Gray and her three best friends
from Bishop Street Orphanage are back and
many new adventures are in store!
Follow Rene D. Schultz on Facebook for more information.

Rene-D-Schultz-Author

A FREE PREVIEW
OF THE
HIGHLY ANTICIPATED
SEQUEL!

# ONE

MAGGIE STOOD UP AND STRETCHED HER ARMS ABOVE her head, trying to relieve the slight ache in her back. She wasn't very tall, but at forty-five, she was still an attractive lady. Her chin-length blonde hair accentuated her beautiful hazel eyes that changed colors depending on her mood. She had been sitting for hours working on her new book. Only, this book was never going to be published or go public. It was a reflection of all the changes in her life over the past three years, since she found her childhood family. It was more like a personal tribute to Lucy, Elizabeth, and Randolph. After all, it was their story, from that first year in the orphanage, to now. And it was going to showcase the incredible differences in their lives after finally getting back together, after a misinterpreted separation of twenty years.

Maggie sat down and leaned her head back. She closed her eyes and began to reflect on her life over the past three years. Maggie, Elizabeth, Lucy, and Randolph's tumultuous childhood in the orphanage was finally put to rest. The calculated lies and deceit of Sister Theresa had torn them apart, leaving them all alone after they left the orphanage to find their way in the world. They had all gone through enough in their childhood to last them a lifetime. Sister Theresa had only increased their insecurities by tearing them apart from the only family they knew. It wasn't until Maggie had learned of Sister Theresa's death and her nightmares came back that she finally decided to search for the reason why they had never contacted each other in almost twenty years.

Elizabeth, her husband, and five children were doing well, enjoying life on the farm. All except her oldest son Randall. He moved from their small farm in North Dakota, and was now living with Maggie in Los Angeles. He was a charming young man who made the Dean's list at UCLA every year, and had set his goal to be a veterinarian. With the help of Maggie, after twenty years of living on the streets in Los Angeles, Lucy's unremitting sobriety had created stability in her life. Then, finally getting her daughter out of foster care had been the catalyst to push her into helping others. She was now the director and headmaster of Safe House and was concentrating on building another shelter to get the runaway children off the streets of Hollywood.

Randolph was still floating between cities, and enjoying the solitude of his ranch in Mexico, and his billion-dollar software company in Silicon Valley. His wealth had imprisoned him into a life of constant bodyguards and limitations. The anonymity on his ranch located in a small town in Mexico, was his only secret reprieve from tabloids and prying eyes.

Maggie's constant friend and outspoken secretary, Denise, was still enjoying marital bliss, along with her two daughters, Briana and Maddie. She was still in the office pushing Maggie to her limits, and after nearly twenty years together, nothing had changed.

Damon, the investigator who Maggie hired to find her friends, was another story in itself....

Maggie opened her eyes and sighed. Three months ago, her new novel had come out and the media blitz had nearly sucked the life out of her. After taking a few years off to solidify her relationships and reorganize her life, she had finally gone back to writing. Fortunately, her time off had only strengthened her creativity and produced a new dimension into her storytelling— romance. Her new book had gone to the top of the New York Times bestselling list in less than two months. It was a little different, and the genre spread out a little more than the stories she had previously written, but the reviewers embraced it with open arms. The novel was about a strong-willed detective that walked on the edge, and at the end, he finally finds romance.

A smile crossed her face and she leaned forward in her seat. How silly she had been to bring a part of her private life into the limelight of her newest novel. Although most authors tended to do that, it was always something Maggie shied away from. For years, she did everything to stay as private as she could. She never fed into the publicity or opened herself up to the tabloids. She had lead a very sheltered existence, filled with an almost nonexistent social life. She had closed herself off from the media that was bent on destroying anyone's reputation they could get their claws into. Except for the past year—she just didn't care anymore. So many things had changed and the tabloids now had a heyday printing trashy rumors about her. She was constantly hounded like an animal, and everything she had cherished privately was now scrutinized by mindless readers of the supermarket gutter press.

Maggie put down her cellphone, leaned over, and pushed the button on her intercom. "Hey, you...."

Denise laughed. "You mean, you're not texting me on my cell? Make up your mind, Maggie—one or the other! Lately, you are driving me totally crazy! You either need to get out of the office more, or take up a new habit, like knitting! This text-buzz, text-buzz, has got to stop!"

Maggie smiled, and said into the box, "Sorry! I'm so confused with all this new technology. Randall keeps pushing me more and more into using my new iPhone, and I keep fighting it tooth and nail! Texting someone across the room is the big thing nowadays with those young kids, but the intercom is easier, with just the push of a button!"

Denise opened Maggie's office door and walked in. She strolled over to her desk and sat down on the chair in front of her. She picked up her hand and wave directly at Maggie. "How about in person? This is even easier than texting or the intercom!"

Maggie gave Denise a big smile and nodded her head. "Much better! How are you feeling?"

Denise shrugged her shoulders. Then she took the Kleenex out of her pocket and blew her nose. "I was up all night with the girls. Briana brought home a cold from school and proudly gave it to the whole family. Schools are a breeding ground for nasty germs that can't wait to infect a whole damn family!"

Maggie scrunched her face in pain when she asked, "Did David get it too?"

"Oh...yeah! He's not a happy camper!" Denise's angry face suddenly burst into laughter, and Maggie joined.

"The lovely perks of having children! And something I don't wish to experience." Maggie continued, "I think Mary Jane is sick, also. Winter is that time of year that all the kids get sick."

Denise sighed. "When Christmas break comes, then maybe we will all be able to stay healthy for a while!"

Maggie's face lit up like a light bulb. "Maybe you should go with David to Hawaii for a break? Beautiful sunny skies, hot humid breezes, and leave the children with Emma."

Denise shook her head. "I gave Emma the holiday off. She's been such a help with the sick kids, and making sure they are well taken care of. David and I love the fact that she comes early in the morning and leaves when one of us gets home. Great idea, Maggie, except David is going crazy at work and can't take off much during the holiday."

Maggie blushed and said, "I'd give you my beach house in Malibu, but I have plans."

Denise smiled and lifted her brows. "Humm...with Damon?"

Maggie reddened again and said, "Yes, Miss Nosy Body! Actually, the whole family is coming for Christmas, like every year. Plus, we have the 'grand opening' of the new shelter for the children. I'm going to give Elizabeth and her family my penthouse and I'll take the beach house."

Denise sat straight up in her chair, threw her arms across the desk and leaned forward. "For cripes sake, how am I being nosy? For two years, I watched him drop by the office just to hang around—and be your friend. Then, last year, I can remember the exact day and exact time he opened the door, paraded by my desk, pushed open your door, and marched right up to you!. I think that was one of the most romantic scenes I have ever witnessed in my whole entire life. It even beat Scarlet O'Hara and Rhett Butler, when he carried her up the stairs in *Gone with the Wind*. And I watch that scene over and over all the time!"

Maggie's face was deep red. "Really...?"

Denise sighed. "Geeez, Maggie, you are one the most naïve people I've ever met!" She continued, "Yes, it was very romantic the way he pulled you out of the chair and planted the biggest, longest kiss any person could ever imagine! And...wasn't it romantic...or a deal breaker for you?" Denise laughed.

Maggie started drawing circles on her blotter with the pen she was holding. "It was something I had secretly dreamed about for years. I was just too shy to initiate any kind of relationship, and too afraid of rejection to pursue it."

Denise sucked in a deep breath and let it out slowly. "Well, thank God he finally grew a set of cojones! Because I was tired of seeing him hang around here waiting for you to give him a sign that you were interested. And I was getting damn tired of watching you moping around like a 'love sick' teenager!"

Maggie's eyes opened wide in surprise. "Was it that bad?"

"Worse!" They both started to laugh.

Denise stood up. She shook her head and clicked her tongue in bewilderment. "I hope you have a very romantic time at the beach house! Was there something you needed when you called me in here?"

Maggie cleared her throat. "Yes! Lucy is looking for volunteers for the 'open house,' at Safe House next week. I thought I would go over tomorrow, and wanted to know if you wanted to join me. She's going tonight to straighten things up, but I'm just too tired."

"I'm going to pass. I have two sick little babies, and one cranky husband at home who need some TLC, and I'm leaving right now to go home to them! Give Lucy a hug for me."

"I will. And in case I haven't said it enough, I will say it once more…. 'Thank you for all your help with the new book. We hit the top of the charts yesterday'!" Maggie and Denise did a fist bump. Then Denise walked out of the office door.

An hour later, Maggie was pulling up into the underground parking of her building. She was exhausted and hungry. Damon had left a text on her phone earlier saying, *'I'm still out of town. I will try to catch the red eye back tonight, hugs.'* Maggie's face lit up with a smile at just the thought of him coming back into town. She missed him and couldn't wait to touch his handsome face or kiss his seductive lips. They had been lovers for the past year and spent most of their time together, when he wasn't busy with his heavy schedule of clientele, or she wasn't on her publicity tour for her newest book. Maggie was in love with him, but had never said those three words out loud. Neither had he. Yet, there was a bond that kept them moving forward with their solid relationship.

Herbie watched as Maggie got out of the car and walked toward him. He hit the elevator button as she approached and stopped next to him. "Evening, Miz

Maggie." His big, toothy smile and eagerness to please was always so endearing to Maggie.

"How's my favorite doorman?" Maggie smiled.

His dark eyes gleamed and his spotlessly clean, dark blue jacket flaunted four rows of shiny brass buttons. The trousers, in the same color, bore the crease of an iron, and the elevator light reflected off of his patent leather shoes. "You's be lookin' jus as tired as me, Miz Maggie. I'z be retirin' real soon hows 'bout yous?"

Maggie touched his wrinkled face and said, "You're such a sweet man. Don't you think now that you are going to be ninety years old, that you deserve to retire next month?"

Maggie wrapped her arms around Herbie and hugged him. He shuffled his thin legs and smiled. "I'll miz you, Miz Maggie."

"I shall miss you, too!"

The elevator doors opened; wearily, Maggie walked inside and waited for the doors to shut. It ascended to the penthouse and the doors opened again. She slowly stepped out of the elevator and walked to her front door. She typed in the passkey number and pushed the door open. Sitting on the foyer table was a large, beautiful arrangement of Maggie's favorite flowers, peonies. Immediately, she could smell something delicious coming from the kitchen. Without even as much time as it took for her heart to beat again, she swiftly walked into the kitchen and threw her arms around the tall, handsome man standing in front of the stove.

She nearly knocked him over from behind. He laughed and said, "Whoa...babe!" He turned around and

8

lifted Maggie up off her feet as they celebrated his homecoming with a long, passionate kiss.

Maggie whispered in his ear, "Welcome home."

Damon pulled her tightly against his body and let his need be known. "Now, this is the way a homecoming should be!"

Maggie laughed and said, "Only in the romance novels...." Then she leaned over to see what was on the stove. "I'm so hungry I could eat a cow! I didn't have lunch today. And I surely didn't expect you to be back early, so it looks like I got two welcome surprises, without another night of eggs and toast!"

Damon shook his head, released her, and started to laugh. "I guess we eat dinner first and then you can show me how really welcome I am!"

Maggie stood on her toes and kissed his cheek. "You're on...." she barely whispered. Then she looked around and asked, "Where's Randall? I haven't seen him most of the week."

"He left a note on the foyer table. Looks like him and his buddies are hitting the fraternity parties tonight and he'll be home in the morning." He made a deep growling sound and pulled her tight against his muscular body again.

Maggie cuddled up to him and looked up with her shining hazel eyes. "Well then, it looks like it's just you and me tonight, big guy!" Unexpectedly, her stomach started to growl.

Damon unwrapped his arms and laughed. He walked over to the stove to plate up what he had prepared. Maggie followed, holding onto the belt loop of his jeans. For some reason tonight, she felt this need to stay connected.

They talked about his trip to Denver over a delicious dinner of rib-eye steaks, sautéed mushrooms, and roasted asparagus. Maggie always loved listening to his client stories and the aggressive way in which he dealt with them. He had been a private investigator for years and was now considered the best in his field, throughout the country. He was always being sought after by the rich and famous, or anyone who could afford his substantial fees. Maggie remembered the day she hired him to locate her three best friends. He had assertively walked into her office, looking like a pirate with his tall, muscular body, and long, rakish black hair. She thought he was a movie star hoping to audition for the movie of her newest book. Not only was she rude and abrasive, she was also sadly mistaken. However, she did wind-up hiring him to find her missing friends. For the next two years, Damon had remained close to Maggie's new family and they continued to be friends. Until that day he stormed into her office, declared his intentions, and planted a slow, passionate kiss on her lips. Maggie was shocked, but when her tumultuous emotional state had finally settled down, their friendship had blossomed into a comfortable relationship. Denise, Elizabeth, and Lucy couldn't be happier. It was Randolph who kept an open eye on Damon to make sure he didn't hurt Maggie.

This was a whole new level for Maggie and Damon. Maggie had never been in a relationship before. Her life had been very reclusive and sterile and consisted of only a few dates. The orphanage had left her with the lack of trust in people and the thought of getting hurt left her frozen in fear. So, with her antisocial lifestyle, only an occasional date had crossed her path. On the other side, Damon had sowed his wild oats during his youth, but as life began to move forward and became more hectic, his time was constantly consumed with his fast-paced business. That day he had responded to Denise's request for investigative services and walked into Maggie's office, his life was turned upside down. He hadn't expected to meet an aloof author with a chip on her shoulder and a viperous tongue that could cut like a sword. This had immediately sparked his interest and continued to surprise him. He was a handsome man who always had women clambering to get his attention. He could have had the pick of anyone, including some of the movie industry's famous starlets. He was picky, and over the years, had withdrawn from the social scene. Nobody had caught his attention the past few years, and he was okay with that. He had a thriving business that kept him traveling all over the world.

That first meeting with Maggie left him guessing about her. Once she hired him, his curiosity began to hit a high note. Although she was reclusive and isolated, he could also see this raw passion she never realized she had. Whenever he got too close, she would close down and flee like a naïve little girl. Then, one day after he obsessed over her passive-aggressive behavior of stubbornness, sarcasm, and emotional shut downs, he marched into her office with every intention to confront her. Only when he grabbed ahold of her shoulders and looked into her surprised eyes, he knew that very second, his life as a wandering loner was over.

After dinner, they settled down on the couch in the family room to watch the news. This was their favorite time together. When everything had slowed down for the day and they could finally just relax. Damon was reclining on the couch and Maggie was curled up next to him. Suddenly, Damon startled Maggie and sat straight up. He immediately grabbed the remote and turned the television volume up louder. Maggie sat up, clutched Damon's hand, and gasped.

A special newsbreak had appeared and a reporter had just announced a shooting. "There is a shooter in the main lobby the 'Safe House,' a well-known rehabilitation center in the heart of Los Angeles. The police have surrounded the area, but we still don't have any word as to what is going on. Shots were fired, but we don't know how many have been wounded, or if anyone has been killed. Stay tuned for updates."

Maggie gasped and her body began to shake as their eyes intently watched the television. Maggie began to panic. "I need to get down there.... Lucy is there tonight, preparing for the 'open house' next week!"

Damon demanded, "Are you sure?" He stood up and pulled Maggie with him. "Let's go...."

Tears began to slide down her cheeks, as the reality of the moment took both of them by surprise. Maggie and Damon were slipping into their coats and walking toward the door, "Please, God, watch over and protect my little Lucy!" Maggie pleaded.

The front door slammed shut . . . .

Find Rene D. Schultz Online

Amazon U.S.	http://goo.gl/6IOaCJ
Amazon U.K.	http://goo.gl/DTdzHx
Barnes & Noble	http://goo.gl/SmkTu01
Goodreads	http://goo.gl/GVoGMv

All titles now available on Apple and Google Books for convenient reading on the go!